Beyond the Grave

Beyond the Grave

Marcia Muller
and
Bill Pronzini

Walker and Company
New York

For Ruth Cavin,
with thanks

First published in the United States of America in 1986 by the Walker Publishing Company, Inc.

Published simultaneously in Canada by John Wiley & Sons, Canada, Limited, Rexdale, Ontario.

Library of Congress Cataloging-in-Publication Data

Muller, Marcia.
   Beyond the grave.

   1. Pronzini, Bill. II. Title.
PS3563.U397B48   1986   813'.54   86-7808
ISBN 0-8027-5651-4

Printed in the United States of America
10 9 8 7 6 5 4 3 2 1

PROLOGUE
1846

FROM WHERE HE stood on the casa's upper gallery, Don Esteban Velasquez commanded a broad view of all that was his. As far as the eye could see were the hills and valleys, creeks, groves of oaks and fruit trees that comprised Rancho Rinconada de los Robles, his grant from the government of Mexico. Below this oak-shaded hill where he had built his hacienda, nestled in one of the little valleys near the westward roadway, stood the adobe buildings of the rancho's pueblo; the cross atop the church of San Anselmo de las Lomas, rising above the stables and garrison and vaqueros' quarters, was like a brand burned in the gray sky by the hand of God. Down there, too, to the rear of the church, was the cemetery where Don Esteban's first wife, Maria Alcazar, and two of his three sons lay at rest beneath the grassy sod.

But it was at none of these things that he stood looking on this drizzly December morning, three days before Christmas. It was at the rider approaching on the main *camino* from the south—a single rider forcing his horse at a gallop along the muddy track, where instead there should have been a long column of men and animals returning without undue haste, in triumph.

The rider was still too far away for Don Esteban to recognize his clothing or his mount. One of the rancho's *soldados*? His *mayordomo*, José Verdugo? No matter. It did not matter. Whoever the rider was, he could only be carrying a message of doom from San Marcos Pass: Don Esteban's plan had failed.

He knew this with a bleak certainty; there could be no other explanation for the lone rider, the thunderous haste. He had known it the moment one of his mestizo servants, having noticed the rider's approach, had summoned him. He had already ordered the servants here to prepare to defend the hacienda. He had already sent word to the remaining few of his men at the pueblo to do

3

likewise there, and to begin evacuating the women and children; and he had requested that Padre Urbano join him immediately.

He had given no thought to escape. This land was his; he had lived here for twenty-five years, and three members of his family were buried here. If he had not been prepared to die defending it, he would not have devised and then sought to carry out his intrigue against the *Americano* troops. He would, instead, have accompanied his young wife, Gloria, and his only living son, the child Felipe, to Mexico City ten months ago, when it had become clear to him, if not to all the other *abajeños,* that war between Mexico and *Los Estados Unidos* was imminent.

What fools those others were! They had shut their minds as well as their eyes to the *Americanos'* desire for the annexation of California. Refused to listen when Don Esteban urged that a well-trained militia be assembled and garrisoned at strategic points throughout the province, rather than relying on the private *soldados* loyal to each don. Refused to listen when he had spoken out in favor of expelling all gringos, not just the troublemakers such as John Fremont. And now it was too late. Now war had been declared. Now the Yanquis had captured General Vallejo at Sonoma and raised a flag, what they called the Bear Flag, proclaiming California a republic. Now Monterey, the provincial capital, had fallen, as had most of the northern half of the province. It was a time for desperate measures if the *abajeños* were to save the southern half.

If the trap at San Marcos Pass had been properly sprung, it would have dealt the advancing Yanqui forces a crippling blow. And by all the saints, it *should* have been properly sprung. Spies had reported the movement of Fremont's batallion on El Camino Real, pointing south for an assault on Santa Barbara. This route, the easiest, would take them through Refugio Pass. But Don Esteban had spread word of an ambush at Gaviota Pass, beyond Refugio: *soldados* from the Santa Barbara garrison waiting to roll boulders down on the *Americanos* as they passed through the narrows. Fremont, believing this falsehood, had diverted his troops away from Refugio to the more rugged route—a brush-grown Indian trail—through San Marcos Pass. It was at San Marcos that the real ambush had been laid, manned by men from Rancho Rinconada de los Robles. Why it had failed to catch the gringos by surprise Don Esteban would soon know.

When the lone rider neared the foot of the hill below, Don

4

Esteban descended from the gallery by way of the courtyard stairs and crossed to the main gate. He said nothing to the three armed guards who waited there in the thin drizzle, watching as he had been watching from above. There was nothing more to be said until the messenger reached them.

But the messenger did not reach them. Halfway up the hill, the plunging horse broke stride, stumbled, pitched the rider as it fell heavily on its side in the thick adobe mud. The animal, so sweat-lathered that its brown coat seemed smeared with white, lay spasming for a few seconds and then was still. The man staggered to his feet, holding his head, swaying with fatigue; Don Esteban, waiting at the gate while the mestizos ran downhill, recognized the wet, strained features of José Verdugo.

The mestizos half carried the *mayordomo* uphill into the court-yard and laid him down beneath the protective overhang of the gallery. Water was brought for him, and when he could speak, the tale he told was this:

The trap had been laid as ordered on the hillside above the San Marcos trail. But it was the men of Don Esteban, not the *Americanos*, who had been the victims of a surprise attack. Scouts had reported Fremont's batallion encamped for the night along Alamo Pintado Creek, in a canyon below the pass; but Fremont had somehow learned of the ambush—from the lips of a traitor, no doubt—and had sent a detachment of perhaps fifty *soldados* on a circuitous route that took them to a position above and behind Don Esteban's forces. A dozen loyalists were killed in the first surprise volley; the rest were routed, run down, and shot or captured. Verdugo had barely managed to escape with his life. He had hidden in a cave until nightfall and then rounded up a horse and raced back here to the hacienda.

Listening to the *mayordomo*'s account, Don Esteban knew that if a traitor had revealed the ambush plan to Fremont, that man would also have revealed the identity of the one who had arranged it. The Yanqui major would not allow such an act to pass unpun-ished. He would dispatch, if he had not already done so, another detachment of troops to arrest Don Esteban, and, if necessary, to lay siege to Rancho Rinconada de los Robles. It was the way of war; Don Esteban would have done the same if their positions were reversed. The *soldados* might arrive today, though it was unlikely they would have ridden all night as Verdugo had done; and if they reached the rancho late in the day, it was also unlikely that they would risk a night skirmish on unfamiliar terrain. Tomorrow, then. Don Esteban and the last of his loyalists would have perhaps twenty-four hours to prepare for the assault.

Men and weapons were too few to mount an adequate defense; he knew this. The *Americanos* would eventually claim a victory. But he would not be alive to see the fall of his rancho. Death was not only preferable, it was to be welcomed. He had no fear of it. His only fear, now, was that his most treasured possessions would become the spoils of war, the playthings of gringos—something that must not be allowed to happen.

Verdugo was being helped to the servants' quarters for food and rest when Padre Urbano arrived in a *carreta* drawn by his old swayback mule. Don Esteban quickly led the priest to his *escritorio* on the upper level, where he explained what had happened at San Marcos Pass. The mendicant listened stoically and offered a prayer when Don Esteban had finished speaking.

"I will not ask you to join the fight against the *Americanos, fray,*" Don Esteban said. "You may leave with the women and children, with my blessing. The decision is yours."

"I will stay," the padre said without hesitation. "It is God's will that I remain with my church."

Don Esteban nodded. He had expected that this would be the mendicant's answer. "I have an important task for you, then. It must be accomplished in all haste and secrecy."

"*Sí,* Don Esteban."

The room was dark, somber except for the fire burning on the hearth grate; the firelight reflected glassily off the rich-grained oak cabinets, made the religious artifacts arranged within them gleam as if with a life of their own. Don Esteban went to the cabinets, stood looking at the artifacts for a moment. Altogether there were two-score of them, gathered on travels to Spain in his early years, to Mexico and throughout California in his later ones. Crucifixes, censers, statues of the Virgin Mary, of the Madonna and Child, of the various saints—all handcrafted of gold and silver, some decorated with precious stones. Holy books encased in bejeweled metal covers. Icons and devotional paintings by El Greco, Francisco de Zurbarán, Jusepe de Ribera. Other items of comparable rarity and value.

He faced Padre Urbano again. "These must not fall into the

hands of Fremont's *soldados,*" he said grimly. "You must find a safe place to hide them."

"At the pueblo?"

"*Sí.* The *Americanos* will not think to look for such treasures there. And quickly, *fray.* We have little time left."

"It will be done. Upon my word as a man of God."

With the padre's help, Don Esteban wrapped each of the artifacts in monk's cloth and carefully placed them inside a large wooden crate brought by one of the servants. A few items of personal value to his wife and son were also wrapped and put into the crate. Two mestizos were then called to carry the crate down to the courtyard and set it in the mendicant's wagon.

"Bring me word when you have found a place," Don Esteban said, drawing the padre aside. "I must leave a record of the location for Doña Gloria and the boy Felipe."

"You will receive me again before dusk, Don Esteban."

"*Bueno.* Before dusk."

Don Esteban watched as the *carreta* clattered down the muddy road to the pueblo. When it disappeared behind a stand of oaks, he returned to the *escritorio* and began to write a letter to his wife and son, one he prayed they would one day read. Once he finished, there would be little else to do except to await Padre Urbano's return. And then to begin the long wait for the coming of Fremont's *soldados.* And then to fight. And then to die as he had lived, as any good caballero lived—with dignity and honor.

The siege began the afternoon of the following day. It was preceded by the arrival of an officer bearing a flag of truce and bringing a formal request for surrender. But surrender meant imprisonment, perhaps the gallows; surrender meant dishonor. Don Esteban refused. A short while later the first shots were fired.

It was a brief skirmish, and a bloody one. The Yanqui detachment numbered one hundred men, heavily armed with rifles and light cannon; there were fewer than twenty men left to defend the rancho, only five of those trained *soldados,* and a shortage of weapons and ammunition. The pueblo, where most of Don Esteban's men were deployed, came under attack first and was quickly overrun and seized. The empty garrison was set ablaze, as were most of the other buildings; the church of San Anselmo de las Lomas was partially destroyed by errant cannon fire. Padre Urbano, the one man of all the rancho's defenders who might have been spared by the invaders, was inside the church, in the path of the cannonball when it shattered the adobe wall. He was killed instantly.

Three dozen troops stormed the hacienda, where Don Esteban awaited them with three mestizos and a pair of matched silver dueling pistols. In the first exchange of fire, Don Esteban fell at the main gate with a bullet in his chest. He, too, died instantly.

There were no survivors.

PART I
1986

ONE

I ALMOST MISSED the auction because of Mama being in the hospital. She'd been rushed there the night before, after collapsing in the recreation center of the mobile-home park where she lives. Her doctor had diagnosed a bleeding ulcer, and they were now running tests to see if she needed an operation. Mama wasn't saying much, but I could tell she thought she was going to die; there was a quiet resignation in her eyes—so dark against her drained face— and her work-worn hands lay still and protectively curled on the coarse hospital blanket.

I might have panicked had it not been for Nick Carillo, Mama's seventy-nine-year-old boyfriend. His manner was relaxed as he lounged on the chair next to her bed, and the smug expression on his bony, tanned face said that he was looking forward to many more years of taking Mama and her diet in hand. Nick is a health nut and constantly lectures both of us about our wicked ways with overly spicy and impure foods. Now he probably envisioned a million occasions upon which to say "I told you so."

But he hadn't started in on it yet, and even though I knew neither Mama nor I would ever hear the end of this episode, I was grateful for his steadying presence. Nick had eleven years on my mother, had been through the countless illnesses of friends and relatives, and was far more realistic than any member of the Oliverez family. When the time for the auction approached and I said maybe I shouldn't go, he told me I was being foolish. "Attending the auction is your responsibility to the museum, Elena," he said, "and besides, your Mama and I will be here when you get back, waiting to hear what treasures you've bid on." So—ignoring Mama's dramatic farewell look—I went.

The sale of old furniture was being held in a cavernous building that used to be an auto showroom, on the frontage road where

Route 101 cuts through Santa Barbara. I'd gone over there the afternoon before—Friday—to preview the items, and there were several I planned to bid on in the hope of acquiring them for the museum. When I arrived there that morning, I parked my car—a vintage VW beetle convertible that I had bought for a song the summer before and was unashamedly proud of—at the far side of the lot where no one could open his door into it and ding its costly yellow paint job. Then I looked in my purse to make sure I had the auction catalog and hurried over to the showroom; the sale was to begin at noon, twelve minutes from now.

Inside, the temperature was at least ten degrees warmer than in the parking lot. Although it was a balmy April day, overhead fans worked sluggishly, and even the most scantily dressed browsers waved catalogs to supplement the fans' ineffectual efforts. Several rows of folding chairs had been set up in the center of the room, in front of a raised platform, and some of the smaller items had been moved up there behind the podium. Other pieces, many of them quite massive, ranged along the sides, where would-be buyers were inspecting them. I took a seat in the front row of chairs and waited for the auction to start.

As director of Santa Barbara's Museum of Mexican Arts, I am not strictly responsible for acquisitions. However, our curator, Rodolfo Lopez—better known as Rudy—had only joined the staff last November, and he was still bogged down in learning the myriad details of the position I'd vacated nearly a year ago when I'd been named director. Rudy was in Los Angeles this weekend attending a big estate auction, and he'd asked me to cover this smaller one here at home. I was only too glad to do so; basically I'm a curator at heart, not an administrator. And the auction promised to be a good one: What Rudy wanted to buy was furniture for a display that would show how Alta Californians had lived in the era of *los ranchos grandes,* and there were several good pieces here that dated from that fabled period. I had my eye on a pair of convent chairs, a hand-carved dining table, and a small marriage coffer. The coffer—a low chest measuring three feet long by two feet tall and incongruously resembling a coffin, which had once contained a bride's dowry—was a particularly fine piece, hewn of dark wood, with a boldly carved crucifix pattern around its edges and hammered brass fittings on the hinged top and on the shallow drawer below the main compartment.

I sat there for a few minutes, feeling beads of sweat break out on my upper lip and forehead and trying not to worry about Mama. An insidious sleepiness crept over me—I'd been up all night at the hospital—and to banish it, I turned my mind to practicalities. Nick would see to Mama's trailer in her absence, so I wouldn't have to deal with that. I hadn't been able to reach my older sister, Carlota, in Minneapolis either last night or this morning; it seemed to me that the last time we'd talked she'd said something about a weekend conference with some fellow sociologists up in Duluth, but I couldn't recall exactly when that was to take place. No matter, I'd try her again anyway before I went back to the hospital. And maybe I should cancel my dinner date with my boyfriend, Dave Kirk— well, tentative date, providing he got back as scheduled from the mysterious trip he'd gone off on four days ago. It was lucky I'd arranged to take the next week off in order to use up some of my accumulated vacation days; before, it had seemed a luxury I could ill afford, but now . . .

A man climbed up on the platform, set a sheaf of papers on the podium, and began to shuffle through them. He was short, some-what tubby, totally bald, and dressed in a red shirt and loud red-and-blue-plaid pants. The auctioneer? I wondered. He wasn't what I had expected. Actually I didn't *know* what I had expected, but this refugee from a golf course wasn't it. As I stared at him, the last-minute browsers began to drift over and find seats, and there were a few moments of chairs scraping and catalogs rustling and people coughing before all quieted down.

Finally the man looked up. He had little piggy eyes and a cheru-bic mouth, and his bald head was shiny with sweat. He surveyed the crowd for a moment and then said, quiet as a college professor, "Good afternoon. My name is Al Doolittle, and I'm your auction-eer here at the Cabrillo Auction Center. Before we get under way with today's sale, I'd like to fill you in on how I'm going to run things."

I stifled a giggle. He reminded me of a waiter in a trendy restau-rant, the kind who introduces himself and then begins to reel off the list of specials that he's frantically memorized fifteen minutes before. Instead of dinner choices, the auctioneer presented us with a set of rules and then began describing Item Number One, a ten-piece lot of Early-American glass novelties that included hats, a lady's slipper, something called a "witch ball," and a milk-glass chicken. I checked the catalog and was disappointed to see that the first of the items I'd marked to bid on—the convent chairs—would not come up until Number Eighteen.

I was not bored in the meantime, though. Al the Auctioneer kept the bidding moving, and after some spirited offers and counteroffers, a dapper-looking gentleman with white hair became the proud possessor of the box of oddly shaped glass objects. I then watched an elderly couple claim an equally aged Singer sewing machine in an oak cabinet. Two obviously gay men chortled over their success in purchasing a Sheraton chest of drawers. A young woman beamed at her new set of pink Depression glassware. A couple barely out of their teens lovingly stroked a carved Chinese chest that I suspected would do duty as a hope chest. When the convent chairs finally came up, I was first with the opening minimum bid of a hundred dollars. However, after several quick exchanges, I was bested by a man in a tan suit. I comforted myself with the thought that anyone with such a cool manner and flinty, appraising eyes could only be an antiques dealer, and thus more practiced at bidding and better financed than I.

Number Twenty-seven, the dining table, also went to the "gentleman in tan," as Al the Auctioneer called him. When I turned to look at the successful bidder, who lounged against a pillar directly behind the last row of chairs, I could have sworn that he smirked at me. I narrowed my eyes and pursed my lips, annoyed. From the types of bids the man in tan was making, he obviously dealt in Hispanic antiques and would probably bid on the marriage coffer, too. *My* marriage coffer. Well, we'd just see if he'd get his hands on that!

When the little chest was brought to the platform for the bidding, I studied its fine carving and lustrous dark wood. The crucifix pattern was sharply defined, and the brass fittings had the natural patina of age. Yes, I wanted this piece for the museum—and I was not going to blunder in as I had before. Cleverly I held back, allowing the man in the tan suit to make the opening move—the minimum bid requested, fifty dollars.

"We have fifty," Al Doolittle said. "Do I hear seventy-five?"

I hesitated, to see if anyone else was interested.

Al said, "Come on, folks, don't get me nervous. We can't let this honey of a chest go for the minimum, now can we?"

"Seventy-five," I said.

14

"We have seventy-five. Do I hear one hundred?"

I glanced back at the man in the tan suit and saw him raise his catalog.

"One hundred now. We have one hundred," Al said. "Let's go for one-twenty-five. Come on, folks, let's get this auction moving."

Casually I raised my catalog.

"The little lady in the front row bids one-twenty-five. Any advance to one-fifty?"

A woman in the third row said "One-thirty-five."

Al looked so stunned that his pudgy features quivered. *"One-thirty-five?* Is that all we hear for this honey of a chest? Come on, let's get this auction *going!"*

"One-fifty," I said.

"Thank you, ma'am. One-fifty, folks. You heard it. Any advance on this bid? Ah, yes, the gentleman in tan is indicating he'll advance to one-seventy-five. Any further advances?"

I looked down at the scribbled notes in my catalog, which said I'd decided not to go higher than two hundred-and-fifty for the marriage coffer. I said, "Two hundred."

Al the Auctioneer looked elated. He bounced up and down on the balls of his feet, his double chins jiggling. "We have two hundred!" Then he turned to the chest and ran his hand over its dark satiny finish. "Look at this piece, folks. It's a beauty. At two hundred, we're practically giving it away." He paused, looked around. "Ah, the gentleman in tan will advance to two-twenty-five."

I turned to look at the man. This time I was sure he smirked. Quickly I said "Two-fifty."

"Now we're going again. Two-fifty. Do I hear an advance to three hundred?"

"Advance," the voice from the back of the room said firmly.

I looked over my shoulder and glared. The man smiled and nodded at me. *No way, mister,* I thought. *There's no way you're getting my marriage coffer.*

I looked back down at the catalog, at the figure "$250" printed in ink. But that figure was based on what I'd decided to pay when I'd hoped to buy not only the chest but also the chairs and dining table. Surely now I could go higher. . . .

"Three-fifty," I said.

Al nodded approvingly, bobbling his chins at me. "The lady in the front row says three-fifty. Do I hear four hundred?"

I sucked in my breath and glanced back at the man in the tan suit. There was no way I could go higher than four hundred.

The man paused for a moment, then smiled at me and remained silent.

I let out my breath in a long sigh.

"Three-seventy-five," a female voice said.

Outraged, I swiveled in my chair. The woman in the third row who had bid earlier—a well-dressed matronly type—sat primly clutching her rolled catalog. I'd done all the work, and now *she* wanted to reap the rewards!

"Four hundred," I said.

This time Al danced a little jig. "The lady in the front row is determined. Do I hear an advance on four hundred?"

Silence.

"This is an extremely fine piece for only four hundred dollars. Do I hear an advance to four-ten?"

The only sound was the whir of the electric ceiling fans.

Al's smile faded. The fleshy folds of his face drooped. He looked like a big baby getting ready to cry. "Do I hear an advance to four-ten?" he repeated.

No one spoke.

Al sighed. "I am going to sell it," he said heavily. "For the second time . . . and the third time . . . and the final time. . . . " Then he looked down at me, and his features did a quick reversal, into a huge, delighted grin.

"Okay, little lady," he said, "you're going to take it away!"

TWO

"AND THEN," I said to Mama, "the dealer had the nerve to come up and congratulate me on my successful bid on the marriage coffer—*even though I had paid too much for it!* Can you imagine?"

Mama's lips twitched in a pale imitation of a smile.

"Dealers," I said in disgust, sounding for all the world like a jaded auction-goer.

Mama was silent.

I frowned and glanced at Nick, who was leaning against the wall next to the window. He shrugged and peered through the slats of the blinds at the parking lot three stories below. Nick didn't look as confident or cheerful as when I'd left for the auction. That worried me more than Mama's unaccustomed silence and was the reason I'd been chattering on about the auction.

It was after four o'clock, and the light that filtered through the blinds had a rich, golden quality. Mama lay on her back, her long gray hair coiled against her pillow, her covers pulled as taut as those on the semiprivate room's other, empty bed. There were flowers on the bureau: a large arrangement of pink and white carnations from Mama's friends at the trailer park, yellow roses from Nick, and my own spray of violets. From time to time Mama's eyes would stray to them, and an expression of bewilderment would cross her face, as if she were wondering how they—and she—came to be here.

The silence in the little white room was making me nervous. I said, "I tried to call Carlota again before I came over here, but she still wasn't home. I think that conference in Duluth *was* this weekend. I could check with University information up there; maybe they'd know—"

"You must not bother Carlota while she is working," Mama said.

"Working!" I laughed, but even to me it sounded hollow. "I know what those sociologists do at their conferences: eat and drink too much, and swap lies about . . . about deviant social groups," I finished lamely.

"Carlota works hard," Mama said.

"Yes, but she also plays hard." My sister is one of the most energetic people I know. She throws herself into everything—teaching, research, writing, beer-drinking—with total abandon. And as proof that this all-or-nothing approach works, she'd earned her Ph.D. in three-and-a-half years and had gone on to a good job at the University of Minnesota. This fall she would be up for her associate professorship, and, true to form, Carlota was fully confident of receiving the promotion.

Mama continued to stare at the ceiling.

I said, "Anyway, when I get hold of her, I'm sure she'll want to come out. It'll be good to see her again—"

"No," Mama said.

"It *won't* be good to see her?"

"I do not want her to come."

"What, you expect her to stay in Minneapolis when you—"

"I do not want her to come." Mama enunciated every word clearly, as if she were speaking to a small child. "Enough fuss has already been made. I do not want Carlota wasting her money on airplane fare."

I glanced at Nick. He shrugged again, his brow furrowed, his eyes watchful.

"If Carlota wants to come," I said, "I don't think we can stop her."

"You will find a way," Mama said.

"*I* will?"

She turned stern eyes to me, and for a moment she looked almost herself. "You will." Then she went back to her contemplation of the ceiling.

I watched her for a moment, and then shifted uncomfortably on the hard chair, looking at my watch. We were waiting for the doctor to arrive and give us the test results. He'd promised to be here at four, but he was late.

Again the silence was making me nervous. Nick was no help; he kept looking out between the slats of the blind, as rapt as if one of the nurses were doing a striptease in the parking lot. After a minute I got up and went to read the card that had come with the flowers from the people at the trailer park. They had all signed it: the

Walters, Mary Jaramillo, Nick's gang of "old fogies" with whom he jogged every morning, even the new park manager. Someone—probably Mary, who was clever with sketching—had drawn a caricature of Mama above the sticky-sweet preprinted get-well message and had written, "We have a beer cooling for you, Gabriela." I was glad that in her retirement my mother had found such staunch friends—to say nothing of a nice boyfriend.

I had just returned to my chair when the doctor, George Ruiz, came in. He was an older man, close to sixty, and I'd known him all my life; Dr. George had delivered both Carlota and me in the back bedroom of the little stucco house where I still lived. He'd made us laugh at our childhood chicken pox bumps, counseled us through the teenage acne stage, and—reluctantly—prescribed the Pill when we'd been in college. Just seeing him standing there in his rumpled white coat, with a stethoscope hanging out of one pocket and his gray hair tousled, made me feel better about Mama. She was in good hands.

Dr. George nodded to Nick and me, then went over to the bed and looked down at Mama. "How are you feeling, Gabriela?"

"All right."

"Mmm. Any pain?"

"No." But her voice was close to a whisper, and her eyes remained fixed on the ceiling. She didn't demand to know when she could go home, or chide him for keeping her here, or do any of the other things I normally would have expected of her.

Dr. George consulted the chart he held and said, "Well, Gabriela, we're going to have to keep you here a little longer. The ulcer is bleeding, and it could perforate. It should be taken care of right away."

Mama turned her head slowly. "You mean, I have to have an operation?"

"Yes, and as soon as possible. I've scheduled it for tomorrow morning."

Mama's face seemed even whiter, her eyes very large. "How did this happen?" she asked. "I've never been sick a day."

"You've had frequent indigestion attacks, haven't you?"

"Yes, but—"

"You've probably had the ulcer for years. A lot of people wrongly attribute the burning sensation it causes to simple indigestion. Have you been constipated?"

Mama glanced at Nick. As far as she was concerned, ladies didn't talk about such things in front of gentlemen—not even close gentlemen friends. "Yes," she finally said.

"Sick to your stomach a lot?" Dr. George asked.

"Well, sometimes."

"You see?"

"I still don't believe it. Isn't an ulcer one of those . . . psychological things you do to yourself?"

"You mean psychosomatic. Stress is a factor in it, yes."

"Then, I can't have one. I don't have any stress."

Dr. George's eyes moved to me, and the laugh lines around them crinkled. "Nonsense, Gabriela. You've had plenty of stress in your time. You raised Elena and Carlota, didn't you?"

"But they're grown now, and all right—so far."

"You see?"

"I don't worry about them. Except when Elena gets mixed up in murder."

"And that's happened twice in the past year. No wonder you have an ulcer."

"Oh," I said, "so now I'm to blame for Mama's condition."

Dr. George grinned. "That's what children are for."

"What, for getting ulcers?"

"No, for blaming our own problems on."

I didn't know how to take that, so I got up and went over by the bureau to sulk. Mama didn't seem to notice.

Dr. George continued to talk with her for a few minutes, describing the procedure and the recovery period. Mama watched the ceiling the whole time; I wasn't sure if she comprehended what he said or not. When he finally left, the silence in the room stretched so taut that I thought I might scream.

Instead I said, "Mama, it won't be so bad. By this time tomorrow it'll be over and . . . "

She looked at me, and I saw bewilderment in her face. "I do not understand how this could happen," she said.

"What do you mean?"

"I have never been sick a day."

"Mama, Dr. George said—"

"I have *never* been sick."

And I have never been able to argue with my mother. I just nodded.

20

"I think," she added, "I would like to be alone now."

"All right," I said.

"Do you want me to stay, Gabriela?" Nick asked.

"Thank you, no. I want to be all alone."

Nick went over and kissed her on the forehead, then crossed to me, put a hand on my shoulder, and began steering me toward the door. "We'll come back after dinner, then."

"No."

He stopped. "Gabriela—"

"No. Come tomorrow before the operation. Tonight I wish to be by myself."

"If that's what you want," Nick said, "we'll wait until then."

We went out and down the hall to the elevator. Nick pushed the button, and we waited in silence. When we had gotten on the car and its doors had shut, I said, "Nick, she's in terrible shape."

He nodded, looking very worried now.

"Nick, what are we going to do?"

"Be here for her tomorrow."

"But—"

"Let it be, Elena. It's out of our hands." He touched my shoulder again, his fingers warm and comforting.

When we stepped out of the hospital into the waning spring sunlight, I said, "What are you going to do now?"

"Go home and have a run. It'll take my mind off things. What about you—what do you plan to do?"

"Go home."

"And . . . ?"

"Just go home."

THREE

I'D PLANNED TO drop the marriage coffer—which at present was wedged into the passenger side of my VW—at the museum before going home. But after leaving the hospital I was much too depressed to bother. Instead, I drove to my house; the chest could spend the night there with me.

The house is an old green stucco in a quiet residential area in the flatlands, below the dividing line where Santa Barbara's terrain and the property values rise. In the hills above me are the comfortable homes with splendid vistas for which the city is renowned. From up there on a clear day you have a sweeping view of the channel and its islands, undimmed by the pall of smog that most people associate with Southern California. In contrast, I don't have any view at all—except for old Mrs. Nunez across the street peering through her curtains, usually at me. But I do have a giant fuchsia plant cascading gracefully over a newly repaired trellis on my front porch, an ancient pepper tree to sit under in the backyard, and five rooms that, while small, are mine alone. Owning the house in which I was born always gives me a comforting sense of roots—and comfort was what I badly needed that night.

When I pulled up, several of the neighborhood kids were taking turns hopping up and down my front walk on a pogo stick. They scattered when I parked in the driveway—I have the reputation of an ogre—but I corralled Donny Hernandez and made him help me carry the little chest inside. Donny is the neighborhood fat kid, and he usually can be found wistfully watching the others, who never ask him to play. I don't waste any sympathy on him, however, because I suspect Donny will eventually have the last laugh; about a year before I'd found him perched in my pepper tree, reading, and after my initial concern for the heavily burdened branch subsided, I noted that his book was a thick paperback on creative investments. Someday, I am sure, Donny will return to the old

23

neighborhood in a fancy car and show everybody that fat can be beautiful.

We set the chest in the living room, and I gave Donny a couple of quarters that would probably become the cornerstone of an impressive blue-chip portfolio. Then I threw open some windows, changed into jeans and a shirt, and returned to look over my new acquisition. It was really a good piece, highly representative of the style favored by the dons and their ladies, and I was sure Rudy Lopcz would be delighted. He and I had worked hard to convince the museum's board of directors to okay the expenditures for the furniture. While the museum had originally been founded to educate Americans on the arts of Mexico, I'd recently decided to gradually shift that emphasis to the arts of Mexican-Americans, and the display of furnishings was one of several planned steps in that direction.

I ran my fingers over the rough-hewn wood of the chest, then lifted its humpbacked lid and looked inside. It was empty except for an old-fashioned, rusted hairpin. Then I tried the shallow drawer below the upper compartment. It was locked, and although it was fitted with a hammered-brass keyhole, I couldn't find any key. Of course that didn't matter for purposes of the museum's display, but it annoyed me all the same. I'd have to call the auction house on Monday and ask if perhaps the key had somehow gotten separated from the chest.

There was a knock on the screen door. I went over and peered through the mesh. Dave Kirk—lieutenant with the Santa Barbara police department and my current boyfriend—stood there. I felt a rush of pleasure and said, "Oh, you're back!"

As soon as Dave stepped inside, I could tell there was something wrong. He didn't kiss me or smile or ask me how I was. In fact, he didn't seem to want to look at me, and his brown eyes were troubled, the set of his mouth grim. When I'd first seen Dave, I'd thought him a nondescript, unreadable Anglo; his appearance was all brown and bland, and his manner—except when crossed, which I had managed to do within a few seconds of our meeting—was mild and low-key. But as our relationship had deepened and we'd become friends and then lovers, I'd learned to read him very well— every nuance of expression, every tone of voice. And what I was reading now was not encouraging.

"How was your trip?" I asked.

"Fine."

"Can I get you a beer?"

"No, thanks." He looked around the room, his eyes briefly stopping at the marriage coffer, but he didn't comment on it. "Listen, Elena," he said after a few seconds, "I really can't stay. I just came over because there's something I have to tell you."

A coldness began to settle on me. It had to be bad news, and I wasn't sure how much more of that I could take today. "Yes?" I said.

"You've probably wondered where I was the last four days."

"The question has crossed my mind, yes."

"I was up in Oregon—Rockaway. It's a small city on the coast."

"Why did you go there?"

He hesitated, and then his jaw became even more set and he went on. "There was a job open. Chief of police. I went up to interview, and they hired me."

"Oh. Well. Congratulations." I was having difficulty taking the information in. Oregon. It seemed very far away. I'd only been there once, on a driving trip with my mother, when she'd insisted on stopping at every myrtlewood factory along Route One. I tried to remember anything else about the state but couldn't. "So, when do you start?" I asked.

"In two weeks. I called the department and gave notice before I drove back down here."

Two weeks! So little time. "Oh," I said. And then I waited. It was several seconds before I realized he hadn't said he was sorry he was moving away, or that he'd miss me, or that I should come up to visit. And when I looked into his chocolate brown eyes, I saw an uncharacteristic nervousness, coupled with a kind of resolve.

He said, "I know this is sudden, Elena, but I think it's the best move for both of us. You and I . . . well, it just hasn't been working out."

I stared at him, a panicky, fluttery feeling in my stomach. "What?"

"I really think it's for the best," he said. "And I also think it would be wise if we didn't see each other again before I leave."

"It hasn't been working out," I repeated flatly.

The tension in his jaw relaxed somewhat. "I'm glad you agree with me."

Was he deliberately misinterpreting my comment? I wondered.

Couldn't he see how stunned I was? What did he mean, anyway—not working out?

Dave went on, "I'll always remember the times we've had together. They've been good times. And I'll always remember you."

I put a hand to my forehead, feeling dizzy and hot and cold at the same time. I wanted to shout, to protest, to insist this couldn't be happening. I wanted to demand explanations: *What* wasn't working out? How long had he felt this way? Was there someone else? But he sounded so definite. And I had my pride. I didn't want to let him see how much he was hurting me.

I said, "Yes, I feel the same way, Dave. And I certainly wish you luck with the new job."

Relief flooded his face then, and he smiled—the warm, crinkly grin I'd always loved. Loved? No . . . yes . . . yes, dammit, I *loved* him! And he was just walking away and leaving me as if I were some casual date.

Tears rose to my eyes, and when Dave saw them, the smile faded. He put out a hand. "Elena, don't."

I brushed at my lashes and looked away, a painting on the wall blurring to a meaningless swirl of colors. I would not let Dave see me cry, would not allow him to know how much pain he was causing me.

"Oh, Dave," I said thickly, "you know I'm no good at saying good-bye. When I was a kid, we'd go to the airport and watch the planes take off, and I'd end up bawling my head off because a bunch of strangers were going away on them."

He laughed, a lightness and freedom in the sound, and I knew he believed me. I was glad I'd lied to him, glad he couldn't know what pain was gathering inside of me.

"You'd better go now," I said.

He stepped forward, took my hand, kissed me on the cheek. Then he turned and went through the screen door. On the front walk, he started to whistle tonelessly.

I backed up, weak-kneed. Sat in my old rocking chair. Waited until I heard his car pull away from the curb. And then I started to cry.

I couldn't understand it. Everything had been fine with us. We hardly ever argued. We'd been good together in bed. We'd laughed and done enjoyable things. My mother and Nick had forgiven him for being an Anglo; all my friends liked him. His friends and colleagues at the department liked me. I was learning to eat pancakes for breakfast; he'd come to appreciate Mexican art. So what on earth had gone wrong? *Why* did he think it wasn't working out?

I sat there gripping the arms of the rocker and crying. In a few minutes my pain over Dave got all mixed up with my worry about Mama, and I rocked and cried and hiccuped and mumbled both of their names. Soon I could feel my eyes becoming hot and swollen. *Maldito!* I tried to stop crying, and when I realized I couldn't, I got up, went into the bathroom, stripped off my clothes, and got into the shower. Under normal circumstances that would have calmed me, but today nothing was normal. But at least I was being ecological, mingling my tears with the city water supply.

After a while the hot water ran out, and so did my tears. I felt dull, shaky, and a little sleepy. As I toweled off and put on my jeans and shirt, I realized I was also ravenously hungry.

In the kitchen, I took out peanut butter and spread it on a banana. After that I had a glass of milk and a cup of spiced apple yogurt. There were English muffins in the freezer; I toasted two of them and ate them with strawberry jam. I contemplated the jug of cheap white wine, but was afraid alcohol might make me cry again. Finally I ate half a cantaloupe and a handful of cashew nuts. Then I went back to the living room and sat down in the rocker.

Well, I told myself, *you've behaved like* un puerco gordo. *Now if you can just get mad and throw something, you'll be on the road to recovery.*

But I couldn't get mad. All I could do was huddle in the chair and feel very small and sad and alone. The sun had gone down, and the room was filled with shadows. I sat there until it was completely dark, and then I got up and turned on a light. And when I did, the marriage coffer caught my eye again.

I went over and stroked it, thinking back to the auction. At the time I'd been worried about Mama, but I'd still enjoyed myself, with no inkling of the further misfortune that was about to befall me. I sniffled, wondering if I'd ever have a good time again—and quickly realized I was being melodramatic.

I opened the lid of the chest, took the rusty hairpin out, and threw it in the wastebasket. There was a lot of dust in the compartment, so I went to the kitchen for a rag and began to clean it out. As I was scrubbing along the rear of the space, the edge of the rag caught on something. I gave it a tug, and it tore. Poking with my fingernail, I removed the fragment of fabric and saw that there was a crack in the wood. Not only had the auction house neglected to tell prospective buyers that the key was missing, but they'd also omitted the fact that the chest had been damaged. I sighed in exasperation and probed with my fingers to see how bad the crack was.

But it wasn't a crack at all; its edges felt smooth, beveled. I pushed my fingernail into it. The nail tore to the quick and I swore, putting my finger in my mouth and tasting blood. After a few seconds, I got my nail clipper from my purse and trimmed the nail's ragged edge, then used the fold-out file portion of the clipper on the crack in the chest. I wiggled it back and forth a little, and then a narrow three-inch-long piece of wood came loose and clattered to the bottom of the compartment.

I dropped the nail clipper next to the wood fragment and pushed my fingers through the little opening. They encountered a cylindrical metal object. When I pulled it out, I saw it was a brass key.

How clever of the cabinetmaker, I thought, and also how typical of furniture of that era. I remembered reading somewhere that the dons had been big on secreting their treasures, tucking away even inconsequential things like this key in well-concealed hidey-holes. Maybe there was more treasure in the drawer.

The thought was a fanciful one, and I expected the drawer to be empty. But when I unlocked it and looked in at a flat brown-leather folder, I started in surprise. I set the key down and took the folder over to my desk to examine it in better light.

The cracked leather was rough-grained, probably cowhide, and the folder had been bound together by a now-frayed brown cord. I opened it and found a sheaf of papers. They were yellowed, on a once-fine vellum letterhead that read in ornate script, "Carpenter and Quincannon, Professional Detective Services, Flood Building, Market Street, San Francisco." Below was what appeared to be a detective's report, dated April 1894. The hand in which it was written was angular and fine, incorporating all the whorls and flourishes popular before the turn of the century.

What a find! I thought. What a fascinating relic of the past! Dave would love this; I should call him—

And then I stopped, remembering I would never call Dave again. Gloom descended on me, threatening to destroy my pleasure in my discovery. To fend it off, I went back to my rocker and began reading.

Report of Investigator John F. Quincannon, in the Matter of Religious Artifacts Belonging to the Family of Don Esteban Velasquez

April 4. The offices of the above were visited by Felipe Velasquez, shortly past noon. Señor Velasquez recounted the facts surrounding his father's death during the Bear Flag Revolution, and stated that a cache of religious artifacts hidden during that time of strife had not been heretofore recovered by his family. However, he said, one artifact had at last been located. He requested aid in obtaining information as to the source of this particular artifact. It was his belief that an investigation might lead to the whereabouts of the remaining pieces.

It was like reading a mystery novel—only this had been written by the detective's own hand and had really happened. My pain over Dave's defection and my worry over Mama receded for the moment, and I quickly turned the page. . . .

PART II
1894

ONE

QUINCANNON WAS ALONE in the offices having his lunch—bread, cheese, strong coffee—and reading a temperance tract, when Señor Felipe Velasquez paid his visit.

It was a rare early-spring day in San Francisco, cloudless and warm. Quincannon had opened the window behind his desk, the one that overlooked Market Street and bore the painted words CARPENTER AND QUINCANNON, PROFESSIONAL DETECTIVE SERVICES. A balmy breeze off the Bay freshened the air in the room, made it seem almost fragrant. The city sounds that drifted in had a quality of sharpness that permitted each to be clearly identified: the passing rumble of a cable car, the clatter of a dray wagon, the calls of vendors hawking fresh oysters and white bay shrimp in the market across the street, the booming horn of one of the fast coastal steamers as it drew into or away from the Embarcadero. The air and the sounds made Quincannon restless. It was much too fine a day to waste indoors. A day, instead, for a carriage ride to Ocean Beach, or a ferry trip to Marin County, or perhaps a stroll in Golden Gate Park—all in the company of an attractive woman. A day that stirred a man's blood and gave rise to amorous thoughts of the mildly indecent sort.

He wondered if Sabina was weakening.

She showed no outward signs of it. Their relationship was to be strictly business, she had said more than once. But she had consented to spend a social evening with him, also more than once, and there was a softness in the way she looked at him sometimes, a softness in her voice even when she rejected his mild advances. Perhaps she *was* weakening. Perhaps underneath her reserve, she felt toward him as he felt toward her and it was only a matter of time before she agreed to become his lover. Or his wife. He had been a firm bachelor all his life; he had considered marriage an unsuitable undertaking for an operative of the United States Secret

Service, a position he had held for fourteen years, and he considered it an equally unsuitable one for a flycop, his new profession for the past five months. Still and all, if it was the only way to possess Sabina; warm, smiling Sabina . . .

Quincannon sighed, ate a wedge of cheese and sourdough, and forced his attention back to the temperance tract. It was another of those written and printed by Ebenezer Talbot, one of the founders of the True Christian Temperance Society. It bore the title "A Bibulous Evening with Satan" and was highly inflammatory in its denunciation of the evils of drink. Two weeks ago, when Sabina had found him reading a different one of Ebenezer's handiworks, "Drunkards and Curs: The Truth About Demon Rum," she had said in surprise, "I must say, John, you're a man of excesses. For more than a year you saturated yourself with alcohol, and now you've joined a temperance union." But this was not the case, as he had explained to her. The other founders of the True Christian Temperance Society had hired him to investigate Ebenezer Talbot, whom they suspected of having embezzled Society funds. Quincannon had subsequently confirmed these suspicions; he had also discovered—and three days ago obtained evidence to prove—that Ebenezer had used his ill-gotten funds to finance the manufacture and distribution of bootleg whiskey to miners in the Mother Lode. Quincannon no longer needed to read temperance tracts, but he found himself buying and reading them just the same—those written by other individuals as well as by the amazing Ebenezer Talbot. They proved to be amusing light reading, a pleasant change from the volumes of poetry and short stories he customarily read for relaxation.

He was absorbed in the tract when the latch clicked and the door opened. He glanced up, expecting to see Sabina. The man who entered was slim, dark, gray-maned, with a neatly trimmed graying beard and the bearing of a Mexican aristocrat. He seemed uncomfortable in a black cutaway coat and matching trousers, as if *charro* garb would be more suited to his temperament; and in his left hand he carried a small carpetbag. His string tie was fastened with a turquoise clip in the shape of a bull's head; his sombrero was studded with silver conchas. The clothing and the turquoise and silver ornamentations suggested that this man, whoever he might be, was not a pauper.

Business at Carpenter and Quincannon, Professional Detective

34

Services had not been so good that Quincannon could afford to be blasé toward a prospective client who was well-dressed and apparently well-heeled. In rapid movements he covered the remains of his lunch with his napkin, opened one of the desk drawers and dropped the temperance tract into it, got to his feet, and came around the desk to greet the visitor.

He was a big man, Quincannon, and his own gray-flecked beard was thick and on the bushy side, giving him the look of a competent and well-mannered freebooter; he towered above the small-statured Mexican. He said, "Welcome, sir. Come right in."

"You are Señor John Quincannon?"

"I am. And you are . . . ?"

"Felipe Antonio Abregon y Velasquez." He spoke English well, with a precision that hinted at culture and breeding, and with a vaguely supercilious inflection. "Your name was given to me by Señor Adams at the California Commercial Bank."

Quincannon didn't know anyone named Adams at the California Commercial Bank. He said, "Yes, of course, Adams—we've been acquainted for years. Won't you have a seat, Señor Velasquez?"

Velasquez sat in one of the padded armchairs that faced the desk, placing the carpetbag on the floor beside him. Quincannon reoccupied his chair, opened the humidor he kept on the desk, and held it out. "Cigar?"

"I will have one of mine."

Velasquez produced a leather case from inside his cutaway coat, extracted a green-tinged cigarillo that he lighted carefully. The smoke he exhaled was rich and fragrant. Quincannon arranged his features into what he calculated to be a servile expression. "How may I help you?" he asked gravely.

"I have come on a matter of the utmost importance to my family," Velasquez said. "Señor Adams said you are known as a man of honor and discretion."

"Honor and discretion. Yes, indeed."

"I hope that is so. You are familiar with the name of Don Esteban Velasquez?"

"Ah, no, I'm afraid not."

"He was my father. In the days of *los ranchos grandes* he owned one of the largest grants in the Santa Ynez Valley, not far from Santa Barbara—Rancho Rinconada de los Robles. I was born there. I still live at the hacienda, what remains of it. But the land

. . . it is a mere fraction of the original grant, all that was left to my family after my father was murdered."

"Murdered?"

"During what you call the Bear Flag Revolution, by a detachment of John Fremont's soldiers." Velasquez said this with such bitterness and hatred that Quincannon wondered if, beneath the gentlemanly exterior, the man harbored a deep resentment toward all Americans.

"I see."

"Do you? Perhaps not. I will tell you the details of my father's death and the destruction of his property. They are important to my reason for coming here."

"By all means, Señor Velasquez."

Velasquez told his story in short, clipped sentences drenched in bitterness. Quincannon was a careful listener, and he thought that the account of the Americans' attack on Rancho Rinconada de los Robles was highly colored and possibly lacking facts as well as perspective. Nevertheless, he found it interesting—particularly so when Velasquez explained about his father's collection of religious artifacts. He took copious notes, as he always did on any investigation, from beginning to end, the easier to order all the facts for the report he would later write.

"The artifacts were hidden somewhere on the rancho," Velasquez said, "either at the hacienda or at the pueblo nearby. If Don Esteban did not hide them himself, he would have entrusted the task to the padre of San Anselmo de las Lomas, the pueblo church. Padre Urbano was also murdered during the siege. There were no survivors, other than the women and children who were evacuated before Fremont's butchers came."

"Were the artifacts later recovered?"

"No, they were not. At least not by members of my family. Their hiding place has never been found."

"But surely your father or the padre provided some sort of written record . . . "

"The day before the attack Don Esteban wrote a letter to my mother in Mexico City. She had taken me there ten months earlier, before the outbreak of war. I have always believed the location of the artifacts was included in this letter. But it never reached my mother. The woman to whom it was entrusted, a mestiza servant, gave it to the captain of a loyalist schooner at Refugio Beach; we

36

later learned the schooner was sunk by an American gunboat before it reached Mexico. The letter was lost with the captain."

"And there was no other record?" Quincannon asked.

"If there was, it was destroyed or confiscated by the revolutionists." Velasquez made an angry slashing gesture with his cigarillo, as if it were a sword aimed downward at John Fremont's neck. "Part of the hacienda and most of the pueblo were blown apart by cannon or damaged by fire."

"Is it possible Fremont's soldiers found the artifacts?"

"Possible, yes. There was much looting done. But my family and our emissaries were unable to locate any of the artifacts, or word of any of them, in nearly fifty years."

"Gold and silver can easily be melted down," Quincannon pointed out.

"Of course. But only half of the artifacts were made of gold and silver. The rest are holy books, devotional paintings, icons. At least some of those should have come to our attention."

"Then, you believe they are still hidden?"

"That has always been my belief, yes. And my mother's, to the day of her death five years ago. Many searches were mounted after the war ended and we returned from Mexico. Our debts were great; we had little money, and the sale of the artifacts would have prevented much of our land from being sold at auction."

"So it would seem they were hidden *too* well."

"So it would seem."

"Perhaps not, though," Quincannon said. "Or am I wrong in assuming one or more of the artifacts have now surfaced? That one, in fact, is in that carpetbag alongside your chair?"

Surprise stiffened Velasquez, bent him forward. "*Diablos!* How do you know this?"

Quincannon said sagely, "An elementary deduction." Not so long ago he had read a volume of detective stories by a British physician named Conan Doyle; Doyle's detective used phrases such as that, and Quincannon liked the sound of them. "You wouldn't have explained about the artifacts if they weren't all or part of your reason for consulting me. Nor would you have brought a carpetbag here unless it contains something you wish to show me. And you could hardly want a private detective to mount a blind search for treasure buried since 1846. The logical conclusion, then, is that one or more of the artifacts have been located and you wish me to

37

investigate the circumstances surrounding the recovery. And to determine if other of the artifacts can also be recovered. Correct?"

Velasquez seemed reluctantly impressed. "That is it exactly," he said. "You *must* be a detective of uncommon skill, señor."

"Others have been kind enough to say so." Quincannon was enjoying himself. Perhaps it was the winy air, the sounds and smells of spring; he felt very self-confident today, in a whimsical sort of way. "Now then, about the recovered artifacts. How many were there?"

"Only one. A statue of the Virgin Mary."

Velasquez lifted the carpetbag, opened it, and took out a large cloth sack closed at the top by a drawstring. The content of the sack was clearly heavy, and Quincannon saw why when it was revealed: the statue was some fourteen inches in height, several inches wide, and made of what appeared to be pure gold, dulled now by age and showing the gouges and scratches of careless handling. Almost reverently Velasquez passed it across the desk. Quincannon turned it over and around in his hands. It was of the Holy Virgin standing in an attitude of prayer, hands below her chin, eyes closed. On the flat bottom of the base, etched into the gold, were the words FRANCISCO PORTOLÁ POR DON ESTEBAN VELASQUEZ, and the date 1843.

At length Quincannon set the statue down on his desk, equidistant between Velasquez and himself. His whimsical feeling had vanished; something about the statue had turned his thoughts serious. Still looking at it, he said, "Where was it found?"

"Here in San Francisco. In a curio shop on McAllister Street owned by a man named Duff."

"Luther Duff?"

"Yes. Do you know him?"

"Only by reputation."

"He is not honest?"

"Occasionally he is," Quincannon said. "Did he contact you about the statue?"

"No, no, it was found in his shop by a man named Barnaby O'Hare."

"And Barnaby O'Hare is—?"

"A historian. He is writing a history of *los ranchos grandes*."

"A friend of yours?"

"Hardly," Velasquez said, as if the very idea of friendship with a

38

gringo offended him. "I permitted him a short stay at Rancho Rinconada de los Robles three months ago and provided him with information for his book."

"Does he reside in San Francisco?"

"No. In Los Angeles. He has been here for two weeks, examining documents and photographs in your Bancroft Library."

"He came upon the statue by accident, then?"

"Yes."

"And notified you immediately?"

"By telegram."

"You'd told him the story of the hidden artifacts?"

Velasquez shrugged. "He knew it when he came to me. It is not common knowledge, but neither is it a secret. My family has spent too much money, and employed too many men, in the search for the artifacts."

"What were your actions when you received Mr. O'Hare's wire?"

"I made immediate arrangements for the statue's purchase."

"With O'Hare?"

"Yes. And with an official of the California Commercial Bank. That was three days ago. I arrived myself only yesterday."

"What was Duff's asking price?"

"Two thousand dollars."

"A pretty sum," Quincannon observed.

"I would have paid twice that amount."

"You are satisfied the statue is authentic?"

"Completely satisfied. The inscription on the base could not have been forged."

"Where did Duff obtain it? Would he say?"

"He claimed it was included in a lot he purchased at auction two years ago in San José. He does not know who owned it or from where it came, he said." Velasquez scowled as he rubbed out the remains of his cigarillo in Quincannon's abalone-shell ashtray. "But from what you have told me about him, he might have lied."

"He might well have. Luther Duff would lie to God Himself for a twenty-dollar gold piece. There are ways of dealing with the likes of Mr. Duff, however—ways of finding out the truth of a matter." Quincannon smiled his capable, reassuring smile. "At which hotel are you stopping, sir?"

"The Bellevue," Velasquez said, "but I have already checked out. Tonight I will be returning to Santa Barbara. As much as I would prefer to remain here until your investigation is completed, there is business that demands my attention at home."

"Will you be traveling by train?"

"Of course."

"Departing when?"

"Seven o'clock."

"I will meet you on the platform at six-thirty," Quincannon promised, "with a report of my talk with Luther Duff and an outline of how I will proceed."

"Bueno."

Contractual matters and the exchange of fifty dollars in greenbacks were quickly consummated. It was while Velasquez was resacking the gold statue of the Virgin Mary that Sabina returned from an errand that had taken her to the Wells Fargo office on Sutter Street.

She appeared pleased to find a new client on the premises and the crisp sheaf of greenbacks on Quincannon's desk. But her pleasure lasted only until Quincannon introduced her as his partner, the Carpenter of Carpenter and Quincannon, Professional Detective Services, and she observed the expression of incredulity on Velasquez's walnut-brown face, heard him say in scornful tones, "Partner? A *woman*?"

Sabina said stiffly, "And why not, Señor Velasquez?"

"Women should not be detectives." He spoke to Quincannon rather than to her, and there was censure in his voice; it was plain he thought less of Quincannon's judgment than he had before Sabina's arrival. "Their place is in the home—"

"Faugh!" Sabina said. "What old-fashioned nonsense! I'll have you know that before Mr. Quincannon and I opened this agency, I was an operative of the Pinkerton Agency in Denver . . . "

"And a fine one she was," Quincannon said. "Progress, Señor Velasquez. Changing times. The new century is only six years hence." He had taken Velasquez's arm and was gently steering him and his carpetbag away from Sabina, toward the door. "There are tasks a woman can perform that a man cannot, even in the detective business. Many such tasks. Surely you understand, a man of your intellect and insight."

"Women have no place in the affairs of men—"

"Thank you so much for placing your trust in me. A decision you won't regret, I assure you. Until six-thirty this evening, then?

40

Good-bye, Señor Velasquez, have a pleasant afternoon." And Quincannon, smiling, nudged him through the door and shut it quickly before Velasquez could offer another comment.

When he looked at Sabina, he saw that there were spots of color on her cheeks the size of silver dollars. She said between her teeth, "What an insufferable, smug, pompous—"

"Now, now. Progressive ideas are foreign to gentlemen of the Mexican aristocracy. Señor Velasquez is a victim of his lineage."

"Señor Velasquez," Sabina said, "is an ass."

Quincannon moved to his desk and gestured at the sheaf of greenbacks. "Fifty dollars, my dear, and the promise of considerably more. He may be an ass, but he isn't a poor one."

"Mm. Just what is it he hired you to do?"

Quincannon explained. Sabina continued to look ruffled and annoyed, but he was not displeased by this. He thought that she was radiant when she was aroused. She was not a beautiful woman, or even a pretty one in any conventional sense; but at thirty-one she possessed a mature attractiveness. There was strength in the shape of her face and mouth, intelligence in eyes the dark color of the sea at dusk. Her hair, layered high on her head and fastened with a jeweled comb (a fashion he found exotic and appealing), shone a sleek blue-black in the sunlight slanting in through the windows at her back. And her figure was a fine, slim one, handsomely draped today in a lacy white shirtwaist and a Balmoral skirt. Looking at her as he spoke, he found his thoughts stirring, shifting again toward those mildly indecent speculations he had indulged in earlier.

"Do you really suppose the statue can be traced to its previous owner?" she asked.

"Perhaps. That depends on what can be learned from Luther Duff."

"You're going to see him now?"

"I am. I should be back by three." He hesitated. "Sabina, have you plans for this evening?"

"Why do you ask?"

"Well, I had in mind dinner at the Old Poodle Dog, opera bouffe at the Tivoli, coffee and cordials at the Hoffman Café—"

"—and a private carriage ride in the moonlight?"

He pretended to be stung. "I had no such intention."

"Didn't you? John, will you never give up?"

"Never. And will you never give in?"

A smile played at the corners of her mouth. The smile encouraged him. He said, "A fine spring evening should not be spent alone in one's rooms."

"What makes you think I plan to spend it alone in my rooms?"

Now he *was* stung. "Who is he?"

"Whom?"

"Your gentleman friend."

She laughed. "His name is John Quincannon and his persistence can be exasperating at times."

"Ah," he said, and smiled. "Ah, but he means well. You'll join me for dinner, then?"

"Yes, but not at the Old Poodle Dog. Such extravagance."

"Nothing is too extravagant for you, my dear."

"John's Grill will be fine."

"And the opera bouffe, the coffee and cordials?"

"Yes. But not the moonlight carriage ride."

"I had no such intention . . . "

"Oh, bosh," she said, but she was still smiling. She turned toward her desk across the room from his. "Go about your business, John, and let me go about mine."

Quincannon plucked his derby off the hat tree by the door, placed it on his head at a jaunty angle, winked at her boldly when he saw that she wasn't looking, and went out to the elevators. He felt fine. There was no longer any doubt in his mind; he was absolutely certain that spring had worked its magic on Sabina just as it had on him.

She *was* weakening. It was only a matter of time.

TWO

QUINCANNON RODE THE streetcar up Market to Van Ness, paused after disembarking to light his pipe, and walked to McAllister Street. There was considerable traffic today, as a result of the fine weather. The broad expanse of Van Ness Avenue was clogged with buggies, surreys, hansom cabs. Men and women in their spring finery strolled the tree-shaded sidewalks. Lovers, some of them, Quincannon noted slyly. He smiled at them, tipped his hat to the ladies. He wished he had thought to bring his stick with him this morning; young blades always carried a stick, and he felt like a young blade again, one with the promise of a clandestine evening just ahead.

No carriage ride in the moonlight, Sabina had said. Ah, but had she *meant* it?

Luther Duff's Curio Shop, as it was unimaginatively called, was in the second block of McAllister west of Van Ness, crowded among similar establishments. A small bell announced his entrance into a gloomy, cluttered interior that smelled of dust, mildew, and slow decay. Only one window was visible, and that so begrimed its glass was opaque; four strategically placed electric lights provided nearly all of the dim illumination. As far as Quincannon could tell, the premises were deserted.

He moved toward the rear, making his way between and around clusters of furniture. He recognized a French cabinet made of ebony panels inlaid with brass, a Spanish refectory table, a Dutch East Indies chest, a Tyrolean pine coffer, a black-lacquered Chinese wardrobe festooned with fire-breathing dragons. Other items caught his attention briefly in passing: a damascened suit of armor, shelves of dust-laden books, several clocks large and small, a trio of odd Aztec fetishes, a stuffed and molting peacock, a set of brightly enameled Japanese dishes, a wavy-bladed Malay kris, a collection of Florentine bronzes, an artillery bugle, a Georgian brass ship's compass, a case of tarnished silverware, a paint-splotched English saddle, an unmarked marble tombstone, and a yellow-varnished portrait of a fat nude woman who would have looked far more aesthetic, he thought, with her clothes on.

At the rear of the shop, a counter ran the full width like a barrier. Behind it was a massive, gilt-trimmed cash register on an oak stand, and behind that was a set of musty damask drapes that curtained off a back alcove. The draperies parted as Quincannon approached the counter and a short, round balding man of about fifty popped out. Even at first glance he was as unappetizing as a tainted oyster. He wore slyness and venality as openly as the garters on his sleeves and the moneylender's eyeshade across his forehead. The suddenness of his appearance made Quincannon think of a troll jumping out in front of an unwary traveler.

"Hello, hello," the troll said. Without his hands touching, he managed to convey the impression of briskly rubbing them together. "What is your pleasure, sir? I have bric-a-brac and curios of every type and description, from every culture and every nation. The new, the old, the mild, the exotic. Something for every taste, sir. And what is yours?"

"I am not a customer," Quincannon said. He made his voice sound gruff, authoritative. "Are you Luther Duff?"

"I am. If you aren't a customer, sir, then—?"

"An operative of the United States Secret Service." Quincannon produced his old Service badge and extended it across the counter, up close to Duff's somewhat warty features. "Boggs is my name, Evander Boggs."

The little troll went pale. He backed off a step, as if the badge were a lethal weapon. "Secret Service?" he said in a different voice. "I don't understand. What do you want with me?"

Instead of answering, Quincannon fixed him with a malevolent look and returned the badge to the pocket of his vicuña chesterfield. If the real Evander Boggs, who had been his superior in the San Francisco field office, knew that he had taken pains not to relinquish the badge upon his resignation from the Service, Boggs's great bulbous nose (one of his friends had once likened him to a keg of whiskey with the nose as its bung) would have glowed like a blacksmith's forge, as it always did when he was enraged. And if he knew that this was not the first time Quincannon had used his name and the badge under false pretenses, he would no doubt suffer an apoplectic seizure. But Quincannon had no intention of telling him. He was rather fond of Boggs, and by not telling him these things, he reasoned, he was safeguarding the old reprobate's health.

Duff said nervously, "Please, Mr. Boggs, what is it you want with me? I've done nothing to attract the attention of the United States government . . . "

"Haven't you?" Quincannon paused, and then said in sharp tones, "What do you know about the counterfeiting of 1840s eagles and half eagles?"

"Counterfeiting? Why . . . why . . . nothing, Mr. Boggs, nothing at all; I swear it!"

"Someone in our fair city has been manufacturing planchets— soldering thin sheets of gold around a piece of silver, so that the edges of the gold enclose the cheaper metal." Such planchets *had* been manufactured, as a matter of fact, but not recently and not in San Francisco. Quincannon had had a hand in ferreting out the koniakers and putting an end to their cleverness. "The five-dollar pieces bear the dates 1844 and 1845; the half eagle carries an 1843 zero mint-mark. You know nothing about any of this, eh, Mr. Duff?"

"No, no, nothing!"

"Both the silver and gold used in the bogus coins appear to have been obtained by melting down stolen valuables," Quincannon said. "Trinkets, statuary, and the like. Statuary in particular."

The troll stared back at him fearfully. "Statuary?"

"Gold statuary. Stolen round and about by thieves and sold to fencemen such as you."

"Fencemen, Mr. Boggs? I don't understand the term."

Quincannon laughed. "Come, come," he said. "The Service knows all about your fencing activities. So do the police. Why deny them?"

"Lies," Duff said. "Slanderous lies. Nothing has ever been proven. I have never once been arrested—"

"Until today, perhaps."

Duff's moist face was now the approximate hue of a blanched almond. "I swear upon my poor mother's grave, I know nothing about the counterfeiting of gold coins!"

"You *do* purchase gold statuary, don't you?"

"Yes. Curios of all types, yes, but never from thieves . . . "

"Do you melt down gold items for any reason?"

"Certainly not, Mr. Boggs. Certainly not."

"Well, then," Quincannon said, and made a sweeping gesture with one arm, "among all these impressive goods there should be at least one gold statue. That stands to reason, eh?"

"It would seem to, but—"

"But, Mr. Duff?"

"I . . . well, I haven't any left, you see . . . "

Quincannon said "Ah" and nodded implacably.

"But I *had* a gold statue until just yesterday. Had it for months, sir. A fine statue of the Virgin Mary."

"Did you, now?"

"Yes, yes. I sold it to the representatives of a Mr. Velasquez, from the southern part of the state. Respected gentlemen, these representatives. One is an official of the California Commercial Bank."

"Have you a record of this transaction?"

"Oh, yes, of course."

"Show it to me."

"Right away. I have it in my office. If you'll wait right here—"

"I will not. I prefer to keep you in sight." Quincannon patted the distinctive bulge under the right side of his coat—his Remington double-action Navy revolver. "Or my *sights,* if necessary," he added meaningfully.

The little troll swallowed, after the fashion of a cow swallowing its cud, and said, "You'll have no trouble from me, sir. I swear it on my poor mother's—"

"Lead on, Mr. Duff."

Duff turned toward the drapery at the rear. There was no break in the wall-to-wall counter that Quincannon could see; he swung himself over it with such quietness and agility that Duff gasped, startled to find him at his heels as he pushed through the drapery. On the other side was an impossibly cluttered office lighted by an electric lamp. Papers spilled off a battered rolltop desk; boxes and wrappings carpeted the floor; two-score different curios were piled in haphazard tiers on a pair of clawfoot tables. But as with many men who kept untidy premises, Duff seemed to know just where everything was. He produced a receipt book from under a mass of paper miscellany on the desk, licked his fingertips, flipped the pages rapidly, and then handed the book to Quincannon.

"There, sir," he said. "One gold statue of the Virgin Mary. Dated yesterday, as you see, and signed by Mr. Adams of the California Commercial Bank."

Quincannon pretended to study the carboned slip. At length he said, "Two thousand dollars is a handsome price."

"Very handsome. The largest single sale I have made this year. The statue was, or I should say is, of pure gold."

"Indeed? And you had this statue in your possession for months, you said?"

"Months, yes. I obtained it late last fall."

"Locally?"

"No. From a gentleman down south."

"Where down south?"

Duff hesitated, then said with some reluctance, "Santa Barbara."

Damn! Quincannon thought. "The gentleman's name?"

Another hesitation, longer this time. Quincannon gave him a steely-eyed look and patted his Remington again. Duff nibbled his lower lip like a rat nibbling cheese, coughed, nibbled some more, sighed, and said with even greater reluctance, "James Evans."

"A curio dealer like yourself?"

"Ah, no, not exactly."

"His business is what, then?"

"He is a . . . well, a procurer of goods for resale."

Quincannon smiled mirthlessly. "A thief, Mr. Duff?"

"No, no, an honest businessman. I do not buy from thieves . . . "

"So you've told me. Did this man Evans supply you with more than one such statue?"

"No. Only the one."

"He had no others?"

"None. I would have purchased them if he had."

"Where did he obtain the Virgin Mary?"

"He didn't reveal his source to me."

"And you have no idea what it was?"

"No, sir, no idea at all."

"Evans resides where in Santa Barbara?"

"On Anacapa Street. Number twelve hundred and six." Duff nibbled again at his lower lip. "Will you be going there to see him?"

"More than likely. The koniakers have a source for gold statuary somewhere in California. It may be that James Evans is not such an honest businessman after all."

"Oh, I'm certain he is," Duff said unconvincingly. "I've dealt with him for years. He is no more a counterfeiter than I am."

Quincannon smiled his mirthless smile and said nothing.

"You do believe me, don't you, Mr. Boggs? Counterfeiting is a fool's game. No, no, I would never cheat the government of our glorious country."

Quincannon maintained his silence a few seconds longer. Then he poked Duff in the chest with his forefinger, so suddenly that the little troll jumped, and said, "For your sake, you had best have told me the whole truth. If I find out you haven't . . . "

"I have, I swear I have. You're not going to arrest me?"

"Not today. But I will if I discover any discrepancy in what you've told me. Or if you make the mistake of sending a wire to James Evans."

"Wire?"

"Warning him about me."

"Oh, I wouldn't do that. No, no, I swear it on my poor—"

"Good-bye, Mr. Duff. For now."

Quincannon went out to the counter, swung himself over it, and quickly left the shop. Fifteen minutes in Luther Duff's company was more than sufficient for any upholder of the law; the stench of the little troll's moral decay was worse than that of his moldering curios. A breath of the fresh spring air was no longer a luxury—it was a necessity.

Quincannon was in somewhat dampened spirits when he returned to the agency offices. The fact that Duff had obtained the Velasquez statue in Santa Barbara—and Quincannon thought he could be believed on that account; Duff had been too frightened to lie—meant that he himself would have to travel south, and soon. And that in turn meant putting his campaign to seduce Sabina in abeyance. Well, no, it wasn't really a campaign of seduction; his intentions were honorable, after all. It was not as if marriage was out of the question, or even undesirable. They shared a partnership already; it was merely a matter of broadening that partnership to include the sharing of a bed. Or an entire household, if necessary. He had nothing against marriage, he truly didn't. He did not even regard it as a final alternative, a last resort. But to be away from Sabina for days, perhaps even weeks, when he was convinced that she was weakening . . . well, it made him feel somewhat subdued, not to say frustrated.

48

He said none of this to her, of course. He merely rendered an account of how he had maneuvered James Evans's name out of Luther Duff—"Sometimes," she said half-reprovingly, "you're too clever for your own good, John," a comment that he ignored—and then he said that he supposed he would have to take tomorrow night's train to Santa Barbara.

Sabina said, "Why tomorrow night's train? Why not tonight's?"

"Tonight's? Have you forgotten our engagement?"

"John, we can dine and have an evening's entertainment when you return. Velasquez is taking tonight's train, isn't he?"

"Yes, but—"

"Well, then? Traveling with him is a good idea. There may be other things he can tell you that will help with your investigation. And when you arrive he can help you find accommodations."

"I have been to Santa Barbara before. I do not need help finding accommodations."

"And," Sabina said, as if he hadn't spoken, "it will prove to him how conscientious you are, increase his confidence in you. This may well be a lengthy investigation; I needn't remind you how important a substantial fee would be to us."

Quincannon said stubbornly, "I do not believe my leaving one day later will make any difference in how Velasquez views me or in the size of our fee. Tomorrow night is soon enough."

"Well, the decision is yours. But you'll dine alone tonight."

"Sabina . . . "

"Business first. Pleasure second."

"Or not at all," he grumbled.

"You'd best go pack a grip," Sabina said. "You'll have enough time to do that and get to the depot on schedule if you leave now."

Quincannon took a cable car up Sutter Street to his rooms, not happily. The sun was shining, the air was like wine, the hot blood of youth flowed through his veins—and he would soon be on his way to Santa Barbara in the company of the gringo-hating son of a Mexican don.

Bah. Humbug.

THREE

IT WAS TWENTY minutes shy of six-thirty when Quincannon, carrying his old warbag, alighted from a hansom cab in front of the Southern Pacific depot at Third and Townsend streets. The area was teeming with hansoms, private carriages, baggage drays, trolleys, and citizens on their way into or out of the depot. It had been seven years since rail service opened between San Francisco and the southland, yet it seemed that more and more people jammed the daily evening train. The Southern Pacific would soon have to provide a second, morning train to accommodate the number of travelers.

He pushed his way inside the depot, waited in line at the ticket window, refused to hear the ticket seller's insistence that no first-class compartments were available, showed his Service badge, showed it again to the stationmaster, said that he was embarking on a special mission at the behest of the governor, and was eventually given the deluxe compartment the line kept available for dignitaries. Free of charge, of course. Ticket in one hand, warbag in the other, he hurried out to the southbound platform and commenced a search for his employer.

The search was neither a long nor a difficult one. He found Felipe Antonio Abregon y Velasquez standing near the boarding plate to one of the first-class cars, in the company of a red-haired, moon-faced young man dressed somewhat foppishly in a plug hat and a double-breasted Prince Albert. Velasquez wore a dour expression that changed not at all when his restless gaze settled on Quincannon. He seemed not to be feeling well.

"Ah, there you are," Quincannon said cheerfully. "*Buenas noches,* Señor Velasquez."

A curt nod. "You are ten minutes late. I do not like to be kept waiting."

"My apologies, sir."

Velasquez grunted, and the grunt evolved into a spasm of coughing that reddened his face.

"Señor Velasquez suffers from travel sickness," the moon-faced young man said. "The fumes from the locomotive affect his lungs."

"Indeed? I'm sorry to hear it."

"It isn't anything serious. Once he is settled in his compartment, he—"

"I do not need you to make my explanations, Señor O'Hare," Velasquez interrupted in irritable tones. "Be good enough to let me speak for myself."

"Oh, of course. I meant no offense."

Quincannon asked the redhead, "You are Barnaby O'Hare?"

"I am." O'Hare wore eyeglasses reminiscent of those favored by Theodore Roosevelt; behind them, overlarge blue eyes studied Quincannon with scholarly intensity, as if he were an object of minor historical interest. "And you are Mr. Quincannon. I must say, I've never met a detective before."

"Nor I a historian."

Velasquez had no patience for polite conversation. He asked Quincannon, "What did you learn from Luther Duff?"

"Your compartment, Señor Velasquez, would be a more private place to discuss such matters."

"Yes, but there is no time. The train will be leaving in a few minutes."

"No matter," Quincannon said. "I'll be accompanying you to Santa Barbara."

Velasquez was surprised; if he had noticed Quincannon's warbag, he had attached no significance to it. He said something in response, but at that moment the locomotive's whistle sounded, and the words were lost in its bleating cry. Great puffs of steam hissed out from under the car, mingling with the black, cinder-laced coal smoke from the stack to form a noxious haze along the platform. Velasquez again began to cough. O'Hare took his arm and assisted him onto the train, Quincannon following.

They made their way along the corridor to a center compartment. A frosted-glass lamp, mounted in a bronze sconce, had already been lighted; its glow reflected in sharp little gleams off the handsome rosewood paneling. Velasquez shook free of O'Hare's grip and sat down near the window. The coughing spell had subsided, but it was plain that his chest continued to bother him.

O'Hare asked solicitously, "Would you like some water? A brandy, perhaps?"

"No, nothing. Be so good as to leave Señor Quincannon and me alone. We have business to discuss."

"Oh, yes, certainly." O'Hare glanced at Quincannon, murmured, "A pleasure," and immediately left the compartment.

"A puppy, that one," Velasquez said. "His tail wags as often as his tongue."

"Puppies can sometimes bite," Quincannon observed.

The rancher made no response to that; the subject of Barnaby O'Hare was of little importance to him. He said, "Well, señor? What of Luther Duff?"

Quincannon told him what he had learned, without explaining how he had learned it. Then he asked, "Is the name James Evans familiar to you?"

"No. I know of no *hombre* named Evans."

"You're certain?"

"Am I an old man with a poor memory? Yes, I'm certain." Velasquez frowned. "How could the statue have been in Santa Barbara all those years with no word of it reaching my ears?"

"Perhaps the statue *wasn't* in Santa Barbara all those years. Evans might have obtained it elsewhere."

"You say 'obtained.' You mean stolen."

"Probably. I'll be a better judge of Evans and his profession after I've met him."

Outside on the platform, the conductor's voice rose in a shout: "All aboard! Last call for embarking passengers! All aboard!" The whistle sounded again, several more times. After less than a minute the car jerked, couplings rattled, and the train began its clattering movement. The smell of coal smoke was thick even in the closed compartment.

"Trains," Velasquez said. "Bah. A man was made to ride live horses, not poisonous iron ones."

Quincannon spent another ten minutes with him, to no benefit whatsoever. Velasquez's travel sickness and dislike of trains had put him in an irascible, contentious mood; and the fact that Quincannon was not Mexican only added to it. When the train neared the sleepy community of San Mateo, he left Velasquez to suffer his own company and sought out his accommodations.

He read for a time from a volume of poems by Wordsworth. He

had three-score volumes of poetry in his rooms in San Francisco, given to him by his mother, and he habitually took one with him whenever he traveled; poetry relaxed him, helped keep his thoughts sharp and orderly. At eight o'clock he went to the dining car, where he ate a huge meal—raw oysters, roast beef, vegetables, sourdough bread, cheese, fresh-churned ice cream. If he had inherited his genteel Southern mother's love for cultural pursuits, he had also inherited his Scottish Presbyterian father's lusty appetites. There was in him a curious mixture of the gentle and the stone-hard, the sensitive and the unyielding. He sometimes thought that was why he had become a better detective than Thomas L. Quincannon, the pride of the nation's capital, the rival of Pinkerton, the founder of the once-respected Quincannon Detective Agency. He knew his limitations, his weaknesses; he had the ability to look at things in different ways, from different points of view. His father had never in his life been wrong, never once changed his mind, was invincible—and had died foolishly, from an assassin's bullet on the Baltimore docks, when he should have been home in bed like other stout, elderly, and gout-ridden men. That would not be his son's fate. John Frederick Quincannon had vowed that he would die in bed, and none too soon, either.

After supper he made his way to the saloon car, with the intention of smoking his pipe out on the observation platform behind. But he spied Barnaby O'Hare sitting alone, nursing a snifter of brandy, and stopped instead at the historian's table.

"Mr. Quincannon, good evening. Will you join me?"

"If you wouldn't mind."

"Not at all. A brandy?"

"Thank you, no. I no longer indulge."

"Oh? Medical reasons?"

"Personal ones. I happen to be a drunkard."

O'Hare seemed taken aback, as much at Quincannon's candor as at the fact itself. "Oh, I see. Well . . . " His voice trailed off, and he studied the contents of his snifter, as if in consultation.

In vino veritas, Quincannon thought, but he did not smile even to himself.

He sat down, produced his pipe and tobacco pouch, and proceeded to load the Turkish latakia mixture he favored into the briar's bowl. When he had the tobacco tamped down to his satisfaction, he lighted it with a sulfur match and said between puffs, "Will you be stopping in Santa Barbara, Mr. O'Hare?"

"Yes, as a matter of fact. I still have people to see in connection with my book."

"A history of *los ranchos grandes,* isn't it?"

O'Hare nodded. "A comprehensive one, I think. I have gathered a wealth of information thus far. Everyone I've spoken to, especially Señor Velasquez and his wife, has been most helpful."

"His wife? I wasn't aware he was married."

"Oh yes. To a woman much younger than he—not that that matters a whit, of course. She also comes from an old Mexican family."

"I see."

"A beautiful woman, Olivia Velasquez," O'Hare said, a trifle wistfully. "Quite intelligent, quite strong-willed."

She would have to be strong-willed, Quincannon thought, to put up with a man of Velasquez's temperament and attitudes toward women. But he said, "I understand you're a teacher by profession," to bring the subject back to O'Hare.

"Yes. A professor of history at the university in Los Angeles. I have a grant to fund my research and writing and a leave of absence from my teaching duties."

"Fascinating topic, history."

"Very. Are you interested in California's past?"

"Indeed I am."

"Any particular facet?"

"The temperance movement," Quincannon said blandly.

"Ah." O'Hare seemed nonplussed again. He lapsed into silence.

Quincannon leaned back with the briar clamped between his teeth, listening to the steady whispering clatter of steel-on-steel. Outside the saloon car windows, the night's blackness was broken now and then by the appearance of individual lights, like fireflies moving through the silky dark, and by strings and blobs of illumination that marked some settlement or other.

At length he said, "Tell me, Mr. O'Hare, how did you happen to come upon the Velasquez statue?"

"Señor Velasquez didn't explain?"

"None of the particulars," Quincannon lied.

"Well, one of my hobbies is visiting curio shops. I find them intriguing; and occasionally one can find old books, maps, journals, and other items of historical interest. San Francisco has many such shops, as I'm sure you know. Luther Duff's was one of several I visited last week."

"What made you examine the statue?"

"Curiosity; nothing more. It is quite a handsome piece. You've seen it?"

"Velasquez showed it to me in my offices."

"Well, you can imagine my surprise," O'Hare said, "when I discovered his father's name engraved in the base. Actually, surprise is too mild a word; I was flabbergasted. I recognized it immediately as one of Don Esteban's long-lost artifacts."

"Did you reveal that fact to Luther Duff?"

"Certainly not."

"You made no effort to purchase the statue?"

"I might have, if I had had the two-thousand-dollar asking price. Not for myself, you understand; I know how much the statue means to Señor Velasquez. As it was, I hurried out and sent a wire informing him of the find."

"Did you ask Duff where he'd obtained it?"

"Oh yes. He said at auction in San José two years ago. How it came to be there, he said, he had no inkling." O'Hare paused for a sip of his brandy. "I expect you were able to extract a different version from him."

"Do you?"

"Else, why would you be on your way to Santa Barbara instead of to San José."

Quincannon smiled around the stem of his pipe. "Whatever I may have learned from Luther Duff is confidential information. You understand, I'm sure."

"Oh, of course. Discretion is an admirable trait in a detective."

"I'm glad you think so."

There was another silence. Quincannon smoked placidly, watching the night glide by outside the windows. After a time O'Hare stirred, finished the last of his brandy, and got to his feet. In the glow of the side lamps, his eyes behind the Roosevelt glasses had the look of peeled grapes.

"If you'll excuse me," he said, "I believe I'll retire. Perhaps we'll see each other again before our arrival."

"If not in Santa Barbara at some point."

"I look forward to it. Good night."

"Good night."

Quincannon lingered after the young historian was gone, to finish his pipe. A waiter approached him and was politely sent away. It was odd, he thought, but after six months of sobriety he no longer had any desire for alcohol. What he had told O'Hare was true: He was a drunkard. During the year prior to those six months, he had besotted himself with liquor. But there had been a reason for it, and that reason was neither a fondness for whiskey nor an inability to control its use. The reason was a woman named Katherine Bennett, a woman he had never met, never spoken to; a pregnant woman in Virginia City, Nevada, who had died—and whose unborn child had also died—with his bullet in her breast.

The shooting of Katherine Bennett had been a tragic accident. It had happened during a gunfight that had erupted when he and a team of local law enforcement officers attempted to arrest two brothers who ran a print shop, for the crime of counterfeiting United States government currency. In the skirmish behind the print shop, one of the brothers had wounded a deputy with a shotgun load of buckshot and then attempted to flee through the rear yards of a row of private houses. Quincannon had shot him, to avoid being shot himself; but one of his bullets had gone wild and found its way into the breast of Katherine Bennett, who had been hanging up wash in the neighboring yard.

A tragic accident, yes, but he had not been able to bear the burden of two innocent lives on his conscience. Guilt had eaten away at him; he had taken to drink to dull the images of that hot September afternoon, the dying screams of Katherine Bennett that echoed and reechoed inside his head. His work had suffered; he had felt incapable of ever turning his weapon against another human being, even to save his own life. Sooner or later Boggs would have been forced to dismiss him from the Service, and he would surely have become lost in a mire of alcohol and guilt if it had not been for two occurrences this past fall.

The first was a counterfeiting case involving coney greenbacks that had been flooding the Pacific Coast from an unknown location. Quincannon had uncovered evidence that indicated the source to be a remote mining town, Silver City, in the Owyhee Mountains of Idaho; and Boggs, being shorthanded, had had no choice but to send him there undercover to investigate.

The second occurrence was his meeting Sabina during the course of that investigation. At first he had been both fascinated and repelled by her, for she bore a superficial resemblance to Katherine Bennett; and she also seemed to be involved in the shady goings-on in and around Silver City. It was only later that he discovered she was neither the milliner she pretended to be nor the criminal he feared her to be, but a "Pink rose"—a female operative of the Pinkerton Agency's Denver branch—on an undercover assignment of her own.

Quincannon had continued his steady, mind-dulling consumption of alcohol while in Silver City, and as a result he had made a foolish mistake that nearly cost Sabina her life. Far-reaching changes had been wrought in him as a result. He had found the strength to stop drinking, to accept his guilt and his dependency on liquor for the senseless, crippling indulgences that they were—indulgences that had almost caused the death of a second innocent woman. And where was the purpose, the atonement, in destroying *himself?* There were things to be done with his special skills, perhaps even lives to save over many years of public service. And indeed, wasn't the ongoing use of those skills a proper memorial to the short and tragic life of Katherine Bennett?

After his return to San Francisco, he had given considerable thought to his future. Alcohol had no part in it—he had had his last drink in Silver City—but he'd decided that Sabina did have. He had asked her by wire if she would consider leaving the Pinkertons and joining him in a brand-new venture, a detective agency wherein they would be equal partners. She had wired back affirmatively. She was a widow—her husband, also a Pinkerton operative, had been killed in the line of duty two years before—and had no family ties in Denver; she, too, was ready for a new beginning. He had given notice to the Service, over Boggs's strenuous objections, and when Sabina arrived in San Francisco, they had pooled their savings and opened Carpenter and Quincannon, Professional Detective Services.

If the agency had not yet prospered, neither was it floundering. If the past five months had had their share of frustrations, they had also had their share of smiles and satisfactions. Life felt and smelled and tasted good again. The past was behind him, trapped in an occasional nightmare, a vagrant thought or feeling like a dark cloud passing across the face of the sun. He was, he had realized not long ago, with no little surprise, a reasonably happy man once more.

Not that he was happy at the present time, however. This train was just not where he wanted to be—especially not after he returned to his compartment and settled himself into the berth the porter had made up for him. There was something about the rhythm and motion of a moving train that made sleeping alone a difficult and depressing state of affairs. . . .

Santa Barbara was a settlement of some five thousand residents, nestled between the Santa Ynez Mountains and the sea. Its primary attraction was its sulfur and mineral springs, whose healthful and curative properties had been bombastically praised by a New York writer named Charles Nordhoff in an 1871 travel guide to California. Ever since, tourists had flocked to Santa Barbara to take the waters—the modern version, Quincannon supposed, of the eternal quest for the fountain of youth.

He had visited the town more than once as an operative of the Secret Service, the last time three years ago on a case that had taken him to the old Ortego rancho outside the neighboring village of Montecito. The hilly land there now belonged to members of a spiritualist colony called Summerland, who believed they could converse with dear-departed friends and relatives through an individual called a medium. Locally the colony was known as "Spookville," and Quincannon had found that appellation all too appropriate. More than one strange thing had happened to him in Spookville, not the least of which was an attempt on his life outside the spiritualists' temple near the beach.

It was midmorning when the train arrived at the main depot at Victoria and Rancheria streets, on Santa Barbara's west side. Well-fed, if not well-rested, Quincannon alighted in the company of Felipe Velasquez and Barnaby O'Hare. The two men had been in the dining car when he entered it at eight o'clock, and he had joined them for breakfast. Velasquez's travel sickness no longer seemed to be plaguing him; he was in better spirits this morning and had eaten the same hearty meal as Quincannon. Their conversation had been polite and limited to neutral topics. No mention had been made of Don Esteban's lost artifacts, and Velasquez had prudently refrained from speaking James Evans's name in front of O'Hare.

Velasquez's intention was to stay the night in Santa Barbara, he said, at the St. Charles Hotel, and then return to Rancho Rinconada de los Robles early the next day. Quincannon asked and was given directions, in the event that he was required to stay in town longer than just one day. He also managed to find out that O'Hare was stopping at the Delgado, a small lodging house on Gutierrez Street. If for any reason another talk with the historian became necessary, he wanted to know where to find him.

Quincannon saw Velasquez into a waiting hack, said good-bye to O'Hare, who set off on foot, and then engaged a hack for himself. It deposited him at the Arlington Hotel on State Street, Santa Barbara's finest hostelry—an elegant three-story building surmounted by a tall, square tower that concealed a water tank, and surrounded by lush gardens. The desk clerk insisted that no rooms were available. Fifteen minutes later, after a private discussion with the manager, Evander Boggs, chief of the Secret Service's San Francisco field office, was personally escorted to a large and comfortable third-floor suite.

Quincannon spent a few minutes refreshing himself, went downstairs again, treated himself to a brace of ten-cent Cuban panatelas at the tobacco counter in the lobby, and strolled outside. There was fine spring weather here, too; instead of taking another hack, he decided to walk to Anacapa Street. He unwrapped one of the cigars, lighted it, and set out to meet James Evans.

What he found at number 1206 Anacapa Street, however, was a German family named Kreutz.

James Evans had not resided there for three months, and neither the Kreutzes nor anyone else in the neighborhood knew what had happened to him.

PART III
1986

ONE

By Sunday noon I was back home from the hospital, relieved in one way and disturbed in another. When Nick and I had arrived there at seven, Mama had already been given something to relax her before surgery. She kept telling me I should go to work, and after the third time I stopped reminding her that I didn't have to go, it was the weekend. She asked Nick about how his run had gone at least seventeen times; since it was a subject that interested him far more than going to work interested me, he replied to each question, dredging up more details to keep her mind off her imminent operation. He was explaining how his buddy Ed's pulled hamstring might keep him out of the Carpinteria Marathon two weeks from now, when they came to take Mama down to surgery.

Then Nick and I went to the cafeteria to wait. While he drank milk and read the Sunday paper, I gulped down what seemed like gallons of black coffee. I'd bought a sweetroll, too, but I couldn't eat it; my huge grief-induced appetite of the night before had vanished and I felt choked up and slightly queasy. Anyway, every time my hand strayed toward the roll, the old health nut's jaw pushed out in a way that made him look like a bulldog.

To keep my mind off what might be going on in the operating room, I thought back to the old detective's report I'd read the night before. It had actually been only a fragment of a report, ending abruptly, as if the rest of it had been lost. I wondered what had happened in—and to—the additional pages. Had John Quincannon found Don Esteban Velasquez's missing artifacts? There was no way of knowing.

Finally Dr. George found us and said the operation had gone well; Mama was on her way to her room from Recovery.

It was when I saw Mama that I started to worry all over again. She was groggy, but I'd expected that. What I hadn't expected was for her to be as closed and unresponsive as she'd been the afternoon before. She held Nick's and my hands and said she was relieved that everything was going to be okay, but she didn't ask when she could go home, or if we'd gotten hold of Carlota yet, or any of the other things that would have made me feel she was really there with us. And when Dr. George said we should go and let her rest, she didn't protest. As we went out, she was staring at the ceiling just as she had been when we'd left the day before.

I tried to talk to Nick about it, but he was looking preoccupied and said something about having errands to run; he left me in the hospital parking lot. His abrupt departure made me feel even more shaky inside. I got into my car and sat there for a few minutes, thinking. All my life I'd depended on Mama, and now she was weak and in need of support herself. And ever since I'd known him, Nick had seemed strong and self-assured, but Mama's illness seemed to have unnerved him. This was, I decided after a few minutes, one of those growing-up experiences when you realize that your elders are not invincible but mere humans who are easily frightened when their increasingly fragile bodies seem to be letting them down. Being able to categorize it that way made the situation a little less threatening but did nothing to comfort me. I've found that coming-of-age events are seldom reassuring until their emotional barbs are blunted by time.

When I got home I thought about having some more coffee, then drank a glass of wine instead. It eased the shakiness somewhat but also made me feel light-headed and curiously directionless. With several hours until I could go back to see Mama again, I prowled the house, straightening a pile of books on the bedside table, putting away a couple of pairs of shoes, washing the few dishes that stood in the sink. I tried Carlota again, and when I got no answer, I decided to pay some bills. But once I was back in the living room, I couldn't make myself sit down. So I paced.

My thoughts kept moving, too: from Mama to Dave; from worry to disbelief. I felt disoriented, and there was a strangeness in my usually familiar surroundings. The living room walls seemed whiter than before; in contrast, the furnishings looked shabbier. I wasn't sure about that painting I'd bought a couple of months ago; it was a primitive, but maybe the technique was amateurish. Even my pottery sun face by an artist named Candelario looked strange to me; its wide red mouth and blazing eyes seemed too intense for a room I'd intended as a restful haven.

Suddenly I had an overpowering impulse to drag all the furniture into the center of the room, pile the smaller things on top of it, and begin rearranging. To resist what could only be a disastrous urge, I finally paused and thumbed through the old detective's report that I'd left on my desk when I'd finished reading it the night before.

After only a few lines, my mind was no longer on my troubles; instead it was with John Quincannon, arriving in the Santa Barbara of those earlier, more tranquil times. There would have been no shopping malls and housing tracts, no cars and trucks and exhaust fumes, no cute boutiques and trendy restaurants and all the other things that were now spoiling the charm of the town. I wished I could see Santa Barbara as Quincannon had seen it; wished I could go along with him as he pursued Don Esteban Velasquez's missing artifacts. It was strange, I thought, how I felt a kinship with the long-deceased detective. I wanted to know more about him, what had happened to him while he was here, how his case had turned out. I was terribly disappointed that the rest of the report was missing.

Paging through the report again, I picked out the name of the church that the Velasquez family had constructed on their rancho— San Anselmo de las Lomas. Saint Anselm of the Hills. There was a little town in the Santa Ynez Valley, northeast of Santa Barbara, called Las Lomas; since the rancho had been located in that same general area, it was probable that its name was an abbreviated version of the church's.

The reason I knew of Las Lomas was that a local historian, Sam Ryder, lived there. Sam had been a student of my mother's professor friend, Ciro Sisneros, and had finished up a book Ciro had been writing when Ciro was murdered last summer. If anyone would know about the Velasquez family and their missing treasure, it would be a historian who practically lived on the site of the old rancho.

I took out the county phone book and checked for a listing for Sam Ryder, but there wasn't any. That really didn't matter, though; Las Lomas was a tiny town, little more than a clearing in the vineyards for which the Santa Ynez Valley was becoming famous. I could drive out there to talk to him, maybe even take a picnic. It would be a good way to keep my mind off Mama and Dave. . . .

But then I sat down in my rocker, my excitement evaporating as quickly as it had come. I didn't want to drive out there alone.

Didn't want to pack a picnic just for myself. What I wanted was to share this interesting discovery. And who I wanted to share it with was Dave. We'd shared so many things, important and unimportant, in the time we'd been together. It didn't feel right. . . .

Basta, Elena, I told myself. There isn't going to be any more sharing with Dave Kirk, so get used to it. If you don't want to go out there alone, get up and call a friend.

I went to the phone and dialed Tina Aguilar, who had been my amiga from grade school to this very day. Tina would enjoy the kind of excursion I was planning, and she was also someone to whom I could talk about what was upsetting me. But Tina's phone rang eleven times before I remembered she'd gone to L.A. for the weekend. Then I called Susana Ibarra, my public relations director at the museum. She was home but about to go sailing with Carlos Bautista, whom she grandly referred to as "my fiancé." It didn't raise my spirits to hear that; Carlos was chairman of our board of directors, very rich, fifty-three-years-old to Susana's nearly eighteen—and my former boyfriend. Never mind that I'd found him boring and stuffy and had failed to be impressed by his money; this was irritating in the extreme.

But surely there was *someone* I knew who would want to go on a picnic. My secretary, Emily Dominguez, and her husband and baby? No, Emily had decided to take her vacation week the same time I did, and they had all gone up to Lindsay to visit her parents. What about Jesse Herrera, the artist who was my closest male friend? No, not him, either. Jesse had recently fallen in love, and all his waking hours were devoted to his pretty Estella. . . .

I could have continued down the list of my friends, but suddenly it seemed like a great deal of effort. Much more effort than it would take to simply throw some cheese and bread and a couple of bottles of Dos Equiis into a sack and set off for the valley alone.

The Santa Ynez Valley contains some of the finest vineyards and cattle graze in California. Flowers are grown there for seed, and all-year-round colorful fields stretch toward the softly rounded hills in wide stripes of red and yellow, blue, pink, and white. There are excellent recreation areas, such as the several-thousand-acre county park at Lake Cachuma, the reservoir that provides Santa Barbara's drinking water, as well as two restored missions, Santa Ynez and La Purisima. And of course there are the historical towns-turned-tourist-traps, such as Solvang. Labeled "Little Denmark," Solvang outdoes Scandinavia with half-timbered buildings, windmills, and thatched roofs with fake storks perched on top; smorgasbords, pastry shops, and souvenir stands abound. Solvang is a must for the type of person who just loves to bring home little plaques for the kitchen that say such things as GOOD FOOD, GOOD MEAT, GOOD GOD, LET'S EAT! But you can't convince me that the people of Danish descent whose forebears settled the area really enjoy being surrounded by all that tackiness—any more than I would want to live in an adobe hut with piñatas hanging on the front porch. The tourist dollar that just keeps flowing in is another matter entirely.

Today I was able to avoid Solvang, turning east toward the hills between Santa Ynez and Los Olivos. The county road to Las Lomas rose gradually into rougher terrain—rocky outcroppings where chaparral gradually gave way to live oak and sycamore. Here and there I glimpsed delicate orange patches of the California poppy, and brown-and-white cattle grazed on the slopes, standing easily on an incline, as if their legs were shorter on one side than on the other. I smiled, remembering how I'd once advanced that fanciful theory to a rather serious, literal-minded man who had brought me out here for a picnic. He had looked at me as if I'd lost my senses, laughed nervously—and never asked me out again.

After about five miles, the road narrowed, its pavement becoming rough and pitted and crumbling away at the shoulders. It wound between rock-strewn hills on which only scrub vegetation and half-dead trees grew, then went up a steep rise. At its top was what remained of a great white birch that looked as if it might have been struck by lightning; its upper branches were jagged and torn, pointing toward the cloud-streaked sky like angry fingers, and on its trunk a weathered sign was nailed. I slowed the car next to it and made out faded green lettering that said Las Lomas was one mile ahead.

From there the road dipped sharply, and on the left, across a gully and through a clump of oaks, I saw a flash of white. I slowed once again, peering through the shadows beneath the trees. The white area was large and rectangular in shape—the wall of a building, perhaps?

It was too soon for me to have reached the village, but this land might have been part of the old rancho, which had spread over many thousands of acres. I looked around for a place to pull off the road, and left the Beetle in a clearing that—from the litter of beer cans and bottles—looked as if it had been used for parking and partying. After stumbling across the rock-strewn gully on the other side of the pavement, I followed an erratic path through the oak trees and came out in a level field of high grass and wildflowers. In the middle of it rose a tall adobe wall, once whitewashed but now begrimed by time and the elements. It was solid, about twenty-five-feet-high, with no doors or windows.

I waded through the knee-high wildflowers, sneezing a couple of times because of the pollen in the air, and went up to the wall. It was genuine adobe, not the stucco that is mainly used today, and I could see the outlines where the bricks had skillfully been joined together. When I touched it, the wall felt rough and sun-warm. I moved along it to the left, peered around, and stopped in surprise.

This wall and about half of the one perpendicular to it on the opposite side were all that remained of the structure. The rest was low weed-choked foundations, laid out in a rectangular pattern. Within them lay more of the kind of debris I'd seen where I left my car, as well as large pieces of half-rotten timber, shards of red tile, a scattering of adobe bricks. The rear wall was scrawled with graffiti, and over it all someone had arched a bright, spray-painted rainbow.

I stepped over the two-foot foundation and picked my way through the rubble and thick vegetation toward the far end of the ruins, stopping to examine a massive piece of wood that bisected the space. It was large enough to have been the main roof beam and was jagged and blackened at both ends. Glancing at the back wall, I noted that it was also black at its top; whatever this structure had been, it had probably burned many years before.

When I reached the foundation at the far end, I saw that it was divided in the center, as if for a wide door. Stepping through the opening, I turned and surveyed the ruins. The rectangular space was about forty feet in length; to my right was a square founda-tion—about ten feet on each side—that adjoined it. There was no way of telling if the side walls of the building had contained windows or not, but what remained of the one on the left was recessed on the interior. The recess reminded me of something. What?

Of course—the apse in a church.

I'd probably stumbled onto the ruins of the church mentioned in

John Quincannon's report—San Anselmo de las Lomas. It would have been similar in style to the Franciscan missions: plain adobe and wood beam, without the elaborate stained glass windows and statuary of the typical Catholic church. The walls would have been whitewashed, the pews simple wooden benches, and any artworks would have been small paintings or statues of the saints. All those things were gone now, of course, destroyed in the fire or stolen. I was surprised that the great roof beam remained—it would make good firewood—but it was massive enough that it would have to be sawed up before it could be moved.

I looked around, feeling the way an archaeologist must after stumbling onto a lost city. I was certain now that this was the site of Rancho Rinconada de los Robles's pueblo—that center of the day-to-day activities of those who worked and lived on the sprawling self-sufficient spread—and as I searched for it, I began to see more evidence. To the right of the church was what appeared to be a graveyard; the tips of a couple of headstones peeked through the tall grass. About thirty feet away, under a big olive tree, was a three-foot-high round structure that looked like a well; probably it had been a *lavandería,* the rancho's equivalent of the town pump, where the laundry was done. When I came to explore the surrounding area—perhaps crossed that dry creek bed to that gnarled apple orchard, or climbed the rocky, oak-crowned knoll off on the right— I might see where the foundations of the stables, outbuildings, vaqueros' quarters, or even the hacienda were.

Had John Quincannon come here and seen these ruins? Had the place been as desolate then as it was now? No, the rancho was still being worked in those days; there would have been some buildings still standing, the hacienda for one. But the church would have been much the same, since it had been destroyed some forty-odd years before Felipe Velasquez had engaged the detective's services.

I narrowed my eyes, squinting at the ruins of the church through my lashes. For a moment I could almost picture it as it had been in the days before the Bear Flag Revolt. It would have been an immaculate white with a red tile roof; a carved wooden or iron cross would have crowned the peak over the heavy double doors. The square structure to the right was undoubtedly the bell tower; it would have risen high above the rooftop, its heavy bell silhouetted against the sky.

It was strange, I thought, that no one had tried to restore this place, or at least make a historical attraction of the ruins. Of course, the revolutionaries had destroyed a great deal of it. And then, it was also well off the beaten tourist track, in a rocky and inhospitable place. Perhaps whoever owned the land now preferred to let the ruins of the rancho lie in peace, visited only by teenagers seeking privacy, and occasional curious people like myself.

A sudden breeze came up, rushing through the nearby orchard and rattling the trees' leaves. The wildflowers that surrounded me rippled with its passage. I looked up at the sky and saw that the streaky clouds were now tinged with gray. The temperature had dropped sharply, as it often does in the hills on uncertain spring days. I shivered, wishing I'd brought a sweater.

The landscape had a bleak aura now, in spite of the still-bright sun; the remaining wall of the church seemed a lonely reminder of an age that was gone and would never come again; the bright colors of the spray-painted rainbow were a mockery of the grandeur these ruins represented.

I crossed my arms, hugging my elbows and feeling my spirits sink. I thought of Dave, the loss of him. And I thought of Mama, her illness that was only a prelude to old age and death. My life had taken a turn in the last two days, a turn that I was powerless to stop.

Always before I'd been the sort of person who fought against changes she didn't like. If there was a problem, I could think it through and fix it. If a situation displeased me, I could twist it around and make it right. But now I felt caught up in a great wave of inevitability, a force as strong as the one that had destroyed the great ranchos and the way of life that the dons had assumed would go on and on forever. Standing in this lonely place among the ruins made me realize for the first time how truly powerless we human beings are.

I stood there for a long time, arms wrapped tightly across my breasts, feeling sorry for myself. But after a while—as it had the night before—my self-pity began to seem ludicrous.

"*Pobrecita* Elena," I said aloud. "You thought you were all grown-up, and now you find there's yet another lesson to be learned."

Then I wiped a couple of tears from my cheeks and made my way back to the car to get my picnic lunch.

70

TWO

BEFORE I COULD carry my picnic lunch back to the ruins of the church, it began to rain, so I gave up on that idea and ate in the car. By the time I had finished and started down the road toward Las Lomas, the sun was out again and a rainbow—delicate translucence that in no way resembled the gaudy imitation on the church wall—arched over the landscape. The tender spring leaves and blossoms were studded with droplets that broke the light into miniature prisms, as if pieces of the rainbow had flaked off and fallen to earth.

The little village of Las Lomas shared none of the beauty of the country around it. It nestled in a valley on the edge of Los Padres National Forest, where the foothills became mountainous and rugged. A ragtag collection of shabby frame and cinder-block buildings sprawled around a town square. Half weeds and half packed earth, the square contained a flagpole without either flag or rigging, a basketball hoop minus a net, and a broken-down green picnic table. A couple of small boys were tossing a baseball around on the dirt section that apparently served as a playground, and an old brown dog lay under the table watching them.

The main road into the town deadended at the square. I turned left and parked in front of one of the few buildings that wasn't in poor repair—a freshly painted white Victorian house with a picket fence and well-tended garden. When I got out of the car and took a closer look, I saw that what grew there was not flowers but vegetables—big spiky-leaved artichoke plants, seedling beans that had already begun to climb a trellis, tomato plants with yellow blossoms. White-flowered strawberry plants were everywhere, like a ground cover. It seemed an efficient and economical use of space, and for a moment I thought of all the room I had in my backyard and how attractive it would look filled with vegetables. Then I remembered last summer's zucchini disaster—zucchini grows like

71

weeds for everybody but me—and dismissed my visions of living off the land.

Back on the corner where the road had entered the town, I'd passed a grocery store with a gas pump out front, and now I started walking back to it. The sign on the cinder-block facade said MARSHALL'S, and there was a bin full of potatoes and onions and some sacks of feed sitting under the overhang of the rusty corrugated iron roof. When I got closer I could see, through the front window, wire racks containing potato chips, other snacks, and packaged baked goods. I opened the screen door and stepped inside.

It was a country store but without the usual charm of such establishments. The wooden floor looked grimy; the light was a peculiar jaundiced yellow; the walls a dirty beige. Rows of shelves stretched from the door to the rear where the refrigerated cases were, but they were half-empty and what canned and boxed goods stood there were in total disorder. To my left was a counter with produce in crates; most of it looked wilted or half-rotten. To my right was a checkout counter, backed by high shelves that held liquor, candy, and cigarettes. An old man with wispy gray hair and a sallow complexion stood behind it, putting a fifth of Old Crow into a paper sack. His customer had his back to me and was slipping a wallet into the hip pocket of his faded jeans. When the screen door flapped shut, the customer glanced over his shoulder; he was about forty, with a suntanned, weathered face and a full head of faded sandy hair. I smiled self-consciously and began turning the rack of snacks to give myself something to do until they'd finished their business.

"There you go, Gray," the man behind the counter said. "Guess that should hold you for a day or two."

"Until tomorrow, at any rate." The younger man's words were joking, but there was an edge to them.

"Well, while the old lady's away.... Hear anything from Georgia lately?"

"I get a letter every week, but it's pretty old news. The dig's up in the mountains, and the mail has to be taken down to Lima to be posted. The mail service from Peru is bad at best."

"Well, that's what you get for marrying a lady archaeologist," the storekeeper said. "Still, I see Dora's helping you out, keeping you fed. You were at her house twice this week for dinner."

72

"You see a lot, Jim." Now the edge was back in the voice of the man called Gray.

"Enough. I see what interests me."

Gray gave a dry, humorless laugh as he went toward the door. "If you can find anything interesting in this town, you're welcome to it." He went out, letting the door slam hard behind him.

I stopped turning the rack and went up to the counter. The storekeeper—Gray had called him Jim—smiled at me, showing crooked, tobacco-stained teeth. "Help you, young lady?"

"I hope so. I'm looking for a man named Sam Ryder."

"Oh, the professor." His grin widened when I looked perplexed. "Oh, that's just what we call him hereabouts. He's the town scholar, unless you count Dora Kingman, lady up the street with the organic garden in her front yard. She writes cookbooks—natural foods, like the hippies eat. But Sam, he's a real writer. Got rooms full of books."

"I see. Can you tell me where he lives?"

"I can show you." He came around the counter and motioned for me to follow him outside. In front of the store he stopped and pointed diagonally across the square. "Over there, third house from the end. Red one with white trim, next to the lapidary."

"The what?"

"Lapidary. Fancy name for a rock shop. Belongs to Gray Hollis, the fellow who was just in here buying booze."

"A rock shop—here? Does he get many customers?"

"What he sells is mostly by mail order. Doesn't make much, but that don't matter. Gray's wife is the one who puts bread on the table—and bourbon in Gray's glass. You probably heard us talking about her; she's with some big expedition that's digging up a city in Peru."

The storekeeper spoke matter-of-factly, as if he were discussing the recent rain shower, but underneath his words I caught a hint of malice. I'd already learned more from him about the residents of Las Lomas than I ever cared to know; heaven only knew what I could find out if I pressed him. But the present-day inhabitants of the area weren't what interested me. I thanked the old man for the directions and set off across the square, thinking that if I lived in the village and had a fondness for bourbon, I'd probably drive all the way into Santa Ynez to do my shopping.

The two houses the old man had pointed out—the one belonging to Gray Hollis and Sam Ryder's—were very different from each other. Hollis's was a rambling brown-frame structure with a glassed-in front porch; there were shelves directly behind the windows, and on them sat polished chunks of rock. A sign on a wrought-iron standard said Las Lomas Lapidary. The front yard was a formal garden centered around a dry fountain and edged with wagon wheels. I guessed this was the creation of Hollis's absent wife, since it was beginning to show signs of neglect.

In contrast, the yard of the small boxcar-red house next door looked as if it had never been touched by human hands. A big pine tree stood in its center; cones and needles littered the ground, fighting with the weeds for dominance. The low iron-mesh fence had bent over in places from the weight of rampaging blackberry vines. I went through the half-open gate and up a narrow path to the sagging cement porch. Two wires extended from the hole where the doorbell should be, so I opened the torn screen door and pounded on the inner one.

The man who answered my knock was short, roly-poly, and had curly bright red hair that was as undisciplined as his front yard. He didn't look like any historian I'd ever seen, but he did look like he ought to be out in the kitchen baking sugar cookies. I stared at him in surprise.

The man didn't seem to share my discomfort. He smiled as if I were an old friend whom he was very glad to see and said, "Hello. Are you looking for me?"

"If you're Sam Ryder."

"That I am. And you are . . . ?"

"Elena Oliverez, Gabriela's daughter."

His smile broadened, making him look like a happy cherub. Although I remembered my mother saying Sam Ryder was in his fifties, he seemed almost boyish, with his plump features, unwrinkled skin, and curiously innocent blue eyes. If I had had to describe him in one word, I would have said "round."

He said, "Well, for heaven's sake. How is Gabriela, anyway? I haven't talked to her since I delivered Ciro Sisneros's book two months ago."

"Right now, she's in the hospital." I felt a sudden rush of guilt; since lunch, I'd put Mama out of my mind. Dave, too, come to think of it.

Sam Ryder's mobile features took a quick downward turn. "The hospital? Nothing serious, I hope?"

"An ulcer. But she's going to be fine."

"Well, that's a relief." He stepped back and motioned for me to come inside. "Forgive me; I shouldn't keep you standing on the porch. I'm addled today—a chapter on Russian and French aggressions in the Pacific Northwest, and it's not going well."

I followed his rotund little figure inside, thinking that even if he didn't look like a historian, he sounded like one. The room he led me into further reinforced the impression: three walls were bookcases floor to ceiling; a long parsons table covered with more books and papers sat under the front window. An electric typewriter hummed noisily on a low stand next to the table, and beside it, a cigarette smoldered in an ashtray. Sam went over and crushed it out, then pressed a button on the machine, and the typewriter went silent.

"I don't want to interrupt your work," I said.

He moved one pudgy hand in a gesture of dismissal. "You're not, really. On top of the Russian and French aggressions, I'm having people for dinner, and I have to start preparing things. You'll stay, won't you?"

"Well . . . " I thought of Mama; Nick had said he would see her around five, and I had promised to come at seven, when he had a meeting to attend—something to do with one of the marathons he was running this spring.

"It's nothing formal," Sam said. "Just a few neighbors stopping in around four. I'd be pleased if you'd join us. Gabriela fed me many times while we were conferring over Ciro's manuscript, and I was never able to return the hospitality. At least allow me to feed her daughter."

"It's just that I have to be in Santa Barbara at seven, to visit Mama in the hospital."

"No problem. You'll have plenty of time to eat and drive back there."

"Then I'll stay."

"Good." He beamed at me, and then started toward the back of the house. "Come keep me company while I get things started."

I followed him to the kitchen, impressed by his easy hospitality. I am a nervous hostess at best—always forgetting to make a dessert, or having the various parts of a meal come to the table at odd intervals—and would never just casually invite an extra guest for dinner. Maybe, I thought, Sam's offhandedness had something to do with living in the country, where people were more easygoing and less suspicious of strangers. But probably it had more to do with having what seemed to be an open and trusting nature.

The kitchen stretched across the entire rear of the house and had big windows overlooking a yard that rivaled the front in untidiness. Sam sat me down in a canvas director's chair with a glass of white wine and began bustling about, assembling bowls and utensils and ingredients on a chopping block, talking the whole time.

"Actually," he said, "I'm glad you interrupted me when you did. This project is becoming a pain in the ass."

"You're working on another book?"

"A text for the Oregon public schools. Updating their state history curriculum. I can't seem to get into it. There's something so *dreary* about a place where it can rain more than a hundred inches a year." Sam took a pottery bowl from the oversize refrigerator and tasted its contents with a wooden spoon, his eyes closed. Making a face, he went to a spice rack that covered almost an entire wall and selected several jars. After dropping pinches of this and that into the bowl, he stirred, tasted it again, smiled, and held out a clean spoon to me. "It's gazpacho. Try it."

I got up and took a sample. It was delicious, with all sorts of delicate flavorings that I couldn't identify.

Sam watched me anxiously. "Okay?"

"Wonderful."

"Thank God. At least I won't catch hell over the soup course."

"Catch hell?"

"From Dora—Dora Kingman. She writes natural foods cookbooks, grows organic vegetables. The only way I can get her to come to dinner is to use her produce and follow her recipes to the letter. That's okay, though, because she knows what she's doing—where food is concerned." He paused, then grinned mischievously. "Besides, what I didn't tell her about was the lasagna and chocolate mousse."

I sat down, smiling politely while I wondered about a dinner made up of those three courses. "Who else is coming besides Dora?" I asked.

"Arturo Melendez—"

"The artist?"

"You know him? Oh, of course—Gabriela mentioned you were director of the Museum of Mexican Arts."

"Yes, but I haven't actually met him yet." I'd heard of Melendez, though; he produced very good primitive oils, and I'd been thinking of contacting him about exhibiting at the museum.

"Well then, seeing him in his natural habitat should be interesting for you. I should warn you . . . "

"Yes?"

He shook his head. "Never mind. Anyway, there's Arturo and Dora and Gray Hollis—"

"The man next door who runs the lapidary."

Sam raised his bushy red eyebrown. "You're pretty well informed about our little social set."

"I saw Mr. Hollis in the store when I stopped to ask where you lived. And the storekeeper—what's his name?"

"Jim Marshall."

"Jim Marshall told me about Mr. Hollis's business."

"His private business, too, no doubt."

"Well . . . yes."

Sam put the bowl of gazpacho back in the refrigerator and took out a covered pan that must have been the forbidden lasagna. "He probably hinted that Gray's the town drunk."

"In a way."

"Well, in a way it's true, ever since his wife left him about six months ago."

"Left him? Marshall said she was on some sort of archaeological expedition in Peru."

"She is, but it still amounts to the same thing. Georgia and Gray don't get along, and I'm convinced she doesn't intend to come back. There are those who hope that's what will happen—but not Gray. And that's why he drinks. He'll probably be squiffed when he comes over here, and that means he and Dora will get into it again. Oh, you're in for a rousing introduction to our little group." Sam didn't look particularly dismayed at the prospect. He popped the lasagna into the oven, then took out a salad spinner, and began to toss lettuce leaves into it.

"Aren't Dora and Gray friends?" I asked. "Jim Marshall mentioned something to him about having dinner at Dora's."

"They are friends. That's why Dora will take off after him about his drinking. She cares what he's doing to himself, but she doesn't

77

realize that often the best way to be a troubled person's friend is to leave him alone." Sam dumped the lettuce into a salad bowl, dropping a few pieces onto the floor. He picked them up, inspected them, shrugged, and tossed them into the bowl. Sam may have been a gourmet cook, but he had a few rough edges, and it made me like him even better.

"But listen," he said, "I've been chattering away at you, and all of a sudden I realize you didn't just drop in out of the blue. No one comes all this way without a reason, and I don't flatter myself enough to believe I'm it."

I smiled and held out my glass when he went to refill it. "In a way, though, you are. I need to talk to a historian, one who knows this area in particular. And I thought that since you live here, you might be able to tell me what I need to know."

"And that is?"

"About the Velasquez rancho, Rancho Rinconada de los Robles— its history and if there are any descendants of the family still living around here."

"You've come to the right man." Sam hefted a chef's knife and began chopping vegetables for the salad. "I find the era of *los ranchos grandes* fascinating, and I've made quite a study of it. The Velasquezes are particularly interesting because of all the obfuscation about their downfall."

"Obfus—?"

"Confusion. Rumors. There's a regular legend grown up about them. More myth than legend, I guess."

This was the kind of thing I was looking for. I waited to hear what he would tell me.

"The Velasquez grant was one of the most profitable of all the ranchos," he went on. "And the family's way of life was one of the most opulent. They raised blooded horses; all the time there were races, with the attendant heavy gambling. Entertainments were lavish—dances, fandangos, weddings. The rancho functioned as a self-sufficient community—they made their own cloth, tallow, raised their own food, even had their own private garrison of soldiers. They didn't need anything or anyone—or so they thought. And they weren't uncultured, either: it's said that Don Esteban Velasquez had an extremely valuable collection of religious art objects."

That would be the artifacts John Quincannon had been hired to find in 1894. "What happened to the rancho?"

"That much we know. It was overrun and partially destroyed by a detachment of soldiers from John Fremont's battalion during the Bear Flag Revolt. Don Esteban himself was killed in the fighting. After that the rancho never fully functioned again, and most of its land was eventually sold off to pay debts."

"Those are facts?"

"Yes."

"Then, what's the legend?"

Sam set his knife down and fumbled in his shirt pocket for a cigarette, his eyes reflective. "The why of it is what we don't know. The Bear-Flaggers didn't just overrun ranchos for amusement. It wasn't that kind of revolt. Why the destruction, then? What did they have against the Velasquezes? You see?"

I nodded. "Do you have a theory?"

"No, not really. I suppose I could formulate any number of them, if I cared to. But as a historian, I've got to stick to facts, and there are too few of them in this case."

I was silent for a moment, wondering if there was anything in John Quincannon's report that might shed light on the matter. If so, I couldn't recall it. "Those ruins up the road a mile or so—are they what's left of the rancho's church, San Anselmo de las Lomas?"

"Yes. And of the pueblo. The church ruins and a few foundations of other buildings are all that remain. The hacienda was on a hill a quarter mile or so to the east, but there's nothing left of that. It burned in a forest fire in the 1920s; the fire also destroyed what little was still standing of the pueblo. The pueblo is supposed to be haunted, you know."

I could understand why people thought so; apparently I wasn't the only one who had been affected by the eerie desolation of the place. I said, "But the Velasquez family still lived at the hacienda after the revolt."

Sam looked curiously at me but didn't ask how I knew that. "Until the turn of the century. Then the last of them moved to Santa Barbara."

"Who owns the land now?"

"The site of the hacienda and the pueblo is still in Velasquez hands. There is a woman in West Los Angeles, I believe, who controls it and prefers to let it lie as is. As I said, the rest was sold off long ago to pay debts."

"Do you know how I can get in touch with this woman?"

Now Sam looked openly curious. "Why?"

"I'll explain. But first—*can* you put me in touch with her?"

"Perhaps. There's an old lady who lives on the other side of the square who was at school with her. I believe they still correspond. She—the old lady—is never home on Sundays; her daughter takes her on an outing then. But I can speak with her tomorrow and then call you." He came around the chopping block and pulled up a companion to my chair. "Now. Why are you so interested? Does it have anything to do with Don Esteban's missing artifacts?"

"You've heard about that, then?"

"Of course. It's a fact, and also part of the lore about the Velasquezes' downfall. It's said that the don hid his collection before Fremont's troops attacked. As far as I know, the artifacts never turned up."

"What do you think happened to them?"

"I would think that would be obvious: Fremont's soldiers got them."

"Don Esteban's son, Felipe, wasn't so sure of that."

Sam raised his eyebrows.

"I found some old papers," I said. "Part of a report made by a detective who was hired by Felipe Velasquez to look for the artifacts. The report tells of the beginning of the search, and now I want to know the end." I went on to give him the particulars of what I'd read.

When I was done, Sam looked excited. "The Velasquez treasure.... So part of it did turn up."

"Yes. But did Quincannon ever find the rest of it? Reading that report was like reading a mystery novel with the last few chapters torn out."

His eyes shone. "What fun! I'd love to see the document."

"I'll be glad to show it to you," I said, "in exchange for your getting the Velasquez woman's address."

"It's a deal." But suddenly he looked wistful.

"What's wrong?"

"Nothing, really. I was just thinking how much more interesting the Velasquezes are than the Russian and French aggressions. You'll be sure to keep me posted on what you find out, won't you?"

"Of course."

"Maybe if you ever do learn how Quincannon's case turned out, I could write it up for a historical journal—if that wouldn't be stealing your material."

"*My* material? What would I do with it? I can't write to save my soul. You're welcome to use it. *If* there's anything to find out—"

A woman's voice, loud and strident, called Sam's name from the front of the house. He frowned in annoyance and said, "It's Dora, fifteen minutes early, as usual. The party's about to begin."

THREE

From the sound of her, plus Sam's previous comments, I'd expected Dora Kingman to be a sour-faced old busybody. The woman who entered the kitchen was not more than thirty, wiry and athletic-looking, with close-cropped black hair and a pert face. She broke into a grin when she saw me and said, "Oh, good, somebody new! What these potlucks need is fresh blood."

Sam made introductions while Dora set a paper sack on the counter and began to unload Tupperware containers in various sizes and shapes. She said, "I'm glad you could join us, Elena. Sam, get off your buns and help me find room for these in the fridge. And what *is* that smell coming from the oven?"

Sam rolled his eyes at me and went over to the refrigerator. He opened its door and started dubiously into its tightly packed depths.

Dora said, "I asked—what's the smell?"

"Lasagna."

"Ahah! Cheating again."

He opened one of the containers she'd brought and sniffed at its contents. "And what's *this* smell?"

"Brown rice with eggplant."

"Ugh. It's all gray and tan."

"To each his own. I knew that except for the gazpacho and salad, you'd cheat, so I brought the things that I like to eat—and that are good for you."

Sam shrugged and stowed the containers away, balancing them one on top of the other. Neither he nor Dora seemed particularly upset with each other; I suspected he "cheated" every time she came to dinner and that she always brought her own food.

The screen door slammed, and footsteps came across the front room. Gray Hollis appeared in the doorway, brown paper bag in hand. Dora turned, and her eyes narrowed as they moved quickly to the bag.

"So, Gray," she said, "what are you contributing tonight?"

He raised the bag, which clearly showed the outline of the bottle within. "Fine bourbon whiskey." As Sam had predicted, Gray was drunk, teetering on the fine line between rigid control and stumbling lack of coordination. He walked to the counter in a marionettelike gait, got a glass from the cabinet, and poured himself a couple of fingers of liquor. Dora glared openly at him. When he took the bottle from the bag, I noticed that it was only two-thirds full.

Dora opened her mouth, but Sam pushed a stack of plates into her hands, saying, "I thought we'd eat outside. You want to set the table?"

Dora glanced back at Gray but carried the plates out a side door to where a picnic table stood in a clearing among the weeds. Gray watched her go with an amused expression, then leaned against the counter and raised his glass in a toast. "Here's to you, Sam. And to our pretty visitor, who I believe I saw in Marshall's earlier."

Sam introduced us, adding that I had come to see him "on a quest of historical importance." Before I could explain, there was a flicker of motion over by the door, and we all turned our heads. A young man stood there, silent as a ghost. He was Chicano, slender to the point of being frail, with thick hair falling to his shoulders.

"Arturo!" Sam said. He went to the counter and poured a big glass of wine. The young man moved gracefully across the room, setting a covered plate on the chopping block. He took the glass wordlessly and retired to one of the director's chairs. I looked at Sam, but he was inspecting the nachos on the plate. Gray had turned and was looking out the window at Dora and sipping bourbon.

Since no one seemed about to introduce me, and Arturo Melendez's silence indicated he might not speak English, I said, "*Yo me llamo* Elena Oliverez."

He acknowledged the words with a slight twitch of his lips that might have been a smile.

I looked at Sam again. He smiled reassuringly and said, "Sorry. That's Arturo Melendez. He's just shy. Will you take the utensils out to Dora for me?"

I got them from the drawer he indicated and went outside. Dora had arranged the plates on the picnic table and was standing next to it, staring sightlessly at a half-dead rosebush. When she heard my footsteps, she turned.

"Oh, Elena, thanks for bringing those out," she said. "I didn't want to go back inside."

"Because of Gray?" I began laying the knives and forks next to the plates.

For a moment she was silent. Then she said in a low, strained voice, "Yes. It's horrible what he's doing to himself. I can't bear to watch."

"I understand his wife has left him."

"Yes, but that's no reason to kill himself with drink. Georgia was a miserable wife. The fights they'd have! She threw a pair of scissors at him once. He's better off without her."

"Maybe that's true, but I suspect he doesn't know that yet."

"He should. I've told him and told him."

And that was your first mistake, I thought. I've never been married, but I've had enough experience with friends who have been to know that no matter how bad a marriage is, a person doesn't want to hear his friends' criticism—at least not until it's completely over for him.

I said, "Did Gray drink a lot before Georgia went to Peru?"

"Hardly at all."

"Then he'll probably stop when he's ready to."

"Do you think so?" There were tears in Dora's eyes, and her small hands were clenched white-knuckled over her breasts.

Por Dios, I thought, she's in love with him. She's the one who Sam meant when he said there were those who hoped Georgia would never come back from Peru. "I'm sure of it," I said firmly. Then, to get her mind off Gray, I said, "Dora, what's wrong with Arturo Melendez?"

"Wrong?"

"He doesn't speak."

Dora shook her head. "Oh, that's just the way Arturo is. He's quiet, and with a stranger here, he's bound to act more shy than usual."

It seemed more than shyness to me; and Dora was so wrapped up in Gray's problems that she didn't make a particularly good observer. I decided to try to draw Arturo out during dinner; he was an exceptionally talented artist, and one who I felt deserved more recognition than he'd gotten.

As things worked out, though, any further conversation with Arturo was impossible. The talk around the picnic table turned into a running argument between Dora and Gray, with Sam desperately introducing neutral topics that both of them ignored. Gray kept the bourbon bottle right beside him, and every time Dora made a critical comment, he refilled his glass; the level of liquor rapidly dropped to less than two inches. When Dora found she couldn't get a rise out of Gray, she started in on Sam's poor eating habits. Arturo ate silently, his eyes cast down and his expression closed, seemingly unaware of what was going on around him.

I was sitting next to him, and I studied him covertly, glad of someone to divert me from the tiresome bickering going on across the table. When he finished what was on his plate, he kept his eyes down, as if the smeared pottery surface was an object of fascination. After a couple of abortive attempts to speak to him about his work, I finally concluded that what I was dealing with was a seriously depressed person.

It wasn't unusual; I'd seen it before in other minority artists. It was a state born of repeatedly having to drag one's emotional guts out and spread them on the canvas, only to later be dismissed as amusingly ethnic but essentially unimportant. Arturo, I decided, had been living in the shadow of the Anglo art establishment for too long, and it was now beginning to erode his personality. It was time he got out into the sun where he would receive recognition for his considerable gifts—and that was something the museum and I could help him with.

By the time dessert was served, the meal had degenerated thoroughly. Sam's beautiful chocolate mousse was greeted with silence. Gray seemed more interested in the remainder of his bourbon. Dora was sulkily spooning out her fresh fruit salad. Arturo declined dessert with a shake of his head. I felt so sorry for Sam that I took an extra-large helping and wolfed it down, in spite of the fact I wasn't really in the mood for sweets.

After Sam finished his mousse, he passed cigarettes around, and everyone but Gray and I lighted up. Gray made a caustic remark to Dora about how health-conscious people shouldn't smoke. She countered by pointing out that at least she didn't quit and then take it up a few days later like he did. Sam watched them anxiously, and I could see he was searching for a way to divert them from what promised to be a full-blown quarrel. Suddenly his face brightened, and he said, "What a dunce I am! I forgot to tell you all the reason Elena has honored us with her presence."

They all looked at him: Gray's eyes were bleary, Dora's impatient, and Arturo's seemed to be looking inward.

"She has made an incredible find." Sam went on, describing in glowing terms John Quincannon's papers and the story they told. No one looked very impressed.

"So, what're you gonna do," Gray said, "go out an' dig up this treasure, get rich?"

His words sounded like an exaggerated parody of a drunk, and I wanted to smile. Controlling the impulse, I said, "I doubt it's still hidden. Probably Quincannon found it and restored it to the family."

"Then why isn't there any record of it?" Sam said.

"Yeah. Just think, Elena," Gray said, "you could have your own li'l arcological expedition right here. I know about those things; I could help you."

Dora glanced anxiously at him.

"Dig it up," he said, waving his glass. "Dig it all up."

"Gray—" Dora said.

"Ah, shaddup."

"Gray!"

"Let Elena talk, will you?"

Quickly I said, "I must admit I did entertain some thoughts of finding the artifacts when I stopped off at the ruins—"

"Gray, you've been a drunk for quite some time now, but you've never been a *rude* drunk—"

He reached agitatedly for his glass and knocked it over. The bourbon flowed across the table and into his lap. "Shit!" he said, and jumped up.

I felt a tug at my sleeve. Arturo was looking shyly at me. "The ruins—you have been there?"

I was surprised. These were the first words he had spoken to me. "Yes, just today."

"I often go there. They are *muy tranquilo*. I like to sit there and imagine how it was in the days when our people were strong and respected."

Respect. *Respeto. Acepción de personas.* In either language, in any shade of meaning, it was a concept my people mentioned time and time again. We had almost wrung the word dry of any significance, almost worn out the idea by talking about it. And had we achieved it? In some areas, perhaps. But not in the really important ways, as evidenced by Arturo and his debilitating depression.

I said to him, "Will you go there with me sometime?"

He hesitated, then nodded. "I should like that."

"*Bueno.* The next time I'm here I'll come for you."

He smiled and dropped his gaze again.

Gray was still mopping at his liquor-soaked jeans, and Dora was still glaring at him, a bright spot of red on either cheek. Sam seemed relieved when I declined another helping of mousse and said I needed to get back to Santa Barbara. I took down his phone number and promised to call him the next afternoon for the information about the Velasquez woman, and then I took my hurried leave.

As I crossed the square, the village was bathed in spring twilight; it softened the more squalid aspects of the shabby buildings, made the trees seem fuller, the vegetation more lush. I caught the faint scent of apple blossoms, the gentle strains of piano music from one of the nearby houses. A dog barked and then was silent. A mother called her child and received a glad answering shout. Las Lomas was the image of peace and tranquillity—which only went to prove how deceptive appearances can be.

FOUR

MONDAY NOON I arrived at the museum, the marriage coffer once more wedged into the passenger side of my car. The parking lot of the nineteenth-century adobe in the city's historical district looked strangely deserted; there were only three cars, all of which belonged to volunteers. Leaving the chest where it was, I entered the building by the door off the loading dock and went down the tiled corridor to the office wing. The secretary's desk across from my office was cleared, the typewriter covered. I stopped and frowned until I remembered that Emily—like me—was on vacation.

Neither Susana Ibarra nor Rudy Lopez were in their cubicles, and the door to the office of Linda Trujillo, our education director, was closed. Where was everyone? I wondered. It was lunchtime, but the staff took their breaks at staggered intervals. Concerned, I made a quick tour of the galleries; they, the gift shop, and the entrance were all manned by our ever-reliable volunteers. It seemed they took their duties more seriously than my staff.

I crossed the inner courtyard, noting that no one had bothered to turn on the water in the little blue-tiled fountain, and checked the office wing again. It turned out Linda was there after all; I could tell by the strains of the classical music she often played while writing copy for the fact sheets we make available to our visitors. But where were Susana and Rudy? Apparently while *el gato* was away, *los ratónes* had decided to play. And *el gato* was not at all pleased with that.

I went into my office and sat down in my padded leather chair, then took John Quincannon's investigative report from my tote bag, and locked it securely in the drawer of my desk. Shortly after I'd been named director, I'd developed the habit of keeping important papers and valuables here at the museum where they were protected by an alarm system, rather than at home. My neighborhood is reasonably crime-free, but there had been just enough

89

break-ins in the last year to make me continue the practice. The report wasn't exactly valuable, but I have a great respect for historical significance, and I didn't want to chance losing it through fire or theft.

Next I reached for a stack of little pink message slips piled on the blotter. The writing on them was Susana's; at least she had not taken the morning off. I thumbed through them, seeing nothing that needed to be tended to immediately. Then I swiveled the chair around and stared through the heavy wrought-iron bars of the window at the azalea plants in the courtyard, thinking about Mama.

I'd talked with Dr. George when I'd gone to the hospital the evening before, and he'd said she was progressing nicely. And Mama had seemed in much better spirits. Nick had finally got hold of Carlota, and she and Mama had had a long phone conversation in which Mama had convinced her not to fly out. I heard all about that and then reciprocated with my story of dinner at Sam Ryder's. Mama was interested enough to ask if Arturo Melendez was single. Yes, I said, and very talented. But was he handsome? she asked. Well, maybe *un poco*. Well, then, she said, did he make any money? Artists, after all. . . .

I'd been glad to close the subject by saying Arturo was as poor as a churchmouse. But then Mama had gotten on the subject of Dave. When was that policeman coming to see her? *Dios* knew she didn't relish the idea of an Anglo son-in-law, but all the same she did enjoy the young man. . . .

I'd put her off by saying Dave was still out of town. Our breakup wasn't something I felt I could discuss right then. It might make Mama feel relieved, because she strongly disapproved of intercultural marriages, but if she saw how hurt I was, she would become upset and then angry—not a good thing so soon after surgery. I have never been good at hiding my feelings from my mother, and she seemed to sense something was wrong, but she just eyed me suspiciously and didn't say anything.

I'd gone home from the hospital yesterday evening feeling sure that Mama was on the road to recovery both physically and emotionally—which was why her state of mind this morning had surprised and dismayed me. She had been back in her stare-at-the-ceiling mood, and even Carlota, who called shortly after I got there, couldn't get through to her. Nick had arrived around eleven-thirty, bringing one of the special thick peach milk shakes she liked, but she'd barely looked at it—or him. It was then that I'd left, because I couldn't bear to watch her withdraw into herself any more, couldn't stand to see the hurt and anxiety on Nick's face.

This wasn't like Mama, not at all. If something was bothering her, she liked to get it right out in the open. I hadn't always appreciated her direct approach, because usually what bothered her was some transgression of mine, but now I would have welcomed it—

There was a knock on my door, and Rudy Lopez spoke my name. I swiveled the chair around. My curator stood in the doorway; tall, stocky, and curly-haired, wearing an outrageously bright purple shirt. His round face was pitted with scars from teenage acne, but when he smiled—as he did now—you didn't notice any imperfection; Rudy's warmth and obvious interest in other people made him nearly handsome. Mama had been very excited when she'd met him, proclaiming him *muy guapo.* And she'd been very disappointed when I'd told her he was gay.

Rudy said, "What are you doing here? This is supposed to be your vacation."

"Yes, and you all seem well aware of that. Where were you?"

"At lunch." He held up his wrist and tapped his watch. "I go from eleven-thirty to twelve-thirty."

It was twelve-twenty-five. I felt ashamed. No wonder my staff sometimes accused me of being a slave driver or, as Susana often put it, *una osa negra*—a black bear. "Well, what about Susana?" I asked defensively. "She's supposed to go from twelve-thirty to one-thirty. Who's taking care of the phones?"

"Susana had an appointment, so Mrs. Ramirez is answering."

"*Por Dios,* Mrs. Ramirez needs all her concentration just to make change when a visitor buys a postcard! What was Susana's appointment, anyway?"

Rudy looked amused. "She went to have her legs waxed."

"What?"

"She was out on Carlos's yacht yesterday, and she noticed they weren't as smooth as she'd like them to be. So one of Carlos's *rico* friends suggested she try waxing—"

I held up a hand. "I don't want to know about it. Susana's getting mighty expensive tastes for the salary we pay her."

"Well, she's going to be a millionaire's wife, so I guess she's practicing."

"Wife? We'll see about that."

"She has a ring."

That startled me. "A ring? She called him her 'fiancé,' but I had no idea it really was that serious."

"She received it this weekend. *Muy grande y caro.*"

"The man's taken leave of his senses!" But Susana hadn't; she was being as pragmatic as ever. She'd been married once before, to a thieving Colombian who had run off to Bogotá when his crimes had caught up with him. Susana, also a native of that country, had chosen to remain in the U.S., in spite of the fact that she had been only sixteen at the time. She would prefer, she had said, to make her way alone here rather than return to "a backward land." So far, she was making her way splendidly.

Rudy shrugged diplomatically. "Time will tell whether it's a good match or not. You still haven't said what you're doing here on your vacation day."

"Oh!" I got up and crossed to the door. "Come on out to my car. I brought a marriage coffer that I found at that auction on Saturday. A very good piece. Did you have any luck in L.A.?"

He waggled a hand from side to side. "*Un pocito.* A couple of chairs. This display is going to be more costly than we'd anticipated, I'm afraid."

"I'm afraid of that, too, from the prices several other pieces brought at the auction I went to. We'll just have to go slowly and buy carefully. Maybe if we assemble an impressive small collection, the board will release more funds. Or perhaps we can interest one of our patrons."

We went out to the parking lot, and Rudy helped me bring in the chest, exclaiming over its fine condition. We carried it down to the basement where the conservation laboratory was, and I left him debating whether he should use an oil soap or some heavier solvent to clean the wood.

Back in my office, I looked at my watch. It was almost one, time to call Sam Ryder for the name and address of the Velasquez descendant. I dialed his number in Las Lomas, but it rang ten times with no answer. After setting the receiver down, I began to doodle on my desk blotter, taking my mind off my troubles by thinking about John Quincannon.

His agency, Carpenter and Quincannon, had had offices in the Flood Building in San Francisco. Was it possible that the firm still existed? The report I'd found had been dated 1894; that would make the agency nearly a hundred years old. Was it possible that Carpenter and Quincannon had remained in business, been passed down to the heirs of either John Quincannon or his partner? If so, how could I find out? Dave would know . . .

And then I remembered that I couldn't ask Dave anything—ever again.

How long would this go on? I wondered. How long before I stopped thinking of Dave as if he were still a part of my life? How many weeks or months before I stopped wanting to ask or tell him things, before I stopped making plans for two when I was only one? I tried to remember the aftermaths of my other love affairs, but the pain of those seemed slight compared to what I was feeling now.

Stop this, I told myself. Think about Quincannon. Who else would know about tracing what happened to his agency? For one thing, there were business directories. I picked up the receiver and called the public library reference desk; they checked the current San Francisco directory for me. There was no listing for Carpenter and Quincannon.

It was disappointing, because it would have been so simple merely to contact the agency, tell them I was doing historical research about one of their former clients. They probably would have been glad to help me; I doubted the reports of the investigation would be considered confidential after all these years.

I wondered what had happened to Quincannon's files. Perhaps the agency had been absorbed by another firm, and the papers still existed in some musty cabinet. Wasn't there a state bureau that could tell me what had happened to the firm? They kept records of businesses even in those days. I'd have to think this through, figure out who to contact. But right now, I'd try Sam again.

This time he was home; he'd been visiting the old lady across the square before, and she'd given him the name of the woman who was descended from the Velasquezes: Mrs. Sofia Manuela, of Manzanita Way in Santa Monica.

"I had the city wrong but was correct about everything else," Sam said. "She is a very old lady, the daughter of Don Esteban's son, Felipe. She does own the land down the road from here and is the last surviving heir, as she was an only child and had no children herself."

Felipe Velasquez's daughter! This woman was not only a family member but someone who might even remember Quincannon's investigation. "Is she willing to talk with me?" I asked.

"My friend said she would welcome the opportunity. Just call and say you got her number from Rosa Jenkins."

I scribbled the name on the blotter and then, to be polite, asked, "Did everyone calm down after I left last night?"

"More or less. Dora stomped off in a huff, forgetting all her Tupperware. Gray went home to pass out. Arturo helped me with the cleaning up."

"I like Arturo very much."

"Me too. I just wish he wasn't so depressed."

"How long has this been going on?"

Sam hesitated. "Six months or more."

"I'm going to try to organize a showing of his work here at the museum. Perhaps it will help if he gets some positive critical attention."

"Maybe." Sam sounded faintly hopeful. He made me promise once more to let him know anything I might find out and then hung up. I depressed the cradle button on the phone and made a call to Santa Monica.

Mrs. Manuela told me—in a voice made high-pitched and tremulous by age—that her friend Rosa Jenkins had already called and mentioned my interest in the Velasquez family. She would be glad to talk with me and had a whole box of papers I might like to look at. When could I be there? she asked.

I said I could leave Santa Barbara right away. Would mid- to late-afternoon be all right?

Any time would be *muy bueno*, she said. She would be expecting me.

FIVE

I FOLLOWED ROUTE 101 along the edge of the ocean, barely taking notice of its placid waters or the blight of the offshore oil drilling platforms. Ventura and Oxnard and Camarillo were soon behind me, and I began the long ascent before the freeway dropped down into the Los Angeles Basin.

This was familiar territory, traveled hundreds of times over the years; I'd often gone to Los Angeles to visit museums and attend plays and concerts. For a while there had been a man I'd stayed with in Redondo Beach. But mostly my journeys south had been to see the Aunts in East L.A.

The Aunts—I always thought of them as capitalized—were Mama's sisters, Margarita and Constanza. There were two other aunts—Florencia and Claudia—who sometimes came for visits from the Mexican state of Sinaloa, but they were unmemorable: silent, faded women who only seemed alive when laughing and chattering behind closed doors with Mama and the Los Angeles Aunts. There were uncles, too—macho men from either side of the border who gathered apart on the front porch of Constanza's little frame house to drink beer and discuss important things in their deep, booming voices. And there were the cousins—the exotic L.A. cousins.

Most of them were older than Carlota and me. Older and more worldly-wise. This was in the last days of the pachuco, that knife-wielding, hip-talking scourge of barrio life in the forties and fifties. My male cousins were a little young to be true pachucos, but they wore the trademark pegged pants and outrageously poufed hair; they called each other *ese* ("man") and *vato* ("dude"), and sometimes they were *bien prendidos,* which translates into "well-lit" and means drunk. Next to them and their hard-faced, gaudily dressed sisters, Carlota and I seemed mere Girl Scouts (which we actually were—Santa Barbara Troop 49).

95

The cousins suffered our presence because—I realize now—we were a perfect audience, easily awed. They would strut up and down the sidewalk, talking of gang fights and marijuana and calling their girlfriends "chicks." And all the time they'd watch Carlota's and my expressions out of the corners of their eyes. It didn't matter to us that these same cousins became peculiarly docile when Tía Margarita would call them in to supper, nor that they would mind their manners at the table as much as we did; we still went back to Santa Barbara with intoxicating visions of big city life dancing in our impressionable little heads.

As the years passed, we went to the Aunts' for different reasons: children's birthday parties gave way to weddings and baptisms, and later there were funerals. And as we grew, Carlota and I went less frequently; when we did, there were fewer cousins on hand. Donny, Margarita's son, had been killed in Vietnam; his brother, Jimmy, was a contractor and now lived in Illinois. Constanza's son, Tom, we didn't speak of; he'd gone to prison many years before. Rosalita had lots of babies, Patty worked as a nurse in San Diego, Josie had a drunken husband, and Lisa had turned out bad. And so it went year after year, the family drifting apart. I supposed it was the American way in the 1980s, but now—as I turned west on the Santa Monica Freeway, rather than going east—I felt a sharp stab of nostalgia for those afternoons on the cracked sidewalks of East L.A.

Manzanita Way turned out to be a block-long street within walking distance of Santa Monica's beach, and it actually had manzanita growing alongside it. The evergreen shrubs were in full bloom, and their waxy bell-like flowers were a subtle contrast to the showier yellow blossoms of the forsythia bushes in many of the yards. The houses were typical California stucco bungalows like my own, but they sat farther back from the street and many were on double lots. Mrs. Manuela's address was 1121A, which meant she probably occupied a cottage behind one of the larger homes. I parked at the curb under a big purple-flowered jacaranda tree and found a concrete path leading between numbers 1121 and 1119. There was a second building back there, built on the style of the main house and containing two units. I knocked on the door of unit A, and it was soon opened by a small, very old white-haired woman in a pink candy-striped dress. Her seamed mouth curved up in a smile when she saw me, and her eyes began to sparkle behind silver-rimmed glasses.

"Señorita Oliverez?" she asked.

"Sí."

"Buenas tardes." She held the screen door open and motioned for me to come in. "Por favor."

I stepped into a tiny living room that was decorated in blue-and-green floral-patterned wallpaper; the furnishings were upholstered in a Wedgwood blue. Two tortoiseshell kittens lay on one cushion of the loveseat, curled in a yin-and-yang position, and a third was licking its paws on a hassock. The room was clean and uncluttered, and everything in it—including Mrs. Manuela—seemed diminutive. I sat down on the love seat at her request, feeling strangely big and awkward, in spite of being a slender five-foot-three.

Mrs. Manuela said, "Lo siento. . . . I am sorry. Do you wish to speak in English?"

In Spanish, I replied, "I am at home in either language."

"Then, we will speak Spanish. As I grow older, I find the language of our people comforts me. In it, I know who I am. And since your interest in my family is what has brought you here, it is fitting." She moved toward a door at the rear of the room. "I have coffee brewing. Will you have some?"

"I'd like that, thank you."

"Then I will bring it. While I am gone, you may make the acquaintance of Laurel and Hardy and Chaplin." She indicated the kittens. "They are Hollywood cats, abandoned there and rescued by a young friend of mine. And they are all comics."

I smiled as she left the room and got up to pat Chaplin, the one who was licking his paws. He may have been a comic, but right now he seemed to have misplaced his sense of humor, because he glared at me and went on licking. I decided not to bother Laurel and Hardy, who were still sleeping.

Mrs. Manuela returned in a few minutes with a pot of coffee and two mugs—blue, like the room. She poured the steaming liquid, handed me one mug, and said, "Do you wish cream or sugar?"

"Neither, thank you."

"Good. You will live a longer life for abstaining."

Por Dios, I thought, she's a health nut like Nick. And—again like him—her appearance indicated she knew what she was talking about. She had to be in her nineties, but she moved like a much younger person.

She sat in a chair opposite the love seat, tasted her coffee, and

97

then nodded approval. "I have a new percolator," she said, "and I am only learning how to use it. This is good, is it not?"

"Very good."

Looking pleased, she set her mug on a coaster on the table beside her and said, "Now. You are interested in my family."

"Yes." I had thought of ways to explain what otherwise seemed like plain nosiness and had come up with a story that had the advantage of being at least partially true. "I am assisting a historian who lives in the village of Las Lomas in writing a paper for a journal."

She nodded. "Mr. Sam Ryder, who is a neighbor of Rosa Jenkins."

"That's right. So far I've done little more than visit the land you own near the village—what remains of the rancho."

Mrs. Manuela's face gentled when I mentioned the rancho, and her eyes softened until they had a misty quality. "Rancho Rinconada de los Robles. The land you speak of is the old pueblo and the site of the hacienda."

"I understand you still own the property."

"Yes. I doubt I could ever bring myself to part with it. But frankly, no one has asked me to. While the rest of the rancho—those portions that were sold off many years ago—is excellent agricultural land, the pueblo itself is good for nothing. Don Esteban Velasquez—my grandfather—built the rancho as he did so as not to waste usable land. The pueblo was in a rocky area, as you have seen; the hacienda stood on a hill above. My father, Felipe Velasquez, claimed that Don Esteban loved the site because it reminded him of his native home in Oaxaca, Mexico."

"Did you live at the hacienda when you were a girl?"

"For a time, yes. But my father died when I was very young, and my mother and I moved to Santa Barbara. I was not there for very long, either. When I became of school age, my mother became concerned about me. I was not a happy child, and did not make friends easily. In fact, my only playmate was Rosa Jenkins—she was Rosa Santiago then, daughter of our servant, Maria. Finally my mother decided to send me to the school my father had attended in Mexico."

Mrs. Manuela paused and smiled faintly. "I was so shy that I would not go alone, so my mother had to send Rosa with me. She received a good education on account of my backwardness, and we have been friends all our lives."

I said, "Why did you and your mother leave the hacienda?"

"It was very lonely there after my father's death. He was a great man, and my mother loved him very much. Maria Santiago once told me that before my father died, my mother was a very strong woman. Too strong, perhaps, because she and my father fought frequently. But after we moved, she became more and more withdrawn and reclusive. I have always suspected that she sent me away because secretly she wanted to be alone."

"What happened to her?"

"She died—those of my generation would say of a broken heart—when I was sixteen and still at school. Although I had seen her only on vacations, I was shattered by the loss. I had no one left in the world but a stuffy old family lawyer who was to dole out what I considered stingy payments from the estate. I started to pine away, as was fashionable with young girls in that day."

The cat on the hassock—Chaplin—stood up and jumped into Mrs. Manuela's lap. She pushed it into a lying-down position and began to stroke it, continuing as if there had been no interruption. "One day, Rosa decided she had had enough of my languishing. She came to me and said, 'Look, we are all alone in the world'— her mother had also recently died—'and we are of age, so let's do something daring. Let's run off to Los Angeles and get jobs and find ourselves husbands.' Naturally I was shocked—but not so shocked that I didn't think about it. And within a week we were on our way north."

I said, "*Did* you get jobs and find husbands?"

She smiled gently. "We did. Not the jobs we'd envisioned, of course; we did not become silent-movie queens. But we did make ends meet, working as shopgirls in the barrio and living in a rooming house run by a kindly woman who liked young girls and looked after them. Rosa met Tom Jenkins first; he was an Anglo, but that didn't matter—Rosa always was daring. Ironically, Tom was from Lompoc, he owned a drugstore there. The store prospered, and he bought her a little summer home in Las Lomas, and when he died, she moved up there for good."

"And you?"

"My husband was called Tom also. We met at a dance and married within a month. Then we moved here because both of us had always wanted to live close to the sea. Tom was a good provider; he worked for a warehouser, the same one for forty years.

We were able to buy this property cheaply, and with his salary and what was left of my family's money and the rental from these units, we had a fine life. My only regret is that we never were able to have children. Tom has been gone sixteen years now, and I miss him as if he had died yesterday."

I felt a sharp twisting sensation deep inside. I hadn't been with Dave long enough that I would still miss him after sixteen years. He hadn't given me the chance.

Mrs. Manuela must have seen the pain on my face, because she said, "What is the trouble?"

"Oh." I made a gesture of dismissal. "Oh, it's nothing."

But she didn't believe me. "Have you been disappointed in love?"

"Well . . . yes."

She shook her head sympathetically. "That is always painful, and when one is young, it is even more so. Time will heal your hurt, however. There will be others for you, and eventually you will find the One."

The One. *That* brought back memories. I pictured the little bedroom Carlota and I had shared—the one that was now my guestroom—and remembered the long-ago nights when we'd been tucked into bed and were supposed to be sleeping. One of us would creep into the other's bed, and we'd pull the covers over our heads so Mama couldn't hear, and then we'd speculate on the men who would one day arrive to claim us. What would their names be? What would they look like? Would they be rich or handsome? And—most important of all—when and where would they appear? We'd been terribly anxious for them to do so, but so far they hadn't—neither for me nor for my sister.

The conversation was making me uncomfortable, so I merely said "I hope so." Then I led the topic back to the reason I had come there. "Mrs. Manuela, what happened to the furnishings that were in the old hacienda?"

For a moment she looked confused. "Oh, of course. My mother took them to our new home in Santa Barbara. After she died, they were placed in storage by the lawyer, and when Tom and I finally bought our house—we lived in the big one up front, I only moved back here and rented that one out after I found I could no longer take care of it properly—when we bought it, the furnishings were shipped to us."

100

"You've sold some of them, haven't you?"

"Only recently. I couldn't keep all of them here, and I decided I should let them go to people who really wanted them."

"Do you remember a marriage coffer, one with a crucifix design around the edges?"

"Why, yes. That was my mother's, her hope chest, as they call it now. I hated to part with it, but the dealer wanted to buy the things in a lot, and the chest was part of it."

"I think you'll be pleased to know it has found a good home." I went on to tell her about my job, the display Rudy Lopez and I were assembling, and the auction.

Mrs. Manuela looked both pleased and interested. "How strange it is that the chest ended up in Santa Barbara once more," she said. "The auction house I sold it to was here in Santa Monica, but I understand they conduct sales in all parts of the state. Is it because of the chest that you and Mr. Ryder became interested in my family?"

"In a way. Mrs. Manuela, what can you tell me about the religious artifacts your grandfather hid during the Bear Flag Revolution?"

The non sequitur didn't seem to surprise her. "Ah, yes—the artifacts. That is part of the family folklore. But how did you learn of them?"

I explained about the detective's report in the marriage coffer. Mrs. Manuela's faded old eyes sparkled with excitement.

"So that was where the key to the chest was," she said. "I never knew about that little compartment. The chest was where my mother kept her important personal papers, and she always locked the drawer, since I was an exceptionally curious child, and not a tidy one when prying into other people's belongings."

"Then, all the years you had it, you were never able to look inside the drawer?"

"No. I thought the key had been lost."

I said, "But you *did* know that your father had hired someone to look for the artifacts."

"No, I am afraid I did not. You must remember that I was very young when he died and we moved from the rancho. And my mother never mentioned anything of the sort."

"Did she speak to you of the artifacts?"

"No, never. What I knew of them came from Maria Santiago."

101

"Perhaps there would be something about them in the box of papers you mentioned on the telephone?"

She smiled, her face a fine web of wrinkles. "Of course. Come with me, please."

She led me through the small dining ell to the door to the bedroom. Inside was a heavily carved canopied bed, obviously one of the furnishings Señora Velasquez had removed from the hacienda. Mrs. Manuela pointed to it. "There is a wooden box under there that contains the papers. Will you bring it out, please?"

I got down on my hands and knees and peered under the overhang of the bedspread. The box was a low one and measured perhaps three by four feet, with an unlocked hasp and brass hinges similar to the fittings on the marriage coffer. I grasped it and pulled; it was heavy and cumbersome but slid easily on the hardwood floor.

Mrs. Manuela said, "The box contains many of my family's papers. The lawyer had it sent down along with the furniture. In those days I was too involved with my life as a newly married woman to go through them, and in later years whenever I started to, I couldn't withstand the pain. You are welcome to look, however. Take all the time you need. I will be in the living room watching the news."

I waited until she had left the room, then raised the heavy lid of the box. A musty odor rose to my nostrils: dust, old paper, and maybe a touch of mold. I sat cross-legged on the floor and slowly went through the box's contents.

There were shabby leather-bound ledgers full of long columns of figures that I supposed told the story of the last days of Rancho Rinconada de los Robles. A sheaf of papers showing transfer of title to various portions of the land was a sad footnote to the numbers. I set aside several bundles of what looked to be personal correspondence, letters written in Spanish in various old-fashioned hands. A Bible was inscribed with the birthdates and death dates of Velasquez family members. I studied it for a few moments, noting that Mrs. Manuela, the last entry of any kind, had been born in 1892. In addition to the record in the Bible, there were a number of *fes de bautismo,* certificates of baptism, and *partidas de defunción,* death certificates.

Stacks of bills from Santa Barbara merchants continued the story of Senõra Velasquez and the young Sofia after they had moved from the hacienda: They were for food, clothing, cordwood, medical attention. There was a deed in the name of Olivia Velasquez to a house on a street not far from mine; evidently the document had not been turned over when the house had been sold after her death. There was also a pair of books in the box: One was a heavy, leather-bound California history in which a page about two-thirds of the way through had been marked with a white silk ribbon. I opened it and saw the name Don Esteban Velasquez. The three-paragraph account praised his bravery as a *soldado* and described the parcel of land granted him by the Mexican government. The other volume turned out not to be a book at all but a photograph album.

I paged through it and found it was only half-full of faded, sepia-toned photographs showing men and women in heavy old-fashioned garments striking the exaggerated, dramatic poses favored in the latter part of the last century. One of the last pictures was of a man in his fifties, a woman half as old, and an infant. The parents stood on a rocky hillock covered with live oak, the child in the mother's arms. When I turned the page, the picture came loose from its hinges, and I saw on the opposite side the notation "Felipe, Olivia, Sofia."

This, then, was the last of the Velasquez family. I held the photograph up and studied the faces of the couple, Felipe's in particular. There was intelligence in his dark eyes and a slightly selfish, aristocratic set to his mouth. As I stared at the faded print, I found myself seeing the man as John Quincannon might have, filling in the gaps that, by its nature, the detective's report did not contain. Finally I set the album aside and began to remove the few items remaining in the box.

One of these was another accounts ledger, and I was about to set it aside when I saw the ragged edges of some yellowed vellum pages protruding from its top. I pulled them out—and recognized John Quincannon's familiar handwriting.

Excited, I dropped the ledger on the floor and glanced through the loose pages; they were wrinkled and torn in places, but they appeared to be a continuation of the detective's report. Somehow they had gotten separated from the first portion and dumped in here with the other family papers. It was a wonder they hadn't been destroyed.

Hurriedly I put the papers on the bed and began to replace the other items in the wooden box. It would be rude, of course, to rush off right away after having imposed on Sofia Manuela and partaken of her hospitality, but I thought she would understand. And I could also plead the necessity of returning to Santa Barbara so I could visit my mother in the hospital.

But Santa Barbara seemed terribly distant at the moment. I didn't want to wait until I got back there to read these reports. And I didn't have to visit Mama tonight anyway; she'd said this morning—ungraciously, I'd thought at the time—that one visit a day would suffice.

I considered what to do for a few moments longer and then made up my mind. First I would take polite leave of Mrs. Manuela, promising her a return visit when I'd looked further into the story of the search for the Velasquez artifacts. Then I'd find a drugstore and buy a toothbrush, toothpaste, and other necessities. And then I'd find a reasonably-priced motel with a coffee shop, get carryout food, and curl up in my room with this second installment of John Quincannon's investigation.

PART IV
1894

ONE

THE CHIEF OF police of Santa Barbara was a robust, bullnecked man with enormous bristling mustaches. His name was Vandermeer. He wore his blue uniform as if it were a West Point dress outfit, stood and sat with such erectness that Quincannon wondered idly if he had a deformed spine, spoke between tight-pursed lips, possessed a fondness for the word "mister," and managed to convey a curious mixture of deference and suspicion in his speech and actions. He studied Quincannon's Secret Service credentials for a full three minutes, scowling all the while and at the last with such ferocity that Quincannon was certain he was about to pronounce them forgeries and hurl their bearer into the nearest cell; then he said in a deferential voice dripping with suspicion, "My office is at the government's disposal, mister. What can I do for you?"

Relieved, Quincannon said, "I'm looking for a man named James Evans, in connection with a counterfeiting case under investigation. The last address I have for him is number twelve hundred-and-six Anacapa Street, this city, but he no longer resides there."

"Evans, eh? Evans." Vandermeer shook his head as if to jog his memory but with such violence that his mustaches cracked like whips—or so Quincannon fancied. "Only one James Evans I know. Burglar and cracksman, among other things. I expect he's your man."

"No doubt," Quincannon said, "if he resided at number twelve hundred-and-six Anacapa Street."

"We'll soon find out, mister. We'll soon find out."

Vandermeer summoned one of his constables, who in turn brought in a thick file on James Evans. The constable's name was Ogilvy, and it developed that he had twice arrested Evans, once on suspicion of breaking-and-entering and once for public drunkenness and lewd and lascivious behavior at the Arroyo Burro hot springs. "Exposed himself to an old lady and two girls of sixteen,"

107

Ogilvy explained. "Waved his pizzle about like it was Old Glory on a parade day. Drew quite a crowd." He paused thoughtfully. "Most of 'em women, as I recall."

Vandermeer was looking through the file. "Last known address, number twelve hundred-and-six Anacapa Street," he said, and then fixed Ogilvy with a suspicious glance. "What happened to Evans? Any idea?"

The constable shook his head. "He seems to have vanished."

"Dropped out of sight, eh?"

"Yes, sir. Not a whisper of him for some time now. Higgins and me went to question him about a robbery two months ago; he'd been gone awhile then."

"Rumors as to where?"

"A passel. Los Angeles, Santa Maria, Los Alamos Valley, half a dozen more. None of 'em confirmed."

Quincannon asked, "Has Evans dropped out of sight before this?"

"A time or two," Ogilvy said. "Gone elsewhere on a job or to hide out from one he pulled here, I'll warrant. But he's always come back sooner or later."

"Good riddance, if he's gone for good this time," Vandermeer said. "Bad apple, that one. Spoiled enough barrels in this town."

Quincannon asked if he could examine the file; Vandermeer, scowling his ferocious scowl, turned it over to him with suspicious deference. Reading through it at the chief's desk, he learned that James Evans had served one three-year sentence at San Quentin for burglary and four shorter sentences at the county jail (one of those for exposing his pizzle at the Arroyo Burro hot springs). Evans had no particular specialities when it came to his choice of victims or the type of goods he stole; he was believed to have robbed the very poor as well as the very rich, and to have pilfered as much as eight thousand dollars and as little as twenty-seven pennies from a child's piggy bank. He had been born in Ohio, had come to California fifteen years ago, and had no known relatives living here. He had never married, or at least had not as far as the police knew. He had only two known acquaintances, Charles Tompkins and Oliver Witherspoon, with each of whom he had been arrested on suspicion of burglary. Quincannon asked about these two men.

"Tompkins is no longer a threat to society," Vandermeer said with tight-lipped satisfaction. "San Quentin is where you'll find him these days. I put him there myself, eight months ago."

"And Witherspoon?"

"Still active, mister. But he won't be for long, by God."

"He lives in Santa Barbara, then?"

"He does," Ogilvy said, "but if you're thinking he'll give you a lead to Evans's whereabouts, Mr. Boggs, I'm afraid you're in for a disappointment. I talked to Witherspoon myself after Evans disappeared. He claims to know nothing and couldn't be budged." The constable tapped his knuckles meaningfully. "Nor persuaded."

"I'll want to see him anyway," Quincannon said. "That is, if you will be so good as to give me his address."

"Certainly, sir." Ogilvy started out.

"One other matter before you go. The reason I'm hunting Evans is that we of the Secret Service believe he is supplying stolen gold statuary to a vicious gang of koniakers, who then melt them down and use the raw metal to mint their counterfeit coins. We—"

"Diabolical scheme," Vandermeer interrupted. He sounded impressed. "Clever swine, eh?"

"Very clever." Quincannon paused to light the second of the two Cuban panatelas he had bought at the Arlington Hotel. "Naturally," he said, "we are anxious to find the source of this stolen statuary. There may be more of it, and if we can prevent any further loss, the Service is of course bound to do so. Confidentially, gentlemen—and it pains me to say it—it may take a while to put the coney gang out of business."

"Expect you're doing your best, mister," Vandermeer said. "The statuary was stolen here, you say?"

"Or the environs. We know for a fact that one of the statues was of the Virgin Mary—approximately fourteen inches in height, sculpted by an artist named Francisco Portolá, and made of pure gold. Was such a statue reported stolen within the past six to eight months?"

"Not to my recollection. Constable?"

"No, sir," Ogilvy said. "But I'll have a look at the theft reports."

Quincannon sat back in the chief's chair and patiently smoked his cigar while Vandermeer stood in a stiff military posture and glowered at nothing in particular. It was no more than ten minutes until Constable Ogilvy returned.

"Well, mister?" Vandermeer asked him.

"Nothing, sir. If a gold statue was pilfered here within the past year, the theft weren't reported to us."

Quincannon sighed. More work for him; and the more difficult his task, the longer it would be before his return to San Francisco. He asked Ogilvy for Oliver Witherspoon's address. The constable gave him two: a boarding house on Arrellaga Street where Witherspoon resided, and a produce warehouse at Gaviota Beach where he was employed on an irregular basis.

"Try the boarding house first, Mr. Boggs," Ogilvy advised. "Ollie Witherspoon only does honest work when he's forced to, and then you can be sure it ain't as honest as it might be."

As Quincannon prepared to take his leave, Vandermeer said, "Keep us apprised of your progress, mister. Let us know if there's anything else we can do. We stand four-square behind the government here in Santa Barbara."

"I'm sure the president will be pleased to hear that."

"The president? You're personally acquainted with Mr. Cleveland?"

Quincannon had never met Grover Cleveland, nor seen eye to eye with him, for that matter. He said, "Oh yes. Grover is a close friend of mine."

"Good man," Vandermeer said suspiciously. "Fine president."

"Indeed he is."

"I voted for him, mister. You can believe that."

Quincannon believed it. He said, "As any right-thinking citizen would."

"You'll give Mr. Cleveland my regards?"

"The moment I see him."

Vandermeer smiled—an occurrence no doubt as rare, Quincannon thought, as a drunken burglar displaying his pizzle for public inspection. And little wonder, too. Now he knew why the chief wore a perpetual scowl and spoke through such tight-pursed lips. Vandermeer possessed an enormous set of teeth any horse in the state would have been proud to call his own.

Oliver Witherspoon was not at his boarding house on Arrellaga Street. He was, in fact, his landlady said with some amazement, working at the produce warehouse at Gaviota Beach.

Quincannon produced another sigh. Times must be difficult in the burglary trade, he reflected, though no more difficult than they

110

were—at least for the moment—in the detective trade. He returned to the Arlington Hotel, where he changed into rougher clothing from his warbag; then he set out again. A block away, on Victoria Street, were the hotel's stables. From the hostler he rented a rather spirited claybank saddle horse and obtained directions to Gaviota Beach.

When he arrived there half an hour later, he found himself not on the Pacific shore, as he had expected, but on that of the Santa Barbara Channel; the ocean was some distance away, around the bend of Point Concepción. A grouping of warehouses, stock pens, and wharves had been built along the beach, and several small coastal freighters were tied up there. Teamsters and stevedores were busily transferring wool and a variety of produce from the warehouses, and cattle from the stock pens, to the waiting ships; profanity rang as loudly in the salt-tanged air as the bawling of livestock. Quincannon found the atmosphere to his liking. He had always loved water—the Potomac and Mississippi Rivers in his youth, the Pacific after his move to California. If he had not become a detective like his father, he felt that he might have taken up the adventurous career of a riverboat pilot or a seafaring man.

He located the nearest produce warehouse, dismounted, and began asking after Oliver Witherspoon. No one at this warehouse knew him, evidently; Quincannon rode to the next. But it was not until he came to the third and last warehouse that his questions produced results. A stevedore directed him around to where a group of men were unloading bales of wool from a Studebaker freight wagon bearing the words SAN JULIAN RANCH on its side panel. One of the men admitted to being Witherspoon, though he did so with reluctance, wariness, and as much suspicion as Chief of Police Vandermeer had displayed.

Quincannon drew him around the corner of the warehouse, to where he had left the claybank horse. Witherspoon was a big man, heavy through the chest and shoulders, with powerful arms and legs; but he had one of the smallest heads Quincannon had ever seen. It put him in mind of a knobbly peanut crowned by a few sparse black fibers and set out upon a hulking rock. The kernels inside the peanut were proportionately small, Quincannon decided after two minutes with the man. So small, in fact, that they could not even be dignified by the term "brain."

"Well?" Witherspoon said in a reedy, goober-sized voice. "Who the gawddam hell are you?"

"The name is Boggs. Down from Frisco."

"Frisco? After what with me?"

"Nothing with you. It's Jimmy Evans I'm after."

"Who?"

"Jimmy Evans. Used to hang his hat on Anacapa Street."

"Don't know any Jimmy Evans."

"Come along now, Ollie. None of that with me. I've got a lay on for Jimmy."

Witherspoon's knobbly face screwed up as if it were being tightened in a vise. He seemed to be trying valiantly to think. At length he said, "Who sent you down from Frisco?"

"Luther Duff."

"Don't know any Luther Duff."

"He knows you, Ollie. How do you suppose I come to have your name and where to look you up?"

More facial contortions. "What's the job for Jimmy?"

"I'll tell that to him."

"Not until I hear it first. Maybe I heard of Luther Duff, but I never heard of nobody named Boggs."

"Where's Jimmy? Close by?"

Witherspoon glared at him and said nothing.

"Wouldn't be on the lammas, would he?"

"I ain't talking," Witherspoon said. "You are. What's your game, Boggs?"

"Mine and Luther's. And Jimmy's, if he wants in."

"Well?"

"Religious statues. Gold ones."

"Huh?"

"Jimmy swiped a gold statue six months ago—the Virgin Mary—and laid it off to Duff. Duff's just sold it to a lad who wants more of the same. He sent me down to . . . Now what's this, Ollie? What's tickled your funny bone?"

Witherspoon was laughing. At least, Quincannon assumed that was what he was doing; the sounds that came out of him were a series of low rumbles and squeaks, as if a herd of mice were tumbling down a coal chute. The sounds continued for another fifteen seconds, at which point Witherspoon ran out of wind. He bent over at the middle, gasped several times, finally caught his

112

breath, coughed explosively, and wiped drool off his mouth with the back of one hairy paw.

"Gawddam," he said. "Gawddam."

"If it's a joke, let me have a laugh, too."

"It's a joke, all right. And gawddam if it ain't on you and Luther Duff."

"How so?"

"There ain't no more of them statues like the one Jimmy swiped. Not where he got it, by Gawd."

"And where was that?"

"Out of a Mex storekeeper's rooms, while the greaser was downstairs sellin' boots and shirts. Now ain't that a gut-buster?"

Quincannon's smile was genuine. "It is that, Ollie; I'll admit it. Where does this Mex live? Here in Santa Barbara?"

"Sure. Jimmy was on the hog at the time; he was only after some fast jack. I wisht I'd seen his face when he come on that statue. He said he like to fell down dead on the spot." The rumbling and squeaking noises started again. "Gawddam," Witherspoon said.

"What was his name?"

"Whose?"

"The Mex storekeeper's."

"Who knows? Don't matter—he ain't got no more of them statues, that's for certain."

"Too bad for Jimmy, then, if he's still on the hog."

"He ain't. He blew wise to a pretty lay down south."

"Is that where he is now?"

Witherspoon's good humor evaporated. "I ain't sayin'. You still after him?"

"Not anymore," Quincannon said. He moved to the claybank, swung himself into the saddle. "When you see him tell him Duff's in the market for the right booty."

"I'll do that. You headin' back to Frisco, Boggs?"

Quincannon said, "Tomorrow, with any luck. Let me give you some advice, Ollie: Never spark a stubborn widow, especially in the spring. It can be damned frustrating." He rode off, leaving Witherspoon once more engaged in the monumental task of trying to produce thought inside a peanut shell.

Chief Vandermeer was gone from the police station when Quincannon paid his second call of the afternoon. Constable Ogilvy, however, was still on duty and as obliging as he had been earlier. He reexamined the local theft reports for the previous six months, and much to Quincannon's relief, found one filed on October 6, 1893, by a man named Luis Cordova who owned a dry-goods store on Cañon Perdido Street and who lived in quarters above it. A gold statue of the Virgin Mary did not appear on the brief list of items stolen, nor did any other kind of statue, religious artifact, or valuable.

"Peculiar, ain't it, Mr. Boggs?" Ogilvy said. "This fellow Cordova lives poor in the Mexican quarter, so what was he doing with an expensive gold statue? And why didn't he report it stolen?"

"Why, indeed?" Quincannon said, and went to find out.

TWO

THE NEIGHBORHOOD IN which Luis Cordova lived and worked was a poor one, as both Witherspoon and Ogilvy had indicated; but it was not without its pride or its zest for life. There was a good deal of activity along Cañon Perdido Street, a good deal of animated conversation flavored with laughter. Inside a cantina someone was playing a guitar with enthusiasm; Quincannon recognized the liquid rhythms of "*Cielito Lindo*" as he passed. The spicy scent of *frijoles* and simmering taco meat floated on the balmy spring air, reminding him that he had not eaten since breakfast.

He dismounted in front of Luis Cordova's dry-goods store and looped the claybank's reins around the tie rail. The building, of wood and adobe, with an upstairs front gallery, was situated at the end of a mixed block of private dwellings and similar small businesses—a harness shop, a feed store, a shabby tonsorial parlor, a greengrocer's. An outside stairway led up along the east wall, giving access to Cordova's upstairs living quarters; a huge olive tree effectively concealed the upper half of the stairs from the street, an arrangement to tempt the black soul of any housebreaker. The westside wall faced on an intersecting street; it was open now and a buckboard had been drawn up near it. Two young men were busily unloading bolts of brightly colored cloth and carrying them into a rear storeroom. Neither man was Luis Cordova; Señor Cordova, Quincannon was told when he approached them, could be found at the front of the shop.

He entered through the front door and was greeted by the not-unpleasant odors of dust, cloth, lye soap, and oiled leather. The interior was well-stocked with a variety of goods, among them simple clothing for men, women, and children, boots and huaraches and high-top shoes, serapés, rebozos, textiles of different types. In the middle of all this, a thin gray-haired man of indeterminate age was having a spirited argument with a fat woman over an inexpensive black mantilla. The woman, as near as Quincannon could tell with his limited command of Spanish, was upset over the fact that the brand-new mantilla had torn the first time she put it on; she wanted it replaced. The man kept insisting that the mantilla had not been damaged at the time of its sale, that he always inspected each item for defects before allowing it to leave the premises.

The argument raged for another five minutes, with neither side gaining an advantage. Finally the fat woman threw up her hands, told the gray-haired man that she would never again buy so much as a button from him, told him further that he was an *hijo de garañón*—son of a jackass—and stormed out. Quincannon smiled at her as she passed, and tipped his hat; he received a milk-curdling glower in return.

The gray-haired man sighed elaborately, as if such altercations offended his sense of propriety. Then he dusted his hands together and moved to where Quincannon waited. If he was surprised to find a gringo in his store, and a gringo who resembled a pirate at that, he gave no indication of it. He said, "*Buenas tardes,* señor. I may help you?"

"If you are Luis Cordova, you may."

"*Sí.* Yes, I am."

"I'd like a word with you about the burglary you suffered six months ago."

"*Qué pasa?* My English, it is not so good. Burglary?"

Quincannon rummaged through his Spanish lexicon and said haltingly, "*Robo con escado. Soy aquí a discutir un ladrón que escala una casa.*"

"Ah, *sí, sí.*" Interest brightened Cordova's swarthy features, but it was outweighed by an odd sort of apprehension. "You are from the *policía?*"

"I represent a man who now possesses one of the items stolen from you," Quincannon said in Spanish.

"What item is that, señor?"

"A gold statue of the Virgin Mary."

Cordova winced as if he had been struck. He backed up a step, put out a defensive hand, and said anxiously, "There must be some mistake, señor. I know nothing of such a statue."

"It was sculpted by Francisco Portolá for Don Esteban Velasquez in 1843. These words and date are engraved in the base."

"I have never seen such a statue."

116

"It was stolen from your rooms."

"No, señor. No . . . "

"A man named James Evans has admitted stealing it from you," Quincannon lied. "In the face of this, do you still deny possessing it?"

Cordova backed up several more steps, shaking his head violently. Fear glistened in his dark eyes; the sweat of it beaded his forehead. Its cause, Quincannon thought, was something profound, to affect the man this way.

He pursued Cordova until the storekeeper's retreat was stayed by a low wooden counter. Then he said with as much portent as he could muster in his halting Spanish, "The rightful owner of the statue is the family of Don Esteban Velasquez in Santa Ynez Valley. It is now in the hands of Felipe Velasquez, Don Esteban's son; he is the man I represent. Are you aware of the statue's history, Señor Cordova?"

Cordova kept shaking his head. His mouth quivered open, but he didn't speak.

"It is one of many artifacts hidden by Don Esteban in 1846, during the war with Mexico. It is the only one that has been found since. Perhaps you know the whereabouts of the others?"

"No, I know nothing . . . "

"How did the statue come into your possession?"

"Please, señor . . . "

"Did you steal it? Are *you* a thief?"

"*Madre de Dios!* No, no . . . "

"Then how did you come to have it?"

"I did not have it, I have never seen such a statue, I know nothing about Don Esteban Velasquez, nothing!" The words burst out of him in a spray of spittle, his voice rising on each one until the last few were a shout. He twisted away to one side, almost upsetting a table stacked with rough-cloth peasant shirts; swung around and pointed a trembling finger at Quincannon. "Go away! Leave my place of business! You are not *policía*; you have no right to remain here without permission. Leave, or I will have you put out by force!"

Quincannon hesitated. "Listen to me, Señor Cordova—"

"No, no, I will not listen! Alfredo! Sebastián! Come in here, quickly!"

A rear door was thrown open, and the two young men ran in from the storeroom. Big, both of them—and strong; Quincannon knew it would be painful to do battle with them, even with his college training in pugilism and even if he had been inclined to a fight, which he wasn't.

He said to Cordova, "Very well. As you wish. But I will soon return, or others will come in my place. The *policía*, perhaps. You cannot hold your silence forever, amigo."

Cordova said nothing. He seemed to have aged several years in the past few minutes, to have become a stooped and shrunken old man; even his clothing seemed to hang on him now, as baggily as on a scarecrow.

"We will know the truth," Quincannon said ominously. "Sooner or later, we will know the truth." He turned on his heel and walked out.

He sat the claybank for a full minute, waiting to see if Cordova would follow after him for any reason. No one followed after him. Finally, feeling disgruntled, he reined the horse around and made for Victoria Street and the Arlington stables.

It had been an odd encounter, he thought as he rode. Cordova had acted as though he were the thief, not the victim. *Had* he stolen the Velasquez statue? If he hadn't, how had it come into his hands? And why was he so afraid to admit to knowledge of it?

A pretty puzzle, to be sure. And one that might not have an easy solution. He had hoped to be on board tomorrow's train for San Francisco; as matters stood now, he would be spending tomorrow—and God knew how many others after it—in Santa Barbara and its environs.

Being a dedicated and conscientious detective had its drawbacks sometimes. Damned if it didn't.

It was dusk when he arrived at the Arlington Hotel. In his suite he changed clothes for the second time, putting on a fine new Cheviot coat, striped trousers, and a French cravat. Downstairs again, he paused to buy two more Cuban panatelas and a freshly blended latakia pipe mixture for his pouch; and then he took himself off to the St. Charles Hotel at State and De La Guerra streets, a few blocks away.

The St. Charles was an older, two-story adobe structure, its upper level girdled by a broad veranda. It was nowise as large or as opulent as the Arlington, but there was an air of comfort and stability about it—a hotel for businessmen and visiting residents of the outlying towns and valleys, rather than for tourists come to town to take the waters, the sights, or other tourists.

When Quincannon asked at the desk for Felipe Velasquez, the clerk directed him to the small, dark bar off the lobby. Inside the bar he found Velasquez sitting alone before the fireplace, elegantly attired in a black, silver-trimmed *charro* outfit, a ruffled shirt, and a string tie with the familiar bull's-head clasp. He was indulging in a before-dinner glass of wine, which seemed to have done nothing to mellow him. He was in one of his dour moods. He greeted Quincannon tersely, invited him to sit down, and demanded to know what progress he had made since their arrival.

"Quite a bit, sir. Quite a bit."

"You have found James Evans?"

"No. But I've found the previous owner of the statue."

"Diablos!" Velasquez sat forward abruptly, almost spilling his wine; the ends of his tie made a sharp clicking noise as they came together, like castanets. "Who is he, this previous owner?"

"A man named Luis Cordova."

"Cordova, Cordova. I know no one by that name."

"He owns a dry-goods store in the Mexican quarter. Evans pilfered the statue from his rooms above the store."

"Only the poor live in the Mexican quarter. How would such a man—"

"—come to have a gold statue worth two thousand dollars? I don't know—yet." Quincannon went on to recount the details of his brief confrontation with Luis Cordova.

Velasquez saw nothing very puzzling in Cordova's behavior. He said angrily, "He must have stolen the statue himself. From someone else, or perhaps even from the place where my father and Padre Urbano hid it."

"He might not have stolen it at all," Quincannon said.

"Nonsense. Why else would he lie to you? Why else would he be so frightened? His actions make no sense unless he is of the same breed as this man Evans."

Quincannon adopted the patient, gently lecturing tone he used on stubborn and narrow-minded individuals. "There may be another explanation, Señor Velasquez. The facts we have now are too few.

We need more information about Cordova, his background and private life, before any definite conclusion can be reached."

"And how will you find out these additional facts?"

"I have my methods."

Velasquez grunted. "How long will these methods take, eh? Days? Weeks?"

"I have only been in Santa Barbara half of one day," Quincannon reminded him, "and already I've accomplished much."

"Bah," Velasquez said, unconvinced. "Put a pistol to Cordova's head; then he will tell you what we want to know."

"I would, if I felt it would accomplish the purpose. But I don't believe it would."

"And why not?"

"It isn't death or violence that Cordova fears. It's something else, something profound."

"What is so profound as death?"

"For most men, nothing. For some men, a great deal."

"Bah. You speak in platitudes."

"And what is a platitude but a common truth?"

Velasquez seemed about to argue further, changed his mind, picked up his wine, and sat peering into its dark red depths for several silent moments. Then he drained the glass, wiped his lips delicately with a lace handkerchief, and said, "Very well. You are the detective, and a competent one, as you have proven. I accept your judgment."

"Thank you."

"But I will not tolerate a long delay in this matter. I must know where Cordova obtained the statue, and as quickly as possible. *Comprende Usted?*"

"Perfectly."

"Bueno." Velasquez consulted a gold, hunting-style pocket watch. "I must leave now; I have a dinner engagement in twenty minutes, with relatives of my wife." He got to his feet.

Quincannon asked, "You still plan to return home tomorrow?"

"Yes. I leave at eight o'clock. And I will expect you at the rancho within three days. If you do not come . . . "

"I'll come. You have my word on that."

Velasquez nodded and took his leave without another word. Quincannon watched him walk out into the lobby, thinking that he did not relish the prospect of a long ride out to Santa Ynez Valley, or the prospect of a day or more under the same roof with Felipe Antonio Abregon y Velasquez. He had a feeling gringos were not treated with much respect at what was left of Rancho Rinconada de los Robles.

THREE

QUINCANNON WANDERED DOWN State Street, marveling at the big electric arc lights set atop tall wooden poles every half block that produced a white glare so bright the thoroughfare was like a strip of noonday cut from the darkness. Santa Barbara, he reflected, was quite a progressive and attractive little community. Still, he preferred San Francisco. Not only did it contain much that satisfied his broad and sometimes eccentric tastes, it also contained Sabina.

Near Stearns Wharf he found a seafood restaurant that served plump raw oysters and a substantial crab bouillabaisse as palatable as any in San Francisco. It was while partaking of such meals as this that he most regretted being a drunkard. A bottle of chilled French chardonnay would have offered an excellent compliment to the bouillabaisse.

He smoked a post-prandial pipe and considered the rest of the evening. The sulfur spring on Burton Mound? He had taken the waters there on his last visit to Santa Barbara—he had needed a little relaxation after his harrowing experience in Spookville—and had found them invigorating. But it was a long way to Burton Mound, as he recalled, he was not sure the spring was open to visitors after dark, and the waters *did* smell unpleasantly of rotten eggs.

A show at Lobero's Opera House? A quiet evening in bed with William Wordsworth? No, neither of those seemed appropriate to his mood. Well then? What *was* appropriate to his mood?

He still had not decided when he left the restaurant. It was a fine night, cool without being chilly, the sky a silky purple-black brimming with stars and a pale white moon that reminded him of the flesh of a woman's thigh. He stood for a moment in wistful contemplation and then sighed and set out aimlessly along Rancheria Street to the north.

He walked for some time, enjoying the feel of the evening and the silvery shimmer of moonlight on the ocean. There were fewer buildings in this direction, and consequently fewer people; the solitude and the quiet were soothing. Ahead and some distance to his left, a narrow strip of beach gleamed an almost luminescent white beyond a fringe of palm trees. It was an attractive sight, and it drew him toward it. He stopped alongside one of the palms and began to pack fresh tobacco into his pipe, watching the waves break gently around the dark remains of a derelict fishing boat that lay humped and half-buried near the water's edge. The beach was deserted. It might have been a beach on some tropical island, one of those where the native women reportedly went about with bare breasts for all eyes to feast upon. He might be alone upon it, with no other human being within miles—except, of course, for a bare-breasted native girl awaiting his return to their palm-roofed hut. . . .

So he was thinking, fancifully enough, when he became aware of the soft shuffle of movement through the sand behind him. He turned just in time to hear a familiar voice say, "Gawddam, if it ain't Mr. Boggs. How are ye this evening, Mr. Boggs?"

Quincannon smiled wryly and without mirth as Oliver Witherspoon and another, smaller man came up to him. Witherspoon was dressed as he had been that afternoon, in teamsters' garb—and the smile he wore with it was no more humorous than Quincannon's, and no friendlier than a shark's. But it was the other man who was responsible for the tension Quincannon felt. In the moonlight he could see a thin, sharp face, like a fox terrier's, but the eyes were shadowed under a cloth cap that covered most of his head. The man stood with his legs slightly apart, one hand out of sight under his coat, Napoleon-fashion. There was no doubt in Quincannon's mind that the hand held a pistol or some other lethal weapon, and that as fast as he himself was on the draw of his Navy revolver, he was at a mortal disadvantage if violence was in the offing.

He said slowly, speaking to Witherspoon but keeping his eyes on the smaller man, "Fancy this. Out for a stroll, are you, Ollie?"

"You might say that. We been followin' you, Boggs."

"Is that so?"

"Ever since you left the Arlington Hotel."

"How did you know I'm stopping at the Arlington?"

Witherspoon tapped the peanut atop his shoulders. "I got brains," he said, lying shamelessly. "I noticed the brand on that horse you

124

was riding this afternoon. Didn't take no time to track it down and find out who done the hiring."

"Very shrewd, Ollie. But why track me down at all? What's the game?"

"That's what *we* want to know."

"We, is it? And who would this gent be?"

"You don't know him?"

"No."

"Well, this here's Jimmy Evans. And he don't know you, either."

Quincannon feigned surprise. "Well, well. I heard you blew wise to better pickings down south, Jimmy."

"I did, but now I'm back." Evans owned a hard, clipped voice as deep as Witherspoon's was thin and reedy. "Ollie's right—I never heard of you. What're you after me for?"

"Luther Duff sent me to look you up."

"The hell he did. I've done business with Luther a lot of years. Nobody works for him; he squeezes a nickel hard enough to make the eagle shit. He wouldn't hire his mother if he had one. And he'd sure never put her up at a fancy hotel like the Arlington."

"The Arlington was my idea. I favor living high."

"On whose jack? Not Luther's."

"Mine."

"Where'd you get it?"

"On the game with Luther. I met him in Frisco a couple of months ago—put him onto a couple of things. Told him I'd double his business inside a year, and he took a flier on me. I've done all right."

"Maybe you have," Evans said, "but not for Luther. He's a wise old bugger—too wise to send a sharpie like you out on a daffy hunt for gold statues. Who are you, Boggs? What's your real game? And damn your eyes, why're you after me?"

"I'm *not* after you, not anymore. I told Ollie—"

"I don't believe it, by God." Evans jerked his hand from under his coat and showed his weapon—a small Colt automatic, by the moonlit looks of it. "I want the truth, Boggs, and I want it fast."

"You've already had it, I tell you."

"Shoot him in the leg, Jimmy," Witherspoon said. "It hurts 'em in the leg real bad. Then they talk so's you won't shoot 'em in the *other* leg."

"No," Quincannon said, "don't shoot me! Don't shoot me!"

125

"Shut up, Boggs."

Evans said, "Somebody might hear the shot."

"Not out here. There's nobody around."

"We're too close to the road."

"Down the beach, then, by that old derelict."

"No!" Quincannon yelled. "No, you can't—!"

Witherspoon cuffed him above the right ear—a casual blow that knocked his head against the palm bole and set up a ringing in both ears. "I told you once, Boggs. Shut up."

"Down the beach it is," Evans said. "Frisk him, Ollie. See if he's heeled."

Witherspoon stepped around behind Quincannon, expertly frisked him, and removed the Remington Navy from its holster. "Nice rod," he said admiringly. "How many muggs you shoot with this, Boggs?"

"None. I never shot nobody with it."

"Well, maybe we'll shoot *you* with it."

"No, no!"

"Shut *up*, I said." He caught Quincannon's shoulder, spun him around, and gave him a shove. "Get movin'."

Quincannon obeyed. He slogged through loose sand until he was fifty yards from the derelict; then the footing became somewhat firmer. The break and roll of the surf was no louder than a whisper, even this close to the water's edge. The night was still except for random sounds in the far distance.

When they got to within a few feet of the derelict, Evans told him to stop. The boat was a big trawler and had been there for some time; there were gaping holes in its hull and what was left of its superstructure, and sand was mounded all around it. The shadows it threw over the moonlit beach were long and deep; Quincannon moved another pace into them before he obeyed Evans's command. He turned to face the two men again.

"All right, you son of a bitch," Evans said, "now you'll tell me your game or by Christ you'll walk with crutches the rest of your days."

"No, please, don't shoot me!" Quincannon sank to his knees in the loose sand and ducked his head between hunched shoulders. "I'll talk, I'll talk, only please don't hurt me!"

Witherspoon made the rumbling and squeaking-mice sound that

126

passed for laughter. "Didn't I tell you, Jimmy? Big as he is, he's a gawddam yellow-back—"

Quincannon reared up and threw a handful of sand into Witherspoon's face. At the same time he hurled another handful of sand into Evans's face. His aim was better with Witherspoon: the sand struck the peanut square on, stung the eyes, and sent him staggering backward, bellowing. Evans managed to avoid most of the handful that was flung his way; he twisted his body to one side, and the Colt automatic made a flat cracking sound. But Quincannon was moving by then, in a forward roll, and the bullet came nowhere close to him. An instant later, before Evans could set himself to fire again, Quincannon's shoulder connected with the little man's legs and pitched him sideways and down on his back. Quincannon rolled atop the thrashing figure, clamped hard fingers around the wrist that held the weapon. With his other hand he cracked Evans smartly on the point of the jaw. Evans said "Uh!" and assumed the flaccid aspect of a pile of seaweed.

Quincannon rolled off him and made an agile move to gain his feet just as Witherspoon, still bellowing, pawing at his eyes with one hand and brandishing a leather cosh with the other, charged him. He ducked away from the first wild swing, or would have if he'd had firmer footing. As it was one boot got mired and the cosh struck him a glancing blow on the left shoulder. The force of it was enough to knock him down, which gave Witherspoon sufficient time to kick him in the shin. This made Quincannon angry. He dodged another wild swing, successfully this time, and delivered a mighty blow to the side of Witherspoon's peanut. Witherspoon grunted and lunged again, unhurt. The head, clearly, was *not* the place to attack if you intended to stretch out the likes of Ollie Witherspoon.

Taking another offensive tack, Quincannon succeeded in knocking the cosh out of Witherspoon's hand on the next swing and then smote him in the stomach. The blow broke him at the middle but it, too, failed to stop him. He struck Quincannon in the chest, once more in the right side; the second punch might have caved in his rib cage if it had come straight on instead of at a glancing angle. This made Quincannon even more angry. To hell with the Marquess of Queensbury, he thought. He ducked another punch, feigned one of his own, and promptly kicked Witherspoon in the crotch with all the force he could muster.

Witherspoon lay down on the sand and commenced screaming. It was an unpleasant noise on such a peaceful night; Quincannon found his Navy revolver in the big man's pocket and used the butt of it on the Witherspoon peanut. Witherspoon stopped screaming immediately. And the night was quiet again except for the soothing whisper of the surf as it rolled in over the beach.

Quincannon limped to the derelict and sat down on a driftwood log that had washed up next to her. His shin hurt where Witherspoon had kicked him; his shoulder hurt and his ribs hurt and the knuckles on his right hand hurt. And as if that wasn't enough, there was a six-inch rend in the sleeve of his new Cheviot coat.

He sat there for five minutes, holding the Navy revolver and alternately looking at the ocean and the two inert forms on the sand a few feet away. Twice during that time he considered going over and presenting each of them with another bruise or two, but he did not give in to the impulses. He was a civilized man, after all, not a ruffian of their ilk. He had no taste for violence. He was a detective who preferred to use his wits, like that fictional fellow in London Conan Doyle wrote about. What was his name? Holmes? Yes, like Sherlock Holmes. Refined. Cerebral. Genteel at heart.

He wondered if he had ruptured Witherspoon. He hoped so. If not, and if Ollie ever came after him again, he would deliver a kick of such magnitude that it would explode the bastard's scrotum like a balloon.

He stood finally and went to where Evans lay and had a look at him. Then he had a look at Witherspoon. Neither man had moved; neither man was likely to move for some time yet. Moonshine showed him where Evans's Colt automatic and his own derby lay. He picked up the gun first, hurled it through one of the holes in the derelict's hull. Then he picked up the derby and clamped it on his head.

"Let that be a lesson to you," he said to the two unconscious felons, and limped away toward Rancheria Street.

Now he knew how he would spend the rest of the evening. He would spend it in bed, nursing his wounds and sleeping. A pox on Charles Nordhoff. Santa Barbara was *not* good for everyone's health, especially not John Frederick Quincannon's.

FOUR

QUINCANNON AWOKE AT dawn—stiff, sore, and in a peevish frame of mind. After ten minutes, restlessness drove him out of bed. He examined himself in the mirror in the adjoining bath and found four bruises, all of them on parts of his anatomy that would be concealed by his clothing. The one on his shin was the largest and tenderest, but it hurt only when he put too much pressure on that foot; he could walk more or less normally. And except for a scratch that was all but lost in the tangle of his beard, his face had miraculously escaped being marked.

The examination buoyed his spirits somewhat, though not enough to put an end to either his cranky mood or his restlessness. Going back to bed was out of the question. Instead he washed, dressed, and went down to the dining room for coffee and hot pastry.

Traffic was sparse and desultory on State Street when he emerged from the hotel and its grounds half an hour later. The rim of the sun was just visible above the Santa Ynez Mountains to the east; the sky still wore a pink flush, like a bride on the morning after her wedding night, and the air was salty and had a crisp bite to it. It was going to be another glorious spring day. At least, Quincannon thought grumpily, insofar as the weather was concerned.

It was too early to conduct business, but he felt that a long, brisk stroll might clear away some of his muscle stiffness and the remnants of a dull headache. He set off down State Street, found himself approaching the St. Charles Hotel, remembered that Felipe Velasquez was due to leave for his ranch at eight o'clock, and consulted his big turnip-shaped watch. Ten minutes before eight. He detoured into the alley that ran behind the St. Charles, looking for the hotel stables. The odors of fresh hay, old leather, and horse manure led him straight to them.

The first person he saw when he got there was Barnaby O'Hare. O'Hare, dressed in riding breeches and an old-fashioned duster, was watching a stablehand saddle a ewe-necked chestnut horse. The historian's presence here surprised Quincannon—and vaguely annoyed him, for no particular reason. There was no sign of Velasquez, although a fine Appaloosa stallion stood waiting nearby, outfitted in a silver-studded bridle and a high-forked Spanish saddle with tasseled stirrup-skirts.

Quincannon was within ten strides of O'Hare before the moon-faced young man glanced up and saw him. "Ah, Mr. Quincannon," he said with a smile. "Have you decided to join us?"

"Us?"

"Señor Velasquez and I. Didn't he tell you I am accompanying him to Rancho Rinconada de los Robles today?"

"No, he didn't."

"Well, one of the men I shall be interviewing for my book is a neighbor of his. And there are geographical details of the old grant that I'll want to reexamine. Señor Velasquez was again kind enough to extend his hospitality for a few days."

Quincannon thought uncharitably: *After you promised him an entire chapter in your book, no doubt.* He said nothing.

"*Will* you be joining us?" O'Hare asked.

"Not today. At the hacienda in a day or two."

"I look forward to it. Perhaps we'll find time for a talk. I find your profession fascinating, and I should like to know more about it—your methods and such."

"If I confided my methods to everyone who wanted to know them," Quincannon said, "then I wouldn't be a very successful detective, would I?"

The rear door of the hotel opened just then and Felipe Velasquez emerged. He, too, wore riding clothes, and a wide-brimmed sombrero. As the rancher approached, Quincannon saw that he looked pale and hung-over this morning. It gave him a perverse pleasure to think of this pompous grandee listing a few degrees to starboard under a burden of too much wine.

"*Buenos días,* Señor Velasquez."

Instead of acknowledging the greeting, Velasquez fixed him with a sharp look. "Have you something new to report?"

"Not as yet—"

"Then why are you here? Why are you not doing what you're being paid to do?"

"May I remind you, sir," Quincannon said, managing—just

barely—to keep the testiness out of his voice, "that it is not yet eight o'clock?"

Velasquez muttered something in Spanish that Quincannon failed to catch but that O'Hare evidently understood; the smile the young man directed at Quincannon was boyishly amused. Velasquez turned his back, went to where the Appaloosa stood, and began checking the fit of its bridle. O'Hare gave his attention to the stablehand, who had finished saddling the chestnut.

Gentlemen, Quincannon thought, *to hell with you both.* And he stalked out to State Street without looking back.

He finished his stroll in a dark humor and returned to the Arlington, where he consumed a breakfast of five eggs, bacon, potatoes, cornbread, orange marmalade, more hot pastry, and more coffee. That improved his mood somewhat. When he considered himself sufficiently fortified, he walked to the stables, hired the same claybank he had ridden yesterday, and trotted away to the Mexican quarter.

Luis Cordova's dry-goods store was not yet open when he arrived; a hand-lettered sign bearing the word CERRADO hung on the front door and was visible from the street. Quincannon turned his horse, came down the opposite side of the block, drew rein in front of the tonsorial parlor. It was open for business, and when he entered, he found a mustachioed barber and no one else—a fact that satisfied him. If anyone knew his neighbors and could be drawn into talking about them, especially when none was around to monitor the conversation, it was a barber. They were a notoriously loquacious breed, no matter what their race or color.

This barber, once he overcame his surprise at having a well-dressed *Americano* for a customer, and once he discovered that Quincannon spoke passable Spanish, proved to be no exception to the rule. His name, he said, was Enrico Garcia. And while he trimmed Quincannon's hair and beard he obligingly answered the questions he was asked about Luis Cordova.

Cordova had operated his dry-goods store at its present location for many years and had lived above it just as long. His widowed and aged mother had lived with him until her death two years ago; he had never married. He was a private man with no close friends in the community, and as such he seldom talked about his background. Garcia thought he had come from the Mexican state of Oaxaca but was not positive. When he spoke of Cordova as a "shrewd businessman," Quincannon took the opportunity to ask if this meant the storekeeper was perhaps a shade dishonest. Garcia's reaction was one of shock. "Oh no, señor," he said. "No. Luis is very religious. He would do nothing to offend God."

He wouldn't, eh? Quincannon thought. Well, that remains to be proved.

He presented the barber with a generous tip and departed neatly trimmed and reeking of bay rum but with little more useful information about Luis Cordova than he'd taken in with him. He was of a mind to find out what other neighborhood residents thought of Cordova, but that intention changed when he again rode past the dry-goods store. It was still closed, the CERRADO sign still in place. He halted in front and checked his turnip watch. After eleven. The store should be open by this time; odd that it wasn't. Had Cordova gone somewhere on an errand? Or had he simply gone—on the fly like a thief in the night?

He dismounted, tied the claybank, and went along the boardwalk to the outside stairs that led to Cordova's rooms above. He waited until a pedestrian and wagon passed and no others were in sight, then climbed the stairs quickly. The branches of the olive tree hung in thick profusion over the landing, so that he was half-hidden among them as he rapped on the door.

There was no answer. He waited for a time and then tried the latch; the door opened under his hand. A sudden feeling of wrongness came to him, followed by a bunching of the muscles in his shoulders and back. He drew his Navy revolver and pushed the door all the way open, holding the pistol up close to his chest.

It looked as though a small whirlwind had been unleashed inside the adobe-walled interior, leaving havoc in its wake. Tables and chairs were overturned; a small oil painting of the Last Supper had been ripped from one wall, a wooden crucifix hung askew on another; shards of broken glass and pottery littered the floor. A kerosene lamp on the mantel above a cold fireplace burned feebly, indicating that there was little fuel remaining in the fount.

Quincannon stepped inside, shutting the door behind him. The rooms were silent except for street noises that filtered in from outside. A pair of bead-curtained archways led to other rooms, one to his left adjacent to the fireplace, the other in the wall directly ahead. He chose the far one first, crossed to it on a zigzag course to avoid stepping on the broken glass and pottery. The beads clicked like the joints of a skeleton when he passed through them.

More havoc had been wrought here, in what appeared to be Cordova's bedroom. Down pillows had been slashed with a knife, spilling feathers that clung to every surface. The mattress had been ripped open to expose its straw entrails. Even some of the bed's leather springs had been hacked through, as if in a frenzy. Bureau drawers had been pulled out and their contents dumped onto the floor. The door to an old scarred wardrobe stood open, revealing a ragbag cluster of torn and wadded clothing within.

For a moment Quincannon stood narrow-eyed, studying this room as he had studied the other; then he backed out, made his way to the second bead-curtained archway. The room beyond, at the rear, was the largest of the three, covering the entire width of the building. It was semidark in there—rattan blinds covered its plate-glass windows—but Quincannon could tell that it was used as a study. He could also tell that it had been ransacked as thoroughly as the other two.

He moved to the nearest of the windows, edged the blind aside, and looked out. A shed, an outhouse, the rear yard and rear wall of a building on the next block—and no people within the range of his vision. He used the drawstring to raise the blind and admit enough light for him to see more clearly.

The room contained a desk, two overturned chairs, an ironbound steamer trunk with its lid open and some of its contents pulled out, a battered refectory table, and a fireplace with the still-smoldering embers of a wood fire on the hearth. Papers were strewn everywhere, along with ledgers and old books and a dozen other items. All the drawers in the desk had been removed and emptied and thrown into a broken pile in one corner. Quincannon started over to the desk, walking carefully—and then stopped after half a dozen paces, when the angle at which he was moving allowed him to see more of the space behind the desk.

The body of a man lay there, half twisted on his back, eyes open and bulging slightly so that they had the look of small boiled onions in the dim light. Luis Cordova hadn't flown anywhere in the night. He would never fly anywhere again.

Scowling now, Quincannon holstered his weapon and went around the desk, knelt alongside the dead man. There were marks on Cordova's throat, gouged half-moons where his assailant's nails had dug into the flesh; but strangulation, Quincannon judged, had not been the cause of death. There was blood in the storekeeper's hair, blood on the floor under his head: a shattered skull, like as not from a repeated pummeling against the floorboards.

The fingers of Cordova's right hand were closed into a fist, and between two of them a ragged triangle of paper was visible. Quincannon caught hold of the hand, found it limp and cold—confirming his suspicion that the man had been dead since last night, at least a dozen hours. He pulled the fingers apart, removed the tiny scrap of paper. He was about to straighten up with it when he noticed something else: a small, shiny piece of metal on the floor near one of the corpse's legs. He picked this up and then returned to the window, where the light was better, to examine both it and the paper scrap.

The piece of metal was half an inch long, slender, conical in shape, and hollow. He had no idea what it was—and yet, it seemed oddly and vaguely familiar. He studied it for several seconds, still could not identify it, and finally slipped it into his coat pocket. He gave his attention to the torn scrap.

It appeared to be the bottom edge of a letter or some other document—quite an old one, judging from the age-yellowed condition of the paper. It contained six complete words, all Spanish, written in a crabbed and perhaps hasty hand, for the letters were ink-smudged and not well-formed. On one line were four words, on the other, two—what appeared to be the last two lines of a page.

más allá del sepulcro
donde Maria

Quincannon's scowl was now as ferocious as Chief of Police Vandermeer's. He put the scrap into the same pocket as the piece of metal and then, methodically, he set about gathering up and examining all the papers scattered on the floor. It took him more than an hour, and there was tension and frustration in him when he finished. The letter or document from which the scrap had been torn was no longer here, which meant that it was now in the possession of Luis Cordova's murderer. There was no question in Quincannon's mind that it was a vital document.

But his search had not been completely fruitless. He thought he knew now who had written the missing document, and why; and he thought he knew, too, how the statue of the Virgin Mary had come into Luis Cordova's possession. Several letters and an inscription in the Cordova family Bible had given him those answers.

Luis Cordova had not been born in Oaxaca, Mexico; he had been born on Rancho Rinconada de los Robles, in the year 1840. His father and mother had both been in the employ of Don Esteban, and the family had lived at the rancho's pueblo. Luis and his mother had fled to Santa Barbara the day before the siege by Fremont's troops, with the other women and children. His father, Tomás, had stayed behind to fight—and to die. It seemed clear now that Tomás Cordova had helped Don Esteban and Padre Urbano secrete the artifacts; it also seemed clear that he was not as trustworthy as they had considered him to be. He had managed to steal the statue of the Virgin Mary and to pass it on to his wife before she and Luis fled. And he had written down for her the location of the remaining artifacts, so that she or Luis might someday return for them. It was this document that was now in the murderer's hands.

But there were still unanswered questions. *Had* Tomás Cordova's wife returned for the cache of artifacts? Or had Luis, when he was old enough? And if they hadn't, for reasons of their own, were the artifacts still in their original hiding place, waiting to be carried away by the man who had killed Luis?

And who was that man? Who had the missing document?

Quincannon continued to scowl. He did not like cases involving murder. Nor was he fond of complex mysteries, as adept as he often was at solving them. Cerebral detection might be child's play for Sherlock Holmes; for John Frederick Quincannon it was damned hard work.

He tucked half a dozen personal letters into his coat pocket for future reference. Then, cautiously, he let himself out of the rooms, pausing among the olive branches to make certain there was no one on the boardwalk or street below before descending. The few people in the vicinity seemed to pay him no attention as he went to his horse, mounted, turned away from the dry-goods store.

Más allá del sepulcro, he was thinking. *Donde Maria.* What was the significance of those two phrases? They were key phrases, he was sure, to the location of the original hiding place of the artifacts—perhaps so vital that without them, the person who had stolen the document would not be able to determine the exact location. *Donde Maria.* Where Maria. Where Maria what? Who *was* Maria?

As he rode back toward the center of town, the first phrase began to haunt him—to repeat itself in his mind in a kind of macabre litany.

Más allá del sepulcro.

Beyond the grave.

PART V
1986

ONE

Más allá del sepulcro. Dondé Maria.

The words repeated in my mind as they must have in John Quincannon's. They echoed as I waited in the strange motel bed for sleep to come. They haunted my troubled dreams. The dreams were peopled by the vague figures of Felipe Velasquez, Luis Cordova, James Evans, Barnaby O'Hare, and Oliver Witherspoon, who spoke and moved and did various things, although I couldn't really see them. The only person who appeared perfectly clear to me was John Quincannon.

I could visualize him: a big man, maybe bearded, with a slightly ruddy complexion, possibly from a fond indulgence in drink. And I could hear him talking over the events that had transpired, speculating on what their significance might be in a low, contemplative voice. By the time the fog-filtered morning light had crept around the poorly fitting motel curtains, Quincannon and I had had quite a talk.

Who had killed Luis Cordova? And what was the meaning of *más allá del sepulcro* and *dondé Maria*? Had Quincannon found out?

I continued mulling over these questions as I drove north toward Santa Barbara. I'd waited until most of the rush hour traffic had cleared before I'd started, but even so, it was slow traveling until I was past Van Nuys. The delay didn't bother me as much as it normally would have, however; I had other things to occupy my mind.

I was terribly disappointed that this second section of Quincannon's report had also ended abruptly. Had still more of it survived? And if so, where was it? Of one thing I was certain: If the report *had* survived to the present day, I would find it one way or another.

At Thousand Oaks, the freeway widened, and I put on speed as I began to descend the Conejo Grade. My attention began to wander further and further from my driving, and I resumed my imaginary dialogue with Quincannon. We discussed the problem of what he and I should do next all the way to Ventura, and it was only when I had to slam on my brakes for a slowdown caused by a closed lane that I realized how strange my internal conversation sounded—even to me.

The truth was, I'd developed an eerie connection to a man who had probably been dead for forty years or more. I wasn't viewing Quincannon or his long-ago investigation as something out of a history book. Instead I was living it along with the detective, at the same time that I was driving on this twentieth-century freeway. I could speak mentally with him, almost see and touch him. It was almost as if John Quincannon were trying to reach out of the past and tell me something.

The thought made me feel strange and a little frightened. I tried to laugh it off, blame it on my heritage from my superstitious ancestors. When that didn't work, I turned the car radio on to a country-and-western station—I'd developed a fondness for that kind of music after a trip last summer to Bakersfield, the self-proclaimed country-and-western capital of California—and tried to take my mind off 1894 by singing along to songs about present-day heartbreak and drunkenness the rest of the way to Santa Barbara.

When I arrived in town, it was time to visit Mama, so I drove directly to the hospital. I'd called her the night before from the motel, and she'd been somewhat short with me. I hoped she'd be in a better mood this morning, and when I first entered her room, it seemed my wish had been granted. She was on the phone, but she ended the conversation quickly and looked up at me with a smile.

"That was Tía Constanza," she said.

"Funny, I was just thinking about her yesterday. How is she?"

"Not so good. Tom is coming out of prison next week, and she doesn't know what to do with him."

"Is he going to live with her?"

"For a while, she says."

"So why does she have to do *anything* with him? Tom's an adult. He needs a place to stay and a job, not a lot of mothering."

Mama glared at me. "You are all alike, aren't you? You think you're so grown-up and wise, but you're really just children inside."

I proved her point by shrugging sullenly, but at the same time I felt a bit of relief. That glare told me Mama was getting better.

"So," she said after a moment, "why did you go to Santa Monica?"

I didn't want to go into the subject of Quincannon and his report right now. If I got started, I might confess about the odd relationship I'd developed with a dead man, and the last thing I needed was my practical, hardheaded mother telling me I was *loca*. "Museum business," I said.

"What? I thought you were on vacation."

"I am, sort of."

"I thought you were going to use the week to relax and spend some time with Dave and see about getting the house painted."

I was silent, fingering the venetian blind cord on the window next to me.

"Well? You know if you don't get that house painted, you could have serious problems. The last time it was done was in 1968. Another winter with the kind of rains we've been having, and you'll see moss growing on it, and next you'll have to replace the stucco—"

"I'll call a couple of painters today."

"I thought you already had an estimate."

"That was over a year ago. Prices have probably gone up. And besides, I'm not sure it was the cheapest one I could have gotten—"

"Cheapest is not always best. What about Dave?"

"What?"

"How come he hasn't been to see me?"

The pathways that my mother's mind follows are twisted and impossible to chart. Suddenly I felt weary and went to sit on the chair by the bed.

"Well," Mama said, "did you have a fight or what?"

"We didn't have a fight. It's just that. . . . " I stopped, feeling trapped by the web of motherhood that they weave and throw over you. "Dave and I broke up."

Mama's brow knit. "Broke up? You broke up with him?"

"He broke up with me."

"Por Dios, por qué?" When Mama gets upset, she usually starts speaking in Spanish.

"He said it wasn't working out. I don't know why."

Mama became silent, picking at the border of the blanket with her fingernails. Then she said, in English again, "I think that should be pretty clear to you."

"What does that mean?"

"Well, take a good look at the two of you. Dave's an Anglo—"

"Mama, you're the only one who thinks that's a problem."

She went on as if I hadn't spoken. "And he was raised different from you. He's from a nice middle-class Anglo family, and they never had trouble making ends meet. He expects different things from life than you do."

"That's not true!"

She sighed. "Oh, Elena, you were always fighting over those differences."

"We were not!"

"Think about it." Mama held up her hand and began to tick items off on her fingers. "Last winter when you went away for five days: You wanted to go to San Francisco, see some shows, eat in some new restaurants. Why? Because those were the things we never could afford to do when you were growing up. But Dave is used to shows and nice restaurants; instead he wanted to go skiing, which is something no Oliverez has ever considered doing. You went to San Francisco, but not until you'd had a terrible battle. And I have a feeling neither of you had much fun. Then, a few months ago, he bought some expensive camera equipment. Remember? You said you thought it was extravagant and unnecessary. So he turned around and told you that he thought your buying the Candelario cloud sculpture to go with the sun face was stupid. You didn't speak for days after that."

It was true, but then Dave had only been learning about Mexican art, and Candelario's works could be a little bizarre. Besides, I'd had no business telling him how to spend his money—and I'd admitted as much.

"Even Christmas was almost spoiled by those differences," Mama added. "Dave told you your tree was gaudy. And he didn't say anything, but when we all went to Jesse Herrera's party, I sensed he was secretly laughing at the *nacimiento*."

I didn't contradict her, because I, too, had sensed that. Jesse's *nacimiento*—the boxlike Christmas scene many of our people place in their front windows—had been especially beautiful, containing not only the traditional manger, but also miniatures of some of

Jesse's own animal creations, the fantastical papier-mâché *camaleones*. One of the highlights of the party had been the adoration of the figure of the Christ child before it was placed in the manger, and I'd felt Dave found it all very foreign. Well, it *was* very Mexican. But very American, too.

"So you see," Mama went on triumphantly, "you and Dave were always having trouble. It comes as no surprise to me that you broke up."

My temper flared at her smug look, but I tried to control it. After all, she was not yet a well woman. "Dave and I never had any serious problems," I said mildly.

"Yes, you did."

"We did not!" So much for mildness.

"You just refuse to see them."

The anger I'd been holding in check broke loose. Why did Mama always have to have the last righteous word? Who was she to talk about refusing to see things? Look at the way she'd been acting since she'd been in the hospital!

I stood up and said, "Is that so? You're a fine one to talk. I'm not the only one in this family who refuses to see the obvious."

"And what do you mean by that?"

"I mean you. You're also denying reality. Ever since you got sick, you've been lying there and acting shocked that you have an ulcer and feeling sorry for yourself. You've been pretending you were never sick before, when you know that just isn't so. And you've been making Nick and Carlota and me miserable. You've got to face facts, Mama—and one of those is that you'll have to take better care of yourself in the future!"

Mama's eyes grew wide, and then she looked down at the covers. Her mouth began to work, and her roughened fingers squeezed together spasmodically.

My anger evaporated. I felt sorry for her, sorry I'd hurt her, and I wanted to take her in my arms and pet her and tell her I didn't mean a word of it.

But I had meant it—as much as she'd meant what she'd said about Dave and me. We'd both needed to say what had been said.

Tears began to slip down Mama's cheeks. Horrified, I turned and fled before I began to cry myself.

TWO

WHEN I LEFT the hospital, I automatically drove toward the museum. But as I waited in a long line of left-turning cars on Route 101 near the central district, I calmed down long enough to take a good look at what I was doing.

I've always been ruled by a tyrannical work ethic, and when I'm upset, I plunge into one chore or another to take my mind off my problems. But this was supposed to be my vacation, and in spite of that I'd already been in to the office once. Today I'd resolved to stay away from the place, and now I reaffirmed that promise to myself. I'd go for a drive instead and try to sort out my feelings about the unhappy events of the last few days. Probably part of the reason I'd flared up at Mama was because I was overworked.

I twisted the wheel of the car to the right and shot out of the turn lane into the path of an oncoming van. Its driver leaned on the horn, and in my rearview mirror, I saw him shake his fist. I made an apologetic gesture with my hand, and he shook his head and mouthed the word "women." But when I moved into the right-hand lane, he passed me and waved.

I followed 101 as it looped around the business district, then got off on Milpas Street and drove up into the hills, following Foothill Road and looking at the nice houses. I thought about my own house and how I really should call some painters. I wondered if I would ever be able to afford to move away from the old neighborhood, buy something higher up with a view; then I wondered if I even wanted to do that. If I had more money, I'd probably just remodel the kitchen and bathroom, maybe build a deck. . . .

Of course I wasn't fooling myself. I hadn't really come up here to lust after the real estate. A mile or so ahead, Foothill intersected with San Marcos Pass Road. And that route would lead to Las Lomas.

I don't normally like to just drop in on people, and I hate for friends to drop in on me. But I sensed Sam Ryder was the type of person who would welcome a surprise visit. Besides, I didn't intend to stay long; I just wanted to ask him a few questions, one of which was where Arturo Melendez lived. Then I'd stop at Arturo's and ask him if he'd like to make the promised pilgrimage to the ruins of Rancho Rinconada de los Robles. While we were there we could discuss a possible showing of his paintings at the museum.

When I arrived, the village once again looked deserted, but its small dwellings and unkempt square seemed more pleasant to me today, as any place will once you know good people who live there. I parked in front of Sam's house and followed the path through the weeds to the porch. Apparently he had heard the car because he came to the door before I knocked.

I started to apologize for not calling first, but he waved the words away and asked if I'd brought Quincannon's report. I gave him the papers I'd found at Mrs. Manuela's and explained about the others being locked up at the museum, where I'd promised myself I wouldn't go today. Sam didn't seem to care that the report wasn't complete; he took the papers in his hands eagerly and motioned for me to come in.

The desk under the front window was messier than it had been on Sunday, and there were file cards strewn all over the floor. Sam had a big smudge of black ink on his chin, and there was a pencil stuck into the tuft of curly red hair above his right ear. He looked up from the report, wrinkled his nose at the room, and took me into the kitchen.

"It's not going well today?" I asked.

"No. I just don't care what the Russians and French did to the Oregonians. Ever since you were here on Sunday I've been haunted by visions of Don Esteban Velasquez and his artifacts." He patted the report and set it down on the chopping block with obvious reluctance.

I said, "Me, too. That's why I'm here. I need some professional advice."

He motioned toward the director's chair I'd occupied on my previous visit. "Glad to help. You want a beer?"

"If you're having one. But I don't want to keep you from your work."

He got out two Budweisers and held up a glass, looking at me questioningly. When I shook my head, he popped the tabs on both

146

cans and handed me one. "The work will keep. It's fourteen to zip in favor of the Russo-French team, and frankly I'm bored with the game." He sat down in the other chair, propping his feet against the chopping block, and added, "Thanks for not insisting on elegance. I hate to wash glasses."

I said, "I should have stayed to help you with the dishes the other night."

"That's okay. I can always count on Arturo for the washing up."

"Speaking of him, one of the things I wanted to ask you is where he lives."

"Diagonally across the square, three doors down from Dora. It's the little log cabin with moss growing all over the roof."

The idea of one of my people living in a log cabin struck me as amusing, and I smiled.

Sam raised an eyebrow.

"Ethnic incongruity," I said.

"Yeah, I know what you mean—he'd look funny in a coonskin cap. What else did you want to see me about? This report?" He motioned at the chopping block.

I summarized what was in the report for him and told him that I hoped there might be more pages in existence. "Is there anyplace that you know of where the files of that detective agency might have ended up?" I asked. "Or is there any organization that could tell me what happened to Carpenter and Quincannon?"

Sam ran a hand over his chin, smudging the ink streak even more, and finally said, "This was a San Francisco agency, right?"

"Yes."

"Offhand, I can think of three places you could try: the California Historical Society branch in San Francisco, the California History Room of the public library there, and the Bancroft Library in Berkeley. But I'd say you're more likely to find the files of a defunct San Francisco business at one of the first two. I know the librarians at both; if you use my name and identify yourself as director of your museum, they'll be more than willing to help you."

He got the names and numbers and told me to use the phone on his desk. I cleared off a space where I could set my notepad in case I needed to write anything down and then called the California History Room at the public library, billing the charges to my home number. As Sam had said, the librarian was very cooperative and took down what information I had; she said she'd call back within the hour. Next I tried the Historical Society; they had a computerized filing system, and after only a few minutes, their librarian told me there was no information on Carpenter and Quincannon, Professional Detective Services.

I decided to wait for the reply from the public library before investing in a call to Berkeley, and Sam and I spent the time drinking another beer and speculating on John Quincannon: what he had been like, how long he had lived, whether he had ever found the Velasquez artifacts. When the phone finally rang, it was my call from San Francisco. The librarian told me she had been able to locate the materials I'd requested. There was a great deal of material from the files of Carpenter and Quincannon, including rough notes for the specific report I was looking for.

What other kinds of materials were there? I asked her. Was there anything of a personal nature, about the detectives themselves?

There were some diaries and private correspondence, she replied, and there might be a photograph or two. Of course I'd be welcome to look at anything they had. Did I plan to come to San Francisco to study the documents?

I hesitated. The trip would take a couple of days, and I didn't feel right about leaving town while Mama was in the hospital— especially since I would have to spend time cosseting her in order to make up for my earlier harsh words. "Is it possible for you to copy the documents and send them to me?" I finally asked.

Now the librarian hesitated. "This is for the Santa Barbara Museum of Mexican Arts?"

"Yes. I'm director there."

Apparently she didn't see anything odd in an art museum requesting that type of historical information, because she said, "Normally we only perform such services for cardholders, and we'd need prepayment, but I think we can make an exception in your case— especially since you were referred by Sam Ryder."

"Thank you. I really appreciate it." Then, even though it was overstepping the bounds of courtesy, I added, "Do you think you could send them Express Mail?"

Again she didn't balk at my request, but merely agreed, saying I'd have the copies tomorrow morning and that an invoice would be enclosed.

I went back to the kitchen and flopped down in the director's chair, toasting Sam with my beer bottle. "Success. She'll put copies of the reports in the mail tonight, express."

"That means that by tomorrow we'll know the end of the saga. Will you bring the papers up here—all of them, including the first ones you found?"

"Right away. We can read the new ones together." I looked at my watch. It was nearly three. Suddenly a flat feeling stole over me, the kind you get when you're anticipating something exciting and then realize how long it's going to be before it happens. Sam must have felt the same way, because he sighed and stood up, looking gloomy.

"Time for the Russian and French aggressions," he said.

"And I think I'll go up to the ruins of the pueblo and commune with the spirits—if any are left there."

He followed me to the front door. "Were you planning to ask Arturo to go along?"

"Yes. How did you know?"

"He told me you had mentioned doing that. He seemed to be looking forward to it." Sam's eyes held a gleam—the same gleam my mother's get when she thinks some man might be interested in me.

I decided to ignore the insinuation and only said, "I'm looking forward to it, too."

After promising a second time to bring the documents up to Las Lomas as soon as they arrived, I said good-bye to Sam and started across the square toward Arturo's log cabin. The day was warm and sunny, the air redolent of spring blossoms and new-mown grass. In the far corner of the weedy, overgrown area, a woman and two small girls squatted on the ground; they had cleared a patch and turned the earth, and the woman was showing the children how to plant seeds. I watched for a moment as they carefully measured out the contents of the little paper packets and placed them in the furrows, patting the dirt over them with chubby hands. I'd done the same thing as a child, and the wait until the first green shoots poked up into view had seemed unbearably long—much as the wait for Carpenter and Quincannon's files did now.

When I was halfway to Arturo's, I saw Gray Hollis come out of Marshall's grocery store clutching a paper bag that showed the outline of a liquor bottle. He walked with his head down, feet scuffing the hard-packed earth, and as he came closer I saw that his chin was stubbled, his hair greasy, his clothes dirty and wrinkled. Hearing my footsteps, he glanced up; his eyes widened in surprise, and then he nodded a curt greeting and kept on going.

I'd known men like Gray Hollis before—some of my relatives and their neighbors in the East L.A. barrio—who had been beaten down by disappointment and poverty or shattered by the loss of a loved one. They'd worked hard at destroying themselves, sinking lower and lower until one day they hit the stony bottom. Then their lives would go one of two ways: Either they'd pick themselves up and start putting themselves together, or—like my cousin Tom, the one who was now getting out of prison—they'd wallow until some final disaster finished them off. I wondered how soon Gray would hit that bottom and which way he would then choose.

As I crossed the street and started along the opposite side, I saw Dora Kingman in her garden. She was standing just behind the picket fence, one hand shading her eyes, looking at Gray's retreating figure. When she saw me, she let her hand drop and gave me a slight, nervous smile. "Elena, how are you? What brings you here?"

"I dropped in on Sam, to give him some documents and ask more advice about the research I'm doing into the Velasquez family. And now I'm on my way to ask Arturo if he wants to go up to the old ruins with me."

Dora frowned. "I think I saw him ride out of town on his motor scooter about an hour ago, but he might be back by now. I don't see *everything* that goes on."

Not everything, I thought, but most things that concern Gray Hollis. "Well, I'll stop by his place anyway."

"Yes, do that. Arturo needs friends; it would help him overcome his shyness if someone took an interest. And when you pass by here again, I'll give you some tomato seedlings. They're quite hardy this year, and I've got more than I need."

I thanked her and continued down the street to where the log cabin stood under a sycamore tree. It was only about twenty-feet-square and looked primitive, with its rough, peeling bark and overgrown roof, but there was a plastic bubble skylight protruding from the mossy vegetation. Like most artists, Arturo might be on the edge of starvation, but what money he made was invested in the practice of his craft; I'd never known a painter yet who would skimp on acquiring the necessary light.

Dora had been right about Arturo not being home. When he

didn't answer my knocks, I gave in to my natural nosiness and went along the side of the cabin and peeked in one window. It was curtained in blue-and-white-checked material that looked like it had once been a tablecloth, but there was a space where the two sides didn't quite meet. Through it I could see a rough pine table covered with painting supplies and an easel that sat directly under the skylight. There was no canvas on the easel, although there were a number of them in varying sizes turned face to the wall. To one side was the edge of what looked like a wood stove, but otherwise I could tell nothing about the interior of the cabin. Probably Arturo lived spartanly; most good artists I knew seemed to care little about creature comforts; the work was the all-important core of their existence.

I turned from the window, realizing I was being as nosy as Dora Kingman, and started back toward Sam's house, where I'd left my car. Fortunately Dora had gone inside, so I wasn't obligated to accept any tomato seedlings, which—hardy or not—would surely die from my inattention. The mother and daughters had finished planting their garden and were observing it with satisfaction, hands on hips, the girls' stances miniature replicas of the woman's. Gray Hollis was nowhere in sight. When I got into my car, I could hear the reluctant tapping of typewriter keys from Sam's front room. I started the VW and drove out of town, leaving Las Lomas to its daily business.

THREE

THE RUINS OF the church of San Anselmo de las Lomas reflected a white-hot glare in the afternoon sun. As I approached the stark adobe wall, I waded through the knee-high wildflowers, smelling their oddly bitter fragrance. It was hushed there on the hill; the only sounds were an occasional birdcall and a constant, reedy whisper as the wind blew through the leaves and tall grass. It had been warm in the village, but now I felt a chill in the air and gripped my bare arms above the elbow, trying to insulate myself.

I rounded the rear wall of the church and stopped by the crumbling foundation, once again attempting to picture the building as it had stood in 1846. The other day, by narrowing my eyes and viewing the scene through the haze of my lashes, I'd been able to raise the walls and bell tower and the cross crowning the red-tiled peak. Today, however, that didn't work; all I saw were the blurred outlines of the church's lonely remains.

A gust of wind swept across the foundations, rippling the vegetation that carpeted the cracked brick of the church floor. It tossed the tall grass in the adjacent graveyard, revealing the weathered granite tips of a few stones. Unbidden, the haunting words that Quincannon had found on the scrap of paper in Luis Cordova's dead hand echoed in my mind: *"Más allá del sepulcro . . . donde Maria. . . . "*

I said them aloud, hearing their compelling rhythm, feeling their shape on my tongue. Released into the silence around me, they reverberated hollowly, and I clutched my elbows tighter, suddenly afraid, as if the words themselves had a dark, magical power. Then I started toward the graveyard.

The largest of the stones—cracked granite crowned with a dirty marble crucifix—marked the resting place of Don Esteban Velasquez. I knelt and brushed aside the thick blades of grass and foxtails so I could read the inscription: EN ESPÍRITU ADMIRABLE. Great in spirit.

153

Several feet away from this stone was another, simpler one: Padre Urbano, UN HOMBRE BUENO Y RELIGIOSO. The date of death on the stone was the same as that on Don Esteban's. There were other graves, also plain ones, with inscriptions such as CRIADO FIEL—faithful servant—and TRABAJADOR BUENO—good worker. And there were two tiny markers, telling of the early deaths of Juan Gerardo and Manuel Nicolás Velasquez—Felipe's brothers, whose names had been inscribed in the family Bible. These reminders of days when many of one's sons and daughters did not survive to adulthood were finely carved, each topped with a marble angel whose chipped, upturned face was meant to inspire hope of a better life *más allá del sepulcro*. I stood staring from one to the other for a long time, the haunting phrases once again pulsing through my brain.

Donde Maria. . . . None of the stones that I had looked at marked the resting place of a woman named Maria. Nor had I found the grave of Felipe Velasquez. Mrs. Manuela had said her father had died when she was quite young, before she and her mother moved to Santa Barbara. It would seem logical for him to be buried here, among his family and servants. I began wading through the weeds, examining the remaining stones. There was still none for a Maria, but finally, on the far right-hand side where the wrought-iron fence leaned at a dejected angle, I found Felipe's: a plain marker, plainer than Padre Urbano's, engraved with only the name. There was no date of birth or death, no inscription extolling the good works he'd done in his lifetime.

The remaining Velasquez family fortunes, I supposed, had taken a swift downward plunge in the years after Quincannon's investigation. Possibly Felipe's attempt to find the missing artifacts had been a last gamble at saving their holdings, and this poor stone was evidence that Quincannon had failed in his search. A sadness descended upon me and I turned, pushing through the grass toward the ruins of the *lavandería* under the big olive tree, some ten yards away.

Halfway there, however, I stopped, feeling a chill between my shoulder blades. It wasn't the kind of cold I'd felt before from the passage of the wind. This was an emotional chill, icy and striking straight to the bone. I whirled and looked back at the church, expecting to see someone there.

154

The church looked the same as before. There was no one, not even a bird, in sight.

I shook my head and kept going, but now the icy feeling intensified. I spun around, thinking someone might be hiding in the ruins, playing games with me. This time I thought I saw a swiftly moving shadow at the jagged corner of the rear wall. I waited, but there was no further motion. It could, I thought, have merely been the sunlight filtering through the leaves of the nearby trees.

What is this, Elena? I asked myself. Perhaps you're afraid of *espectros*. Ghosts. Don Esteban and the padre and Felipe. The men and women and children who died here during the days of *los ranchos grandes,* and those who fell before Fremont's troops. Perhaps, like Quincannon, they're trying to tell you something.

The idea of ghosts was one I would normally have dismissed as ridiculous. Ghosts belonged to *el Día de los Muertos,* November second, when my people bring bread, food, drink, candles, and flowers to the cemeteries in honor of our departed loved ones. On that night the ghosts are supposed to come and feast, to visit their friends and relatives who have been left behind. But most people like me don't really believe that—any more than I believed that ghosts could stalk ruined churchyards in the middle of this bright spring afternoon.

But then, I reminded myself, people like me didn't normally hold conversations with a long-dead Anglo detective.

Forcefully, I pushed the idea of haunts from my mind and continued past the *lavandería,* planning to look for more foundations, perhaps those of the stables, and—farther up on the distant hill—the hacienda itself. My problem, I thought, was that I was too sensitive to atmosphere, too easily swayed by my imagination—

Then I felt it again. The chill returned, this time spreading over my whole body, raising goose bumps on my arms and legs. I whirled once more and was sure I saw a shadow by the back wall of the church. Without considering what I'd do if I found someone there, I began running toward it.

The tall weeds caught at the legs of my jeans. I jammed my foot against some hard, protruding object and stumbled. I jumped over the foundation and skirted the massive charred roof beam. On the other side of what was left of the right-hand wall, my foot hit a patch of crumbled red tile, and I slipped to the ground. Pushing myself up with both hands, I lurched around the rear of the ruins.

No one was there. Not a blade of grass moved. Not a flower was trampled.

I scanned the area between me and the road; the grove of oak trees looked as if no one had passed through it in centuries; the fields and orchard lay similarly untouched. I listened, but the only sound was the shriek of a nearby jay.

I stood there for a moment, feeling foolish, ashamed at having let my overactive imagination panic me. The chill was gone from my shoulder blades. I was certain no one watched me now.

I continued looking around. Nothing moved, except for a few errant wildflowers. Then I lowered my gaze to the ground. There was a place where the grass was bent, as if someone had been standing on it quite recently. And in among the trampled green stalks lay a foreign object. A cigarette butt—or more accurately, a cigarette filter tip. It had been burned all the way down, singeing the white porous material.

I went over and picked it up; it was still warm. The paper that might have identified the brand was completely burned; this could be any kind of cigarette with a white filter.

I stood with the butt pinched between my thumb and forefinger, staring at the landscape, which once again seemed ominous. The chill I'd felt had not been a product of my imagination; it had not been caused by the wandering of ghosts. A very real flesh-and-blood person who smoked filter-tipped cigarettes had been hiding behind this wall observing me. A person who for some reason had chosen not to reveal himself.

Somehow, I thought, I'd have preferred a ghost.

FOUR

AFTER MY RETURN from Las Lomas, I spent a restless evening prowling around the house. I went from room to room, straightening a picture here, pinching off straggly shoots of a houseplant there, feeling out of sorts and purposeless and, above all, a stranger in my own home. It wasn't the same kind of alienation that had assailed me the other day, when I'd felt like piling all the furniture in the middle of the room and then rearranging it. That had been a simple reaction of emotional shock and anxiety. But *this:* It was as if I were viewing my surroundings through someone else's eyes, seeing them as someone from not only another place but another time.

"And why not?" I asked aloud, stopping myself in the act of reducing my already-ailing Swedish ivy to a mere twig. "You've been living on close terms with John Quincannon for a couple of days now. Why wouldn't you begin to see things as he might?"

I pulled my hand away from the abused plant and went to sit on the sofa, propping my feet on the coffee table and crossing my arms over my breasts. There was a stack of books on the cushion next to me—illustrated volumes on old Spanish church architecture that I'd pulled off the shelves of my personal art library with the idea that one of them might contain a drawing of San Anselmo de las Lomas. I glanced at them and then looked away.

San Anselmo de las Lomas. The image of the ruins and the vestiges of the eerie feelings I'd experienced there that afternoon haunted me, haunted me almost as much as the phrase that still echoed in my mind:

Más allá del sepulcro.

Perhaps, I thought, those strange feelings had been nothing more than the by-product of this uncanny identification I had developed with the long-dead San Francisco detective. Maybe all they proved was the power of suggestion upon an overactive imagination. Or if I were superstitious—and I am descended from an extremely superstitious people—I might say that I had picked up the vibrations from an unpleasant experience Quincannon had had on that spot. If the detective had gone to the pueblo, felt he was being watched, perhaps even encountered danger, as he had on the beach with Oliver Witherspoon and James Evans. . . .

"You're not thinking clearly, Elena," I said aloud. "What about the freshly smoked cigarette?" As I thought of it, I shivered—and realized I would greatly prefer any number of supernatural experiences to the very real and possibly threatening one of having someone watch me from among those ruins.

I'd faced much more disagreeable situations than that in the past year, however. And I knew that the only reasonable way to deal with them was with cool thinking and logic. I now made myself examine the problem more rationally than I had earlier on the drive home from Las Lomas.

The cigarette could have been smoked and dropped there by any number of persons—both known and unknown to me. The obvious assumption was that it was a stranger, someone who frequented the place and had been surprised to find me there. A hiker who lived in the area, perhaps; or one of the teenagers who used the place to party and had spray-painted the rainbow on the church's wall. A teenager would naturally have wanted to keep out of sight—why risk an encounter with an unfamiliar adult? A lone hiker probably preferred his solitude and wouldn't have seen the need for conversation with me—after all, it was more or less a public place, and I had as much right to be there as anyone else. But wouldn't a hiker or a teenager have merely gone away? Why wait and watch from behind that wall for the length of time I'd sensed someone's eyes on me? And why disappear when I approached?

The person's secretive behavior was what made me think it must have been someone known to me, who hadn't wanted to encounter me at the ruins. But who? The only thing I knew for sure was that he or she was a smoker. In today's health-conscious society, that fact should have narrowed the possibilities greatly, but from what I recalled, no one in Las Lomas was concerned with that aspect of his health.

Sam Ryder smoked constantly. I could picture him, gray plumes curling from his nostrils as he talked. He'd even had a cigarette going in an ashtray on the chopping block when he'd prepared the salad for the dinner party. After dinner, when he'd passed cigarettes around, Arturo had taken one. And Dora—a surprise in one so conscious of the other substances she took into her body. Gray had turned down the offer, but his abstinence apparently was an off-and-on thing; Dora had chided him for repeatedly quitting and starting up again, and I suspected he may have refused just so he could act self-righteous and annoy her.

And that was the sum total of my acquaintances in the village. Well, not really, if you counted Jim Marshall, the gossipy old man who ran the general store. Did he smoke? Probably; his teeth were tobacco-stained. And he was the type to hide and observe someone in hopes of adding to his store of rumor.

Of those people, who had known I planned to revisit the site of the old pueblo? Sam, of course. And Dora; I'd told her. Gray would naturally have access to anything Dora knew. Jim Marshall? Any of the three could have mentioned me to him in passing. What about Arturo? He had been off somewhere on his motor scooter.

Like Jim Marshall, Arturo was a perfect candidate for the role of watcher, although not for the same reasons; the artist would have hesitated to approach me out of shyness, perhaps hidden behind the wall debating whether or not to reveal himself. And when I'd run in his direction, his natural inclination would have been to flee.

"Maldito!" I said aloud. So much for logical thinking. All the process had done for me was point up that it could have been *anyone* behind that wall.

How to narrow it down? I wondered. There was, of course, tangible evidence—the cigarette butt. I got up and went to get my purse, extracted the butt from the change compartment of my wallet, where I'd put it for safekeeping. It was an ordinary white filter tip, the tobacco and paper burned down so that the manufacturer's stamp had been destroyed. A police laboratory could easily analyze what brand it was, but that didn't help me; I didn't have access to such a facility. Had I still been seeing Dave, I might have been able to cajole him into having it analyzed for me. But right now Dave was probably packing his expensive camera gear and video recording equipment and skiis in preparation for his new life, which—he thought—would work out so much better without me. . . .

Camera gear and video equipment and skiis. Maybe Mama *did* have a point after all.

I turned my mind away from Dave and back to the question of

the cigarette butt. Surprisingly, doing that didn't take nearly the effort it would have the day before.

In lieu of having a lab identify the cigarette brand, was there anything I could do? I supposed I could drive up to Las Lomas and examine everyone's cigarettes, to see if they smoked cork- or filter-tipped. But that wasn't really a very definitive test, and what about Gray, who probably bummed his smokes?

I had to face it: My clue wasn't much of a clue at all. And what did it really matter, anyway, that someone had been watching me at those ruins? Any menace was probably all in my mind.

Weary of playing detective, I glanced at my watch. Quarter to ten; much too late to call Mama. I'd stayed away from the hospital this evening, hadn't even attempted to phone her. Why? Because I was still angry with her? No, because I was more than a little ashamed of my behavior this past morning. I'd make it up to her tomorrow; we'd talk and all would be forgiven. *Dios gracias,* I thought as I reached for one of the books on church architecture, that I do not come from a family of grudge-holders!

The volume I selected was one that incorporated modern photographs of those Spanish churches that had survived to the present day—mainly mission churches—with reproductions of old drawings of those that had fallen to ruins. I paused at pictures of one of my favorite missions, San Juan Capistrano, its stately bell tower reflected in the fountain of its inner courtyard; then I turned the pages until I came to another favorite, the ornate altar of Mission Santa Barbara. The architecture of the California missions is basically simple: soft arches, clean roof lines, graceful form embodied in plain wood, adobe, and tile. It is only in the most holy sanctuary that austerity gives way to splendor, to wooden and gilt and stone embellishments whose only purpose is the glorification of God.

Near the end of the book I found what I was seeking—pen-and-ink drawings of San Anselmo de las Lomas. The church was much as I'd reconstructed it in my mind: even more austere than that of the missions, with a plain iron cross topping its peaked roof and a square tower containing one great bell. The sketches of the interior showed a long, windowless nave; its huge main beam—the same one that now lay charred and rotting on the ground—ran the length of the structure and was intersected by dozens of smaller cross beams. The altar was very plain: rough-hewn dark wood, with two tall *candeleros* upon it and a carved crucifix above. Unlike many of the churches, there were no niches bearing statues in the wall on either side of the altar; the apses I'd observed in the side walls of the ruins would have served that function. The artist had indicated the apses with areas of shadowing, but the angle from which the drawing had been made had prevented him from showing what was in them.

I looked up from the drawing and closed my eyes, picturing the little church where the Aunts and their families had worshipped in the East L.A. barrio. It had been a poor church, more like the simple ones of *los ranchos grandes* than St. Joseph's, which Carlota and I had attended in Santa Barbara, and it, too, had had apses on either side of the altar. To the right as one faced the congregation had been the Virgin Mary, where she customarily is. To the left. . . . I couldn't remember. Not that it mattered; it just pointed up how much my concern for things Catholic had dwindled since I'd stopped going to church. Not that I didn't still consider myself a Catholic; I had been baptized one, and I supposed one day I would receive the Church's last rites. I had no quarrel with the Church, had not ceased attending Mass for any particular reason. I had merely stopped going, caught up in the pleasures and concerns of my day-to-day life. . . .

The phone rang, making me start and clutch the art book harder. Then I laughed at my jumpiness and set the book aside, going to answer eagerly. The voice on the other end of the line was Sam Ryder's—and he was very agitated.

"Elena," he said, "Elena, I can't believe this has happened!"

"What's wrong?"

"The report—Quincannon's report—that you gave me this afternoon: It's gone!"

"Gone? How?"

"Someone broke into the house while I was down in Santa Ynez, doing my weekly shopping at Safeway. I've looked everywhere, but I can't find the report. It's the only thing missing."

I felt a brief sinking at the loss of the documents I'd gone to such lengths to find, but then I said, "The *only* thing? Sam, you must have misplaced it. No one breaks into a house to steal a hundred-year-old detective's report—"

"Elena, the back door had been forced. And things had been moved around on my desk, as if someone had searched carefully."

I was silent, picturing the messy desk and wondering how he could know that things had been moved.

As if he could read my thoughts, Sam said, "It may not look like it, but I know where every piece of paper on that desk is. They've been disturbed. But there's a jar of spare change that I keep right next to the pencil sharpener that wasn't touched, and whoever it was didn't bother with the TV or the stereo."

I frowned. It *did* sound like a burglary with a specific purpose.

"Elena?" Sam said.

"I'm here. Did you call the sheriff's department?"

"Didn't seem much point in it. They've got more important crimes to worry about than the theft of an old document. But *why* would anybody take such a thing?"

"I don't know."

"It just doesn't make sense."

"No, it doesn't." I was silent for a moment, then said, "Look, Sam, had you already read the papers?"

"Yes. I saved them until I'd finished my afternoon's stint of work."

"Then, it doesn't really matter that they were taken." It did; I hated to lose the documents, but it wouldn't help Sam for me to say so. "Why don't you just fix the lock on your door and try to relax? The thief got what he wanted, so there's not much chance he'll be back."

"I wish there were. I'd fix the son-of-a-bitch—"

"Sam, just take it easy. Maybe we'll get the report back. And in the meantime, we've got another installment coming. I'll be up tomorrow as soon as it arrives."

Sam sounded somewhat cheered by that, and after a few pleasantries he hung up, leaving me to my now-uneasy solitude.

I went to the sofa and sat down again, but made no attempt to go on reading. This latest development, I thought, would tend to prove that the menace I'd felt at the ruins of San Anselmo de las Lomas was real and that the watcher was no mere hiker or teenager. Someone was interested in my research into the Velasquez family—interested enough to follow and observe and, later, to break into Sam's house and steal the documents I'd brought him. Who? Why? What possible connection could there be between a nearly hundred-year-old mystery and present events in Las Lomas?

I could think of one thing: If Quincannon had not found the

Velasquez treasure, perhaps someone else had, recently. Perhaps that person was now trying to keep the fact from becoming public, so he would not have to turn the artifacts over to Sofia Manuela, the heir. That was the logical explanation, but it didn't feel right to me.

Feelings. I smiled wryly, and I went about the house, turning out lights and preparing for bed. Mama was always having feelings. She'd give me a dark look—the kind that indicated there were horrors standing in the wings just waiting to go onstage—and say, "I have a feeling. . . . " And then she'd present the latest dire possibility. I'd scoff at her premonitions, but more often than not they'd be right. And now I was having feelings, too. Perhaps, I thought, I was more my mother's child than I realized.

FIVE

THE NEXT MORNING I went to my office at the museum to wait for the Express Mail package from the San Francisco library. As soon as I got there I checked to see if the first installment of Quincannon's report was still in my desk drawer where I'd locked it two days before. There was no reason it shouldn't have been there, but I felt a quick sense of relief at the sight of its cracked leather cover.

It was now a little after nine, and around me I could hear the museum coming alive. We don't open to the public until ten, but already the staff was arriving, and preparations for the day were under way. Camilla, the volunteer who tends the gardens, was watering the azalea bushes in the little courtyard outside my office window. The phones had begun to ring, and I heard the voice of Susana Ibarra—who had volunteered to handle them in my secretary's absence—answering in cheerful tones. Doors slammed, voices called out greetings, and from the cart that sat outside my door came the smell of freshly brewing coffee. My stomach gave a hopeful growl, and I wondered if anyone had thought to buy doughnuts or sweetrolls this morning.

I was about to go out and investigate when Susana appeared in the doorway. She is an extremely pretty girl with black hair that flows nearly to her waist, and she habitually wears short, brightly colored dresses that accentuate her good legs and tiny waist. Susana, whose first job at the museum had been as my secretary, had turned into an excellent public relations director and all-around trouble-shooter. I alternately took pride in her newly developed skill at dealing diplomatically with people and became nervous at her ambitiousness. At one time, in fact, I'd suspected her of having designs on my job; as it turned out, they were only directed at my then-boyfriend, Carlos Bautista.

Today Susana's silk dress was a warm tangerine color, and a

matching band held her hair back from her forehead. Her long fingernails also matched; I noticed that right away because she had her hands pressed to her breastbone in a peculiarly breathless gesture. I was about to ask her if she was in danger of choking and if so, should I summon someone who knew the Heimlich maneuver, when I saw the ring.

Such a ring would have been hard to miss even if Susana had not been so intent on displaying it. It was a diamond, one huge square-cut stone surrounded by at least a dozen smaller ones. *Por Dios*, I thought, she must feel as if she's carrying a baseball around! That stone has to be at least three carats.

Susana said, "It's three point seven-five carats."

I said, "Oh."

"Of course, the small diamonds bring the total to around five."

"That's pretty impressive."

Susana frowned, dropping her hands to her sides. "What's wrong, Elena?" she asked. "Aren't you glad for me?" There was no gloating or cattiness in her voice; when Susana was happy, she genuinely wanted everybody to share in it.

"Of course I am!" I got up, went around the desk, and hugged her, then examined and exclaimed over the ring. Susana beamed and blushed, and let loose one of her piercing giggles. Then she went to get coffee for us to drink while she told me about her wedding plans.

I sat down in my desk chair, still a little stunned. Rudy had forewarned me about the ring, but I certainly hadn't expected anything of that size, and seeing it gave Susana's engagement to Carlos an overwhelming reality. Was I jealous? I wondered. No, not of her winning Carlos. He was my own discarded suitor; in fact, my standing him up one night was what had thrown him into Susana's arms. No, I wasn't jealous. I just wished this had come at a better time, when I could listen to her plans secure in the knowledge that somebody loved me, too.

By the time Susana returned with the coffee, I had composed my face into what I hoped was a pleased, anticipatory expression. Susana, for all her youth and self-absorption, is not insensitive, however, and she fussed over me a little, setting the coffee carefully on a napkin and going back to get a better sweetroll because the one she'd brought me was missing some of its sugary topping. Her solicitude only made me more determined not to let her realize how low I felt.

Finally she sat down across the desk from me, her hands clasped around her shapely knees, the ring positioned so it caught the light from the window behind me. "The wedding," she said, "is to be on September fourth—my birthday."

She would be all of eighteen, I thought. And Carlos was fifty-three. My preoccupation with my own feelings quickly evaporated and was replaced by a greater concern for Susana. How could such a marriage work, given the vast age difference? Carlos had seemed old to *me*. . . .

"We do not wish to have a large wedding," Susana went on. "I had that with my first marriage, in Bogotá. I did not enjoy it." She paused, then wrinkled her nose. "Of course, I did not enjoy the marriage, either."

I smiled faintly. Tony Ibarra, Susana's first husband, had been a smirking, pretentious man who always reminded me of what used to be called a "lounge lizard." By the time she had seen through him, he had proven himself to be much worse—an embezzler.

"So," Susana said, "it will be a simple ceremony with only our close friends present. And I wish you to be my maid of honor!"

From the way she beamed at me, I knew she thought she was presenting me with a precious gift. I forced a smile and said, "Why, Susana, I'm honored."

She brushed the words away with a gesture of her left hand that sent out a shower of sparkles. "I would have no one else. When I was starting over all alone in this country, you gave me a chance to prove myself. Not many would have done that—not after the way I aided my husband in his wickedness. I have never really expressed it, but I am very grateful, Elena."

Touched, I searched for words, but Susana went on. "There is only one problem. I must ask you—do you easily become seasick?"

I stared at her.

"The reason I ask is that the wedding is to be held on Carlos's yacht. We want something different from the usual type of ceremony."

Something different in a wedding: It seemed to be the California dream. People got married on beaches and in redwood groves, in hot-air balloons and on ski lifts. The settings and ceremonies were ingenious, while the marriages that resulted were often drearily the same. And now Susana and Carlos would formalize their union on the high seas. A weariness settled over me, and suddenly I wished I could say I turned green at the slightest ripple. But I couldn't do that; I have the world's steadiest pair of sea legs, and Carlos knew that from the numerous hours we'd spent together on that same yacht. "No," I said, "I don't get seasick."

"*Bueno!*" Susana clapped her hands together. I realized we'd be treated to many dramatic hand gestures before she got used to that ring.

She reached for a pen and a legal pad that lay on my desk, then said, "Now we can go on with the planning. I think pink for your dress. Or perhaps yellow—something to express the joy of the occasion."

I look like the devil in yellow, and I hate pink. "Fine," I said. "You choose."

"And roses for the bouquet. In colors to match the dress."

Roses make me sneeze. "Whatever you think best. But what will you be wearing?"

"A long dress." She paused. "Oh, you mean the color. Well, certainly not white. But ivory, perhaps. A color that is only a *little* tainted." And then she giggled so loudly I winced.

If Susana was going to be a millionaire's wife, I thought, we'd have to work on that giggle. Perhaps I could train her. . . . But how? I'd ask Mama. She had spent years trying to turn Carlota and me into ladies and—at least with my sister—had been moderately successful.

I was about to ask about the food and the guest list when Rudy Lopez poked his head through the door. Today his shirt was a hideous bright orange. Perhaps I could train *him*, too. . . .

"Elena," he said, "there's an Express Mail package here for you." He held up a thick brown envelope bearing a blue-and-orange label that went surprisingly well with his shirt.

I jumped up and went to take it from him. "Thanks. The reason I came in was to pick this up."

Rudy looked disappointed. "Oh, I thought you might be here all day."

"Why?"

"There are some invoices I need to go over with you. And Linda said something about needing your approval on the copy for the display of Chiapas textiles before she can send it to the typesetter."

168

Susana added, "And I would like your advice on the fall advertising campaign. I am having a difficult time deciding which publications to use."

I sighed and looked down at the envelope, feeling trapped by the demands of other people. I was needed here at the museum; I had to stop at the hospital and see Mama; and I'd promised Sam Ryder I'd bring the documents to Las Lomas and read them with him. Finally I said, "I can remain here until quarter to eleven. You may decide among yourselves who gets to see me first."

Of course, the next hour was not long enough to solve everyone's problems, and I had to promise to call Susana at home that evening—both to discuss the ad campaign and make more plans for the wedding. Then, when I arrived at the hospital, I found Mama was not in her room; she was having a number of tests run, the nurse informed me, and it would be better if I came back in the late afternoon. Fuming, I drove to Las Lomas, only to find that Sam wasn't at home.

I stood on his front porch clutching the precious envelope and debating what to do for a moment. After making the long drive up here, I hated to turn around and go back to Santa Barbara. Besides, Sam might return at any moment. Would it be cheating on my promise that we'd read the documents together if I started without him? I wondered. Of course not; Sam wasn't a child; he'd understand my eagerness.

I considered sitting down on the porch steps, but the cement would be cold, and anyway, after my experience yesterday at the ruins, I felt uncomfortable about reading there, where all the town could see me. I was about to go sit in my car when I remembered the picnic table where we'd had dinner on Sunday night; it was reasonably isolated, screened by scraggly rosebushes.

I went around the house and sat down there in the weedy bower. Tearing the envelope open with eager fingers, I pulled out its contents and spread them on the table. What appeared to be Xeroxes of the personal correspondence and diaries I set aside for later. The notes made for the report of the Velasquez investigation were what I wanted, and I began to read them first.

PART VI
1894

ONE

AT THE ARLINGTON stables Quincannon made arrangements to hire the claybank horse for several days. Then he returned to the hotel, changed into riding clothes, packed his warbag, and had a brief consultation with the manager, in which he said that he was going away for a few days on "grave government business" but that he might need accommodations again on his return. The manager assured him that the suite he had occupied would be held for him until further notice.

From the hotel he went to the telegraph office, where he sent a brief wire to Sabina telling her where he was going and that his investigation might require him to spend several more days in this area. He omitted any details; they would only have given her cause for concern.

He rode out of Santa Barbara to the north. When he reached Goleta he followed the old stagecoach road up into the foothills. A sea wind had sprung up at the lower elevations, but it died away as he climbed toward San Marcos Pass; the sun was warm on his back. The pungent smells of oak, madrone, pepper, filled his nostrils. In different circumstances he might have enjoyed the ride, the countryside. As it was, the murder of Luis Cordova fretted his mind— that, and the Spanish phrases on the paper scrap in his pocket.

Más allá del sepulcro. Beyond the grave.

Donde Maria. Where Maria . . .

Half a mile above a sprawling cattle ranch, the road devolved into a bare-rock slope so steep the road-builders had had to chisel deep grooves into the stone in order to keep coaches and horses from slipping on both ascent and descent. There were two sets of ruts, one worn so deep from use that it was now virtually impassable. Quincannon took the claybank up the second set, a slow process that consumed considerable time. The sun was falling toward the sea when he finally crested the ridge and arrived at a way station called Summit House.

He stopped there long enough to water himself and his horse and to find out the locations of and distances between subsequent stage stops. Then he paid a toll of twenty-five cents for passage through a locked gate barring the road, not without reluctance—private toll roads annoyed him—and pressed on up a steep canyon to the summit. On the north side of the mountains was another station, Cold Spring Tavern. There was still an hour of daylight left when he reached it; but it was a long ride down into the Santa Ynez Valley to the next way station, and it would be foolish to travel unfamiliar mountain terrain after dark.

He put up at Cold Spring Tavern for the night, paying two dollars for a plate of beans and "beef" (the meat tasted suspiciously goatish) and for the privilege of sharing a straw mattress with a variety of tiny crawling vermin. By the light of a kerosene lamp he recorded in his notebook the details of what had taken place in Santa Barbara. Then he studied the half-dozen letters he had taken from Luis Cordova's study and the hollow, conical piece of metal he had found near the body. The careful examination yielded no more information than the earlier, cursory one had. The letter gave him no definite idea of where the Velasquez artifacts had been secreted, nor any clue as to whether Luis or his mother had ever returned to the rancho to steal some or all of them. And while the piece of metal still seemed familiar to him, he was still unable to identify it or to say where he might have seen it before. Had Cordova's murderer lost it? Or had it belonged to Cordova himself?

At length, frustrated, he blew out the lamp and lay waiting for sleep. But his mind would not close down; and he was too stiff and sore from the fight with Evans and Witherspoon, and from his long ride, to force his body to relax. It was a long while before mind and body finally yielded.

When he awoke at dawn he was even stiffer, he itched all over, and his humor was as bleak as the sudden overcast that had settled above the mountains during the night. He washed in cold water, drank several cups of hot, bad coffee, disdained breakfast because he could smell it cooking, and set out again within the hour. The morning was raw, lashed by a chill wind that bit through his clothing, seemed to build a thin layer of ice on his skin. All at once the balmy spring weather of San Francisco and Santa Barbara had become a memory. It was as if he had been thrust backward in time, to the middle of winter. Cold enough to snow, he thought sourly. Bah.

He made his way down the north slopes into the Santa Ynez Valley. After fording a shallow river, he passed a third way station—Ballard's Adobe—and eventually came to the settlement of Los Olivos. There was a hotel in the settlement; he wondered if Felipe Velasquez and Barnaby O'Hare had stopped there for the night, or if they had ridden straight on to Rancho Rinconada de los Robles. In either case they had no doubt passed a better night than he had.

The road led him up Alamo Pintado Canyon, traversed rolling grasslands studded with fat cattle, then entered another canyon—Foxen Canyon, if he remembered correctly—where he soon encountered one of the stage line's Concord coaches bound from Santa Maria to Santa Barbara. Twenty minutes after that he came on the off-road, marked by a pair of giant laurels, that Velasquez had told him led to Rancho Rinconada de los Robles.

Several small ranches fanned out along this road, parcels of hilly cattle graze that had once been part of Don Esteban's vast holdings. Herds of white-faced cattle speckled the landscape; there were occasional flocks of sheep as well. He came on ranch wagons, buggies, cowhands on horseback—considerably more traffic, it seemed, than there had been on the stage road. It was well past noon when he topped a rise and saw, finally, a mile or so in the distance, the wooded hill on which the buildings of the Velasquez hacienda stood outlined against the dull gray sky. From here he could also see, at an angle to his right and perhaps a quarter mile this side of the hill, the ruins of the old pueblo and Padre Urbano's church, San Anselmo de las Lomas.

Quincannon rode toward the hacienda. But instead of proceeding there directly, he veered off on a grass-choked wagon track, obviously little used these days, that took him to the pueblo. It was much larger than he had expected. Once it had contained at least two dozen buildings—the church; a *convento* adjacent to it, where the padre had lived; dwellings for vaqueros and for laborers and their families; a garrison for the rancho's private militia; stables, workshops, and storehouses. Here and there was evidence of tanning vats, racks for drying cowhides, a blacksmith's forge, big adobe kilns for the baking of bread and the making of pottery. Beyond the church was an overgrown graveyard. And beyond the workshops an orchard of apple and pear trees stretched in thick profusion alongside a stream swollen from the winter rains.

But it was a ghost pueblo now, allowed to remain in ruin as a bitter monument to the siege of 1846 in which Don Esteban and so many others had lost their lives. A few of the buildings were still intact, but most showed the scars of battle and the ravages of time: fire-blackened beams, cannon-shattered walls, piles of crumbled adobe-brick and masonry. High grass and wind-tangles of brush and wild patches of prickly-pear cactus obscured and half concealed much of the ruins, so that the details of the pueblo's configuration were blurred and Quincannon was unable to visualize exactly how it had looked half a century ago.

It was a desolate spot—all the more so on a gray day like this one, with the wind blowing cold and making odd little murmuring noises among the decaying remains. Anyone who knew its history and who possessed a superstitious nature would shy clear of it, he thought. It was the kind of place that would have a local reputation as being haunted by the souls of those who had died here. The vague supernatural aura troubled him not at all. He had long ago decided that if he ever came face-to-face with a ghost, he would no doubt turn tail and run; but until that happened he was not going to worry about the existence of spooks and apparitions and things that went bump in the night.

He dismounted near the church, leaving the claybank to feed in a clump of sweet grass. This was where Padre Urbano had died, according to Velasquez—and little wonder. Cannonballs had smashed two of its walls to rubble, and fire had gutted much of the interior; no one who had been caught inside could have survived. The iron cross atop the roof still stood, but it was canted sharply now, as if from the weight of years, and it was only a matter of time before what remained of the roof gave way and the cross and the other walls came tumbling down.

Curiosity took him into the shell of the church. Rubble littered the floor: crumbled and shattered brick, burned wood, twigs and other things brought by a thousand winds. In a jumble of collapsed timbers that might once have been the bell tower, he saw the cracked and rusted remains of the bell—forever mute because its clapper was gone. Grass grew up through cracks in the floor; moss carpeted some of the bricks. He moved through what was left of

176

rows of simple wooden pews, toward an all-but-obliterated altar. In front and to the left of the foremost pew, the toe of his boot stubbed against a chunk of adobe; when he glanced down he thought he saw words etched into a large stone slab. He sat on his heels, scraped away grass and moss and rubble until he could read what was written there.

FRAY JULIO DEL PRADO
1751–1826
HOMBRE DE DIOS

Hombre de Dios. Man of God. The mendicant who had preceded Urbano as the padre of San Anselmo de las Lomas, no doubt; men of the cloth, Quincannon remembered, were sometimes interred in the floors of their churches. He wondered if Fray Del Prado had died here, too—more peaceably than Padre Urbano. But it was a vaguely depressing thought, and he didn't dwell on it.

Neither did he linger at the tombstone or inside the ravaged church. It was a different grave that interested him, one containing the mortal remains of someone named Maria. *Más allá del sepulcro.* Beyond the grave. *Donde Maria.* Where Maria. Beyond the grave where Maria someone lies? That was the logical interpretation of the sentence fragments on the torn scrap.

He went out into the graveyard at the rear. This was the only part of the pueblo that showed signs of care and attention. Encroaching vegetation had been cleared away from the score of graves, and each one was marked by an engraved tombstone. He prowled among them, looking at the inscriptions. The largest stone towered above the final resting place of Don Esteban, and he found where Padre Urbano had been buried. He also found one inscribed with the name Maria Alcazar and the dates 1799–1827. Was this the Maria referred to in Tomás Cordova's document—this the grave beyond which the artifacts had been hidden? But if so . . . how far beyond it? In what direction? There was no way of knowing without the rest of the document.

Well, there were consolations. The person who had killed to get that document might not be able to decipher it without those two key phrases, *más allá del sepulcro* and *donde Maria.* And that person hadn't been here yet in any case; the graves and the surrounding terrain showed no signs of recent trespass. No one had been here, it seemed, in weeks.

Quincannon returned to where he had left his horse, mounted, and rode back to the main road. He was chilled, tired, and ravenously hungry. He wanted nothing so much now as a warm fire, a cup of decent coffee, and any sort of hot food that did not contain meat from the carcass of a goat. Everything else could wait, including what he hoped would be an illuminating discussion with Felipe Antonio Abregon y Velasquez.

The road was deserted and remained that way for the last quarter mile of his journey: he saw no human being anywhere, not even as he climbed the oak-laden hill toward the open gates of the hacienda. The house and its immediate outbuildings were in good repair, freshly whitewashed and with new-tiled roofs; but there was an air of emptiness about them, at least from a distance, as if they, too, had been abandoned long ago. Quincannon found himself wondering if Velasquez and O'Hare had even arrived yet, or if for some reason they had been delayed and he was reaching the hacienda ahead of them.

Through the open gates he could see most of the courtyard, and it appeared to be deserted. But then, when he was almost to the entrance, two young men appeared suddenly from inside, one from behind each of the gate halves—so suddenly that they startled him, made him draw sharp rein. Both men were Mexican, or perhaps mestizo, and roughly dressed. They came in quick, agile movements, like trained soldiers, one to each side of him.

"That is far enough, señor," the bigger of the two said. "Remain where you are. Do not move."

Quincannon sat still, staring down at them in amazement. He had expected a cool welcome and a certain lack of hospitality at the Velasquez hacienda, but he had not expected to be greeted by a pair of grimly leveled rifles—to find himself facing what had the ominous look of a two-man firing squad.

TWO

THE BIGGER MAN gestured with his rifle, a Henry that was at least as old as he was. He said, "Who are you, senor? What is your business here?"

"My name is John Quincannon. I've come to see Felipe Velasquez."

"You are known to him?"

"Yes."

"He expects you?"

"Yes. Is he here?"

The question went unanswered. Instead the two riflemen exchanged a few words of rapid, slurred Spanish that Quincannon couldn't follow. The bigger one said to him, "You will wait with Pablo," and turned on his heel and disappeared inside the courtyard.

Quincannon waited under the watchful eye of the one named Pablo. The eye was full of dark and malignant glints, as if Pablo would like nothing better than to shoot several holes in him. Pablo, it seemed, liked gringos even less than his employer did. That being the case, Quincannon sat very still and maintained a neutral expression that revealed none of his irritation.

The wait was a short one. The other rifleman returned in less than five minutes, with Velasquez beside him. The lord of the manor wore a *charro* outfit, less elegant and ornate than the one two nights ago in Santa Barbara, and an irascible expression. In Spanish he said to Pablo, "Lower your weapon," and Pablo obediently complied, though not without an air of disappointment. Then in English he said to Quincannon, "I did not expect you for at least another day."

"Obviously not. Don't I warrant an apology?"

"Apology?"

179

"For the rough greeting by your two sentries, if that's what they are. Why the rifles?"

"There has been trouble in the valley," Velasquez said. "Rustlers. And the wife of one of the other ranchers was attacked in her home by a stranger, a gringo. Precautions must be taken against such animals."

"Apology accepted," Quincannon said dryly.

Velasquez grunted. "There is a reason you have come so soon?"

"A very good reason."

"We will discuss it in private. Dismount and come with me. Pablo and Emilio will see to your horse."

Quincannon swung down, handed the reins to Emilio, and followed Velasquez into the courtyard. The ranch house enclosed it on two sides, but one of the wings seemed foreshortened; Quincannon had the impression that the house had been much larger when Don Esteban ruled the hacienda. Much of it had been damaged during the siege, no doubt, and never rebuilt. The other two courtyard walls were ten-feet-high, made of thick adobe brick, and covered with layers of vines and climbing roses. Another arched gateway, the gates on this one locked in place, bisected the rearmost wall. From beyond that wall, distantly, Quincannon could now hear the faint lowing of cattle, the sporadic shouts of cowhands at work.

Velasquez wanted to talk immediately in his study, but Quincannon was having none of that. After his reception at the gate, he was not inclined to be deferential. He insisted on hot coffee and hot food first, preferably in front of a hot fire. Grumbling, Velasquez led him past a pair of outdoor baking ovens and into an open arcade that connected the main house with one of its smaller adjuncts. This turned out to be the kitchen, where a fat Mexican woman worked industriously over a nickel-plated stove. The stove was the only modern convenience in the big, too-warm room; everything else—tables, cupboards, wall oven, larder—seemed to be leftovers from Don Esteban's day.

"You will eat here," Velasquez said. "There is no fire, but as you can tell, the room is quite warm."

Quincannon said wryly, "Is this where all your guests take their meals? Or only the *Americanos?*"

"Your levity is ill-timed, señor." Velasquez issued instructions to the cook, said to Quincannon, "I will return when you have eaten," and took his leave.

Nettled, Quincannon warmed himself before one of the brick-heated ovens while the fat woman prepared coffee and a plate of meat and beans—simple fare, as befitted servants and lower-caste gringo detectives. He ate at a bulky trestle table. By the time he had finished, the heat in the kitchen had raised his body temperature by several degrees and started him sweating. He was in no mood to be trifled with when Velasquez returned.

Fortunately the rancher made no remarks. He said only "Now we will talk" and presented his back for Quincannon to follow out of the kitchen, along the arcade, and up an outside staircase to the house's upper level.

From the gallery Quincannon could see beyond the courtyard walls to where a series of barns, bunkhouses, stables, corrals, and cattle pens stretched away along the flattish crown of the hill and down its gently sloping backside. Rancho Rinconada de los Robles may have been a shadow of what it was in the days of *los ranchos grandes,* but it was still a large and impressive spread. At least a dozen men were visible in the vicinity of the corrals and stock pens. From the size and number of the buildings, Quincannon estimated the total work force at thirty or more.

They entered the house through a thick oaken door. A large, cheerful parlor opened to the left, windowed on two sides, with a log fire blazing on its hearth. Two people occupied it—a slender, dark woman in her late twenties, dressed in an old-fashioned, lace-trimmed black dress and a black mantilla, and a little girl perhaps two years of age. Quincannon stopped to look in at them. Velasquez, who had started toward a room on the opposite side, reversed himself with a look of annoyance.

Quincannon said, "Aren't you going to introduce me?"

The woman heard and looked up, which left Velasquez with a choice between further rudeness and at least a show of good manners. He chose good manners, evidently for the woman's sake. She was his wife, Doña Olivia, he said; and the child was Sofia, his daughter. He spoke their names in a protective way and with more gentleness than Quincannon had believed he possessed. His eyes seemed to say, almost challengingly, "Now do you understand why I have posted armed guards at the gates?"

Barnaby O'Hare had said that Mrs. Velasquez was a beautiful woman. Quincannon could understand why—she presented a striking physical presence—but he did not agree with the assessment.

There was a haughtiness about her, an air of aristocratic superiority, that he found unappetizing; and her eyes were cool, distant, with no hint of the fabled Latin passion. He preferred women who mixed warmth with their self-possession—women like Sabina.

Doña Olivia was polite enough, but he sensed that she was no more fond of *Americanos* than her husband. They made an ideal couple, he thought. He wondered if Velasquez had confided in her about his hiring of a detective and decided that the answer was yes; she seemed to know Quincannon's name. She was the type of woman, he judged, who would always insist on knowing her husband's business, and the business of everyone with whom either of them came in close contact.

"Will you be dining with us this evening, Señor Quincannon?" she asked.

"It would please me to do so," he answered before Velasquez could speak. And added perversely, "Your husband has invited me to be your guest for a few days."

"You are welcome, of course." She shifted her cool, black-eyed gaze to her husband. "When you and Señor Quincannon have finished your business, please come to me in the parlor. There is a matter we must discuss."

Quincannon thought: A matter named John Quincannon, no doubt. He felt like smiling at Velasquez and gave in to the impulse. The look he received in return was withering.

Velasquez said to his wife, "As soon as we are finished, Doña Olivia," allowed Quincannon and the woman to exchange a polite parting, and then ushered him into a smallish, oak-paneled study. When the door was shut, he let his anger show; his eyes glinted with sparks of light as he said, "You presume a great deal, señor. A great deal."

"Do I? Perhaps you'd care to terminate my employment, then?" Quincannon had had about all he could tolerate of Velasquez's superciliousness and bigotry. "Pay me what you owe for services already rendered, and I will be more than happy to vacate your house and your land."

Velasquez glared at him for a moment. Then, abruptly, he turned and crossed the room to a window set beside a broad rolltop desk. He stood silent and rigid, staring out at the gray afternoon.

Quincannon let the silence build; he wanted Velasquez to be the first to speak. He packed his pipe and lighted it. The study, like the parlor occupied by Velasquez's wife and daughter, was furnished in the dark, ornate Spanish style of a bygone age. The old-fashioned way in which he and his family were dressed, the house and its atmosphere of faded elegance, had a pathetic quality. The Velasquezes lived in the past, sought to recapture the lost days of the Spanish aristocracy; they succeeded only in making an enemy of the present.

At least two minutes passed before Velasquez turned from the window. The anger was gone; his face was set in grim, tired lines. In that moment he seemed somehow old, not so much an anachronism as a man whose time has come and gone—a man with nothing left to make of his life. And no desires save one: the recovery of his father's lost treasure.

He said, "Why are you here? What has happened in Santa Barbara?"

"Luis Cordova is dead. Murdered two nights ago. Whoever killed him took papers that may reveal the original hiding place of the artifacts."

Velasquez showed no reaction. He stood a moment longer, then turned and shuffled to a chair before the room's cold fireplace, sat down in it, and looked at his hands as if he were a Gypsy seeking his fortune in their seams and creases. At length he said, "How do you know all this?"

"I found the body."

"And the police—did you inform them?"

"No. They'll find out soon enough."

"What *did* you do?"

"Left Santa Barbara immediately to come here. I suspect the murderer did the same."

"You believe the artifacts are still hidden? That Cordova did not steal them?"

"There is no evidence that he stole them. Or that anyone else did."

"But the statue of the Virgin Mary—how did that come into his hands?"

Quincannon explained about Tomás Cordova and his legacy. Velasquez's anger returned as he listened; a small, bright hatred seemed to flicker like firelight over his features. "A filthy traitor, this Tomás Cordova," he said broodingly. "If Don Esteban had discovered his treachery, he would have died in agony."

183

"Perhaps that's how he did die, and only one day later."

Velasquez made a guttural noise and looked again at his hands.

Quincannon said, "There was something Luis Cordova's murderer overlooked, something I found in the corpse's hand."

Velasquez's head jerked up. "What did you find?"

"A scrap of paper, torn from a document I believe was written by Tomás Cordova and given to his wife before she and Luis fled the rancho. A document describing the location of the artifacts."

"Ah. You found no other part of this document?"

"No. Just the scrap."

"It has words on it, this scrap?"

"Yes."

Quincannon took the torn corner from his pocket, moved over to hand it to his employer. Velasquez studied it eagerly, his brow furrowed in concentration.

"*Más allá del sepulcro,*" he said. "In English—"

" 'Beyond the grave.' "

"*Sí.* 'Beyond the grave.' "

"Does the phrase mean anything to you?"

"No. Except that there is a graveyard behind the church of San Anselmo de las Lomas . . . "

"I know, I stopped there briefly on my way here. Who was Maria Alcazar?"

"My father's first wife. She died in childbirth."

"She appears to be the only 'Maria' buried there. Which would make her grave the one referred to in Tomás Cordova's document."

"Yes," Velasquez said, "but that fact by itself tells me nothing. What are the other directions? Without the document—"

"The document can be found."

"Can it?" Velasquez seemed to doubt that; there was an undercurrent of despair in his voice. "You have no idea who took it from Cordova's study?"

"Not yet. One possibility is James Evans. I had an altercation with him the night of the murder; and he knew then of my interest in Cordova and the statue of the Virgin Mary." Quincannon made a second withdrawal from his pocket, held out the slender piece of metal for the rancher to examine. "I found this near Cordova's body. If it belongs to the murderer, it may help identify him."

Velasquez stared at the little hollow cone. "What is it?"

"I wish I knew. I've seen it before—I know I have—but I can't remember where. It isn't at all familiar to you?"

"No."

Quincannon reclaimed it and the paper scrap and repocketed them. His pipe had gone out; he turned to the fireplace to knock out the dottle. When he turned back again, Velasquez was on his feet.

"What are your plans, Señor Quincannon? How will you proceed with your investigation?"

"Then I am still in your employ?"

"Of course." Velasquez dismissed the matter with an impatient gesture, as if it had never been open to question.

Quincannon said in his best Sherlock Holmes manner, "In the absence of definite information I will proceed on the basis of two assumptions. One, that the murderer believes the remaining artifacts are still where your father and Padre Urbano secreted them. Two, that he will come to the pueblo to search for them. I intend to be there when he arrives."

"You will maintain a vigil?"

"A daytime vigil—he won't go to the pueblo at night. There is no moon, and he dare not show a light that might be seen from up here."

Velasquez nodded. "You will do this alone?"

"One man can lie in wait more safely than two or three."

"When do you begin?"

"Tomorrow morning. There is less than an hour of daylight left today; and I saw no indication that our man has yet been to the pueblo. Tomorrow will be soon enough."

"Very well."

"One thing, Señor Velasquez," Quincannon said. "I may be here for some time. During my stay I suggest you at least pretend to treat me as an invited guest. It will make matters easier for both of us. Agreed?"

Purse-lipped, Velasquez said, "Agreed."

Quincannon was given accommodations on the lower floor of the house—perhaps not the best guest room the hacienda had to offer but a comfortable one nonetheless. He permitted himself a two-hour nap on its tolerably soft bed, during which he dreamed of

Sabina. She called him "dear" twice in the course of the dream and kissed him once, and he awoke refreshed and in much better spirits.

He washed in a pannikin of water brought by one of the servants and changed into his only clean clothing—a nobby, dressy, all-wool brown-and-gray-mixed cassimere suit with a diagonal Cheviot pattern that made him look (or so Sabina had said, much to his satisfaction) like a gay young blade. He was just knotting his cravat when the servant returned to conduct him upstairs to the dining room.

Dinner was a somber affair. There were just the three of them; Barnaby O'Hare had left that morning for an overnight visit to the Alvarado ranch, some distance away. Velasquez was moody and had little to say. His wife made polite conversation for the most part, although from time to time she asked probing little questions that told Quincannon her husband had indeed informed her of recent developments in Santa Barbara. The food, at least—a spicy beef stew, tortillas, fresh vegetables—was good enough so that Quincannon indulged in a second helping. It seemed to him that he deserved it.

He and Velasquez had coffee and cigars in the parlor. The rancher also had several glasses of *aguardiente,* which only served to deepen his dark mood. Unlike his wife, he had nothing more to say about Luis Cordova's murder or the words on the paper scrap, which suited Quincannon. Constant reiteration and speculation served no useful purpose, only led to a heightening of frustration.

He was back in his room by nine o'clock, his mood once more as grim as Velasquez's. He did not like the man or his wife, or the style in which they lived, or Rancho Rinconada de los Robles; he longed to be gone from here, to be back among people who lived in the present instead of the long-dead past. If Cordova's murderer did not come soon . . .

But he would. He had killed to find out the location of the artifacts; he would not wait long to come after them.

Quincannon undressed and went to bed. By the light of a coal-oil lamp he tried to read from the volume of poems by Wordsworth; but he had no interest in poetry this evening, took no enjoyment in Wordsworth's bleak, episodic reminiscences of his childhood and his residence at Cambridge. He closed the book finally, put it aside. And in spite of himself, he again took out the conical piece of metal

186

and turned it over in his hand, holding the object so that the lamplight glinted off its shiny surface.

He knew what it was. Hell and damnation, he was morally certain he knew what it was.

What *was* it?

THREE

IT WAS ANOTHER cold, gray day that Quincannon awoke to—a worse day than the previous one, in fact, because of a blustery wind and a wet, swirling ground mist. The prospect of spending eight or nine hours out in weather such as this was enough to try the sweet disposition of a saint. And he was no saint, God knew; it made *him* feel low and irritable and very sorry for himself.

He dressed as warmly as the contents of his warbag would allow, drew on a pair of wool-lined gloves, and left his room. Half a dozen men and women moved about the courtyard, performing a variety of early morning tasks; the two guards, Pablo and Emilio, were at their watch posts on the main gate. Out at the corrals the ranch hands were evidently engaged in the branding of calves: he could hear the animals' frightened bawling, smell the faint drifting odors of chaparral fires, hot metal, and singed hair. He entered the kitchen, where he drank several cups of coffee and ate a huge breakfast to build up his strength for the day's ordeal. He also convinced the fat cook to prepare him a meal of tortillas and fried meat that he could take with him.

In the courtyard again he stopped one of the servants and sent the man to saddle and fetch his horse. There had been no sign of Velasquez this morning, and Quincannon wanted to talk to him again before he left for the pueblo. He approached another servant, sent this one upstairs with a message. When the servant reappeared on the upper gallery, the ranch owner was with him; Velasquez came down alone and crossed to where Quincannon waited by one of the baking ovens.

Quincannon had not passed a restful night, but it seemed obvious that Velasquez hadn't slept at all. He appeared haggard and sunken-eyed, moved like a battle-weary soldier from a vanquished army. One look at him answered the question in Quincannon's mind and kept him from asking it aloud. Velasquez had no more idea this

189

morning than he had had last night of the possible whereabouts of Don Esteban's artifacts.

"You have something to tell me, Señor Quincannon?"

"No. Just that I'm about to leave for the pueblo."

"Then you have not yet identified the piece of metal you showed me?"

"Not yet. But I will."

"I have no doubt of it." But Velasquez's eyes were bleak, his voice listless. "Where will you make your vigil? You have a place in mind?"

"Not as yet. I'll find one that commands a clear view of the graveyard."

"There is high ground to the south of the creek and the orchard, a knoll topped by two large oaks. All of the pueblo can be seen from there."

"Good. I may need a spyglass, though."

"I will have one brought for you."

"You might also instruct your guards to listen for gunfire," Quincannon said. "If they hear any, it will mean trouble and they should come pronto."

"They will be told."

The servant arrived from the stables with Quincannon's claybank. Another brought an old Mexican spyglass in a worn leather case. Velasquez had nothing more to say; he stood hunched and silent as Quincannon mounted his horse. There was an air of resignation about him, as if he felt the mission would ultimately prove futile; as if he retained little hope that his father's artifacts would ever be found.

Quincannon rode out through the gate, down the hill to where another road branched to the south. He turned there, so as to loop around on the far side of the ruins and approach them through the orchard and along the stream. He had gone perhaps a fifth of a mile and was about to leave the road and strike out across a section of rumpled pastureland, when a rider appeared around a bend a hundred yards ahead. Warily Quincannon slowed the claybank to a walk. He did not wish to be seen riding cross-country toward the pueblo; and he wanted a look at the rider in any case, in the event it was someone other than a local rancher or cowhand.

And it was: the man astride the approaching chestnut was Barnaby O'Hare.

O'Hare recognized him at the same time; his moon face registered surprise that modulated into a smile as he drew rein. "Mr. Quincannon," he said. "Well, this is an unexpected pleasure."

"Yes, isn't it?" Quincannon said without enthusiasm.

"I didn't expect you for another day or two. But you're going the wrong way, you know; the Velasquez hacienda is the one on that hill behind you."

"I am aware of that. I've just come from there."

"You have? When did you arrive?"

"Yesterday afternoon."

"Really? But I understood you had two or three days' business in Santa Barbara . . . "

"My business is here now," Quincannon said shortly. "Now if you'll excuse me, I'll get on with it."

"You wouldn't be riding to the Alvarado rancho, would you? I've just come from there."

"No, I wouldn't."

"Well . . . that is where this road leads, you know."

Quincannon said nothing, pointedly. He would have liked to lean over and knock O'Hare off his horse. For some reason the man brought out uncharitable feelings in him.

O'Hare gave him a knowing look. "On the trail of something, eh?" he said. "Detective work for Señor Velasquez?"

"In a manner of speaking."

"Well, I won't pry," O'Hare said. "Won't detain you any longer, either. But I would consider it a personal favor if you'd confide in me later on. *Hasta la vista*, Mr. Quincannon."

And a good day to you, too, you horse's ass, Quincannon thought.

O'Hare lifted a hand and continued on his way. Quincannon rode on a short way himself, looking back over his shoulder as he went. When O'Hare had passed from sight he swung the claybank off the road, cut back at an angle through a screen of trees to where the rain-swollen creek meandered among a series of low, rolling hillocks.

He followed the stream until he came in sight of the orchard that marked the pueblo's eastern perimeter. Then he veered away from it to the south, skirted a tangle of wild blackberry bushes and the shoulder of another hillock. Layers of mist undulated above a section of marshy lowland beyond. And beyond that was yet another hillock, this one crowned by a pair of huge black oaks: his reckoning

191

had been correct. He negotiated the bog and rode halfway up the gentle slope of the hill, at which point he picketed the claybank. He went the rest of the way on foot.

From atop the knoll, as Velasquez had said he would, he had a fine clear view of the pueblo. He could also see portions of the main road to Rancho Rinconada de los Robles, the one he had traveled yesterday; and at an angle behind him, part of the hacienda was likewise visible. All in all, it was a better vantage point than he had hoped for.

He scanned the ruins with his naked eye, saw nothing out of the ordinary. He scanned them again with the spyglass, paying particular attention to the graveyard behind the ravaged church. There was no sign of disturbance in the area, no indication that anyone had been there since his visit yesterday afternoon.

Half a dozen large rocks were scattered through the high grass between the oaks. One of these, shielded by low-hanging branches, had a kind of natural bench on its near side. He had brought the claybank's saddle blanket with him, and he spread this out over the bench to insulate his backside from the cold dampness of the stone. When he sat down he found that he could see over the top of the rock with no difficulty. And he was satisfied that no one could see him from down below.

He settled in to wait. The shape of the rock gave him some protection from the wind, but the cold seeped in through his clothing, his gloves, his boots. As did the damp, even though most of the ground mist was beginning to evaporate. He shifted position constantly, first in an effort to make himself comfortable and then to keep the muscles in his legs and arms from stiffening.

He had been there an hour and a quarter when he spied movement on the main road beyond the pueblo. He caught up the glass, fitted it to his eye. A light spring wagon had come rolling down the hill from the hacienda and was proceeding westward. He lost sight of it for a time, picked it up again as it emerged from behind a wall of trees, and saw that there were three people on the high seat. Two of them were Velasquez's wife and young daughter, both wrapped in heavy ponchos, the child cradled in her mother's arms. The third person, the one driving the wagon, was Emilio, one of the guards who had been posted at the main gate.

Quincannon's beard bristled, and his face shaped itself into a piratical glower. The woman and child were probably on their way to visit a neighbor, he thought, and Velasquez had detailed Emilio to protect them. But had he put anyone on the gate in the man's place? What if there was trouble here and this poor half-frozen gringo detective needed more help than Pablo alone could give? Had Velasquez given any thought to *that* before he permitted his family to go gallivanting through the countryside?

The wagon disappeared completely between two hills. Quincannon lowered the glass and ducked his head turtle-fashion into the collar of his coat. He was feeling sorry for himself again. What sort of miserable job was this for a detective of his experience and talents? There was no dignity in it, by God. No dignity at all. He decided he would charge Velasquez double the agency's fee—*triple* the agency's fee if he were forced to spend more than one day out here in the cold, risking a serious case of the grippe on top of everything else. That made him feel a little better. There was a certain warmth in the prospect of a large sum of money. Not that he was the greedy sort, a common money-grubber. Perish the thought. But a man had to be compensated for his sacrifices in some way, didn't he?

More time passed. The sky began to darken; the wind gathered strength, and the air took on a moist, metallic smell. To the west, above the Santa Ynez Mountains, gangrenous thunderheads had begun to mass like soldiers assembling for an attack. Two hours, perhaps three, and the heavens would open up and dump forth enough water to drown any man fool enough to still be sitting behind a rock on a knoll, accumulating chilblains and flirting with the grippe.

Well, he *wouldn't* still be sitting here when the storm broke. Luis Cordova's murderer was not going to be out digging up buried treasure in a thunderstorm and neither was the man who would eventually bring him to justice. Enough was enough. He would wait one more hour, perhaps an hour and a half if those thunderheads took their time sallying forth for the deluge. Then he would ride back to the hacienda and spend the day in front of a blazing fire, drinking hot coffee and thinking about Sabina.

Ah, Sabina. He should have been thinking about her all along. Money was a warming thought, a certain consolation, but a woman of Sabina's—

Something slashed by his head, making noise like a disturbed hornet, and ricocheted off the rock with a hollow ringing whine. Stone chips flew, stinging his cheek as he lunged sideways, propelled by reflex and instinct, and sprawled out face-down in the high grass. The not-so-distant thunder roll of that first shot reached his ears just before the second bullet plowed a furrow in the turf a few inches beyond his outflung left arm.

He hauled the arm in and scrabbled and rolled forward, downhill toward the creek, tugging frantically at the glove on his right hand. A rock gouged him in the side with such sharpness that for an instant he thought he had been shot; realized he hadn't been when he heard the third bullet, riding the echoes of the second, spang into another rock behind and away from him. He fetched up at a tangle of brush and deadfall limbs and crawled into it, fumbling the Remington out of the holster at his belt. He lay there panting, not moving, trying to pinpoint the location of the shots as the echoes of the third one died away.

It was quiet for a time—a breathless, electric quiet broken only by the ragged murmur of his breathing. Then he heard sounds, wary shuffling movement in the grass not far off. He listened, turning his head in quadrants, trying to see out through the brush. His assailant—and there was only one, he was certain of that—was invisible to him, but now he knew the man's approximate location: over on the north side of the knoll, moving uphill along its shoulder on a course parallel to where he lay.

There was nothing for him to do but lie still and wait. The sniper hadn't seen him burrow up in the brush; if he had, there would have been more shots. For all the man knew, one of his bullets had found its mark, and his target was already dead or mortally wounded. As long as the assailant maintained a high opinion of his own marksmanship, Quincannon had a chance. And how long he maintained it depended on how well Quincannon played possum.

The sounds of movement stopped somewhere above—on top of the knoll, he thought, by one of the oaks. A rotting log blocked his view, and he didn't dare shift position to gain a better vantage point; as quiet as it was, and as close as the sniper was, the slightest noise would betray the fact that he was still alive. He forced himself to remain motionless. There was cold sweat on his body now; the skin along his back rippled and crawled. If the man up there saw him and decided to fire again, to make sure of his kill. . . .

A long, agonizing minute crept away. Then, mercifully, the shuffling movements started again—slow, measured steps coming downhill toward the deadfall. No more than thirty feet away . . . no more than twenty-five . . . no more than twenty—

There was a sudden sharp crack as the man's foot came down on a piece of brittle wood, a sound as loud in that electric stillness as a pistol shot. Quincannon reacted without thinking, again on reflex and instinct; he had one move, one chance, and there would be no better time for it. He shoved off the ground with his left hand, reared up on his knees with the Remington jabbing through the brush in front of him. The assailant had startled himself by stepping on the stick or twig, had looked down automatically at his feet; and that made him vulnerable. By the time he heard and saw Quincannon, brought his rifle to bear, it was too late for him to do anything but die.

Quincannon shot him twice. Would have shot him three times except that the third bullet hit the rifle just as it discharged, sent it spinning free, and rendered the return shot harmless. The man twisted, toppled, skidded downward on his face to within a few feet of the deadfall—a dead fall of his own.

Shakily Quincannon gained his feet. The Remington felt heavy and slippery in his fingers; there was a brassy taste in his mouth. He took several deep breaths, extricated himself from the brush, moved up to where the sniper lay. He turned the man over with his foot, looked down into blank staring eyes and a familiar countenance. He was not surprised at the sniper's identity. He should have been, at least a little, but he wasn't. The only emotion he felt was a dull, smoldering anger.

The man who had tried to kill him was Pablo, the other guard on the hacienda gate.

FOUR

QUINCANNON HOLSTERED HIS revolver, stepped around the body of the dead mestizo, and climbed to the crest of the knoll. The anger continued to smolder in him; he used it like fuel to burn away the cold and the aftermath of sudden violence.

The claybank horse, frightened by the shooting, had pulled loose of its picket and run off into the marsh, where it had come close to getting itself mired. He went down there, spoke gently to the animal to keep it still, finally succeeded in catching the reins and leading it out to firmer ground. Then he mounted, turned to the north, forded the creek, and veered overland through the orchard. When he reached the main road, he kicked the horse into a hard gallop all the way uphill to the hacienda.

There were no guards on the gate when he clattered through. He drew sharp rein, swung down. The door to one of the house's ground-floor rooms opened and Barnaby O'Hare appeared, drawn by the noise of his arrival. O'Hare came out into the courtyard. And the expression on Quincannon's face, the damp and grass-stained condition of his clothing, seemed to startle him.

"Mr. Quincannon, what on earth—"

"Where is Velasquez?"

"Why . . . I don't know. I haven't seen him for the past hour. Has something happened? You look—"

Quincannon pivoted away from him, hurried up the stairs to the second-floor gallery. There was no one in the parlor when he entered; the house seemed unnaturally quiet. He drew his revolver again, went to the closed door to Velasquez's study, and threw it open—standing back and to one side as he did so, out of the line of fire from within.

But there seemed to be no need for his caution or his weapon. Velasquez sat unarmed in the chair before the fire, his hands on his knees; he turned his head at the sudden opening of the door but

197

made no other movement. His posture was that of an old man, a cripple incapable of movement without assistance. Firelight flickered over his face, creating shadows and highlights that gave his skin the look of tallow about to melt.

"So," he said in a thin, dead voice. "Pablo did not succeed."

Quincannon entered the study, shut the door behind him. He might have holstered his pistol then, but he didn't; he let it hang down at his side instead. There was no trust left in him today, not even of his own perceptions.

"Pablo is dead. You should have sent more than one man."

"It does not matter now."

"No? Why doesn't it?"

"Time," Velasquez said. "Time."

"It has run out for you, if that's what you mean."

"Run out. Yes."

"But you didn't think so earlier, when you gave Pablo his orders."

Velasquez lifted one hand, let it fall again to his knee. "I believed then that your death would give me a little more of it—a little more time."

"Because I was close to the truth," Quincannon said bitterly. "And the truth is you killed Luis Cordova and stole the document his father wrote. No one has ever been after Don Esteban's artifacts but you."

"Stole the document? No, señor. It is rightfully mine, as the artifacts are rightfully mine."

"Was it also your right to take Cordova's life?"

"I did not mean to kill him. I went to talk to him, nothing more. I was afraid your way would be too slow. But he was very frightened, and I was very angry. He told what his father had done; he gave me the traitor's letter—all but the last page. He said the last page had been lost years ago. I didn't believe him then. I struck him. He fought me in his fear; it must have been then that he tore off the scrap you found. It was only after I returned to the St. Charles that I noticed it was missing. But I did not think it was in his hand; I thought it had also been lost years ago."

Quincannon felt in his coat pocket. The slender metal cone was still there, and he drew it out. "Cordova tore this from you, too," he said. "From one end of the string tie you were wearing that night. I noticed the tie in the bar at the St. Charles; the ends clicked together once when you moved."

"I knew you would remember what it was and where you had seen it. It was only a matter of time." The ghost of a mirthless smile played at the edges of Velasquez's mouth. "Time," he said again.

Quincannon said, "I should have known all along it was you. I should have known for certain yesterday afternoon. Here, in this room, you asked if I had any idea who had taken the document from Cordova's study. But I said nothing to you about a study; I said only that I had found Cordova dead in his lodgings."

A small fit of coughing seized Velasquez. When it ended, he said, "You are a good detective. If you weren't—"

"If I weren't, you wouldn't have tried to have me killed."

"A desperate measure. But I told you: it was only for time that I did it. Now . . . " He shrugged emptily. "Now, it does not matter. It was all for nothing. There can never be enough time."

"Why do you keep talking about time?"

"I am dying," Velasquez said without inflection. "The doctor in Santa Barbara . . . it was him I saw that night, before I went to Cordova's. . . . He told me I have only a short while to live. A few weeks, no more." He coughed again. "Cancer, señor. Now do you understand?"

Some of the anger went out of Quincannon. He moved closer to Velasquez, into the warmth of the fire. The Remington felt heavy in his hand, but still he did not pouch it. "Yes," he said, "now I understand."

"It was not for me that I wished to recover the artifacts. It was for my wife and daughter. This ranch is not so successful as it might appear. There are debts . . . too many debts. Doña Olivia will be forced to sell after I am gone. Rancho Rinconada de los Robles will be no more."

"The artifacts may still be recovered—"

"No, they will not be. They are lost forever."

"Why do you say that?"

"Because of the missing page. Luis Cordova did not have it; I would have found it if he had, or you would have. He did not lie. It *was* lost."

"The rest of the letter isn't enough? Not even with the words on the torn corner?"

"No. Last night, all night, I studied the two pages. The missing directions cannot be reconstructed." Contempt animated Velasquez's voice as he continued. "Most of the letter is an apology to the traitor's wife. He was sorry he had stolen the statue of the Virgin Mary. He was sorry for his betrayal of Don Esteban. He begged her and God to forgive him. He did this terrible thing only for her sake and that of his child."

"Just as you did a terrible thing for the sake of your wife and child," Quincannon said. "Is there really so much difference between you and Tomás Cordova?"

"A foolish question. I am not a traitor."

"What are you, then? A martyr like you believe your father to be?"

"I am Felipe, son of Don Esteban. I have given him a small measure of vengeance."

A coldness like the touch of dead fingers brushed Quincannon's neck. There was no longer any anger left in him. He felt nothing toward the dying man in the chair, not even pity.

"You're proud of what you've done," he said flatly. "There is not a shred of remorse in you, is there."

"Remorse? Why should there be? I ended the life of a traitor's son—a coward and a thief himself. He kept the statue all those years. He did not return it to my family. He did not give us the traitor's letter."

"Perhaps he was ashamed."

"Bah. It is we who were shamed by him and his father."

"And Pablo? Do you feel remorse for him? Or don't you admit he died because of you?"

"He died because he was loyal," Velasquez said. "As Don Esteban's servants died for him. His death is an honorable one."

"What would mine have been? Would you have found honor in murdering me, too?"

Velasquez made no reply. But none was needed: Quincannon knew the answer. He was a gringo, and in the eyes of Felipe Antonio Abregon y Velasquez, son of Don Esteban the martyred nobleman, all gringos were the enemy. Use one if it suits one purpose; kill one if it suits another. There is never any regret in the death of an enemy.

A silence built between them. Velasquez stared into the fire with his dull, empty eyes. Outside, the wind began to buffet the house, rattling shutters; it would not be long before the storm broke. The air in the room, Quincannon thought, was like the air outside: heavy, oppressive, static with an aura of repressed violence. He

200

found it difficult to breathe, as if there were no longer enough oxygen—or enough space—for the two of them to share.

Velasquez seemed to feel the same sense of suffocation. He said without turning his head, "I would like to be alone now, señor. You will please leave for a few minutes."

A thought entered Quincannon's mind, made him hesitate. But only for a moment. He refused to take hold of the thought, let it slide away into a recess of his consciousness. He backed to the door, not looking anymore at the dying man in the chair, and left the study. And it was not until he closed the door that he finally holstered his revolver.

Barnaby O'Hare was waiting when he stepped out onto the gallery. The historian's moon face was troubled. "Is everything all right, Mr. Quincannon?"

Quincannon said nothing. He moved to the railing, stood staring into the courtyard. The day had turned very dark; the sky overhead boiled with thick, black-veined clouds. As he watched, the first drops of rain began to pelt down.

Beside him O'Hare said diffidently, "Mr. Quincannon?"

"Yes. Everything is all right."

"You seemed so upset a few minutes ago . . . "

"I was. Not any longer."

"Then you found Señor Velasquez?"

"I found him."

"He isn't ill, is he?" O'Hare asked. And when Quincannon didn't answer, "I've been afraid he might be. He wouldn't speak to me when I returned. He . . . well, he acted strangely. He sent his wife and daughter away, you know."

"Yes, I know."

"Did he tell you why?"

"No," Quincannon said. "But I know why now."

"Perhaps he needs a doctor . . . "

"There is nothing a doctor can do for him. Nothing anyone can do."

Lightning flashed in the distance; thunder cracked. Quincannon watched the rain, listening.

Inside the house, inside the study, there was a noise like a small sharp echo of the thunder: a single pistol shot.

O'Hare said, "Oh my God!" and ran for the door. Quincannon stayed where he was and watched the rain, no longer listening.

PART VII
1986

ONE

I set the photostats of Quincannon's notes aside and sat staring at a spider that was spinning a web on one of Sam's straggly rosebushes. This final installment of the detective's story had left me with a curious and conflicting assortment of emotions.

Disappointment, of course, because for all his efforts he had not uncovered the hiding place of the Velasquez treasure. Sorrow, for the participants in the tragedy that had befallen the once-proud family. It was a sorrow that extended to the dead: to Felipe Velasquez, whose life had been twisted and finally destroyed by his obsession with finding the missing artifacts; to his wife, Olivia, the innocent bystander. But I particularly felt a keen sympathy for the still-living Sofia Manuela: From the way she had spoken of her father, the "great man," it was apparent her mother had not told her that Felipe had died a suicide and a murderer. But I wondered if at some point Sofia *had* found out at least part of it; if perhaps that knowledge—rather than sentiment—was why she could never bear to look through the papers in the wooden box she kept under her bed.

To me, Felipe Velasquez had been a strange man. We were of the same culture, descended from the same people, but his attitude of hatred and superiority toward Anglos was something I couldn't fathom—even for those times. Of course I'd felt some resentment of Anglos in my lifetime; it hadn't been easy growing up in Santa Barbara, where even the poorest of them seemed to have so much; I still hurt when I remembered running home from school in tears because a classmate had taunted me about my mother cleaning *her* mother's house for a living. But hate Anglos? Feel inferior or superior to them? No. Maybe the difference between me and Felipe Velasquez—besides the obvious one of time and circumstances— was that I hadn't been raised to hate.

In spite of my sadness and disappointment over the outcome of

205

Quincannon's case, I also felt an even greater excitement than before. In his informal notes, there had been more richness of detail, and he had indulged in a fair amount of speculation; it was as if he'd used these notes to order his thoughts before setting down the bare and still-confusing facts for the final time. Reading them, it was easy to sense Quincannon's anger and frustration.

The question of the whereabouts of those artifacts remained as nagging and tantalizing as when the case had begun. It was clear from Tomás Cordova's letter that they had been buried somewhere near Maria Alcazar's—Don Esteban's first wife's—grave, but her headstone had never been located, and the rancho's pueblo had been thoroughly searched by the family in the years after Fremont's troops had destroyed it, with no trace of the treasure ever turning up.

Where *was* the treasure, then, if not somewhere in the pueblo? Had it been taken away by Luis Cordova or his mother? No, there was absolutely no evidence of that. And—unlike Quincannon, who I assumed was not Catholic from the way he had phrased certain things in his report—I was not surprised that the Cordovas had not used the knowledge passed along in Tomás's letter or turned the information over to the Velasquez family. Shame would have prevented both actions. As described in the detective's words, Luis and his mother were extremely religious, the staunchest of Mexican Catholics. They would no more have stolen religious artifacts than they would have spit on the statue of the Virgin Mary that Tomás had taken, and they would certainly not have desecrated a grave-yard looking for them. Nor would they have allowed outsiders—especially the Velasquezes—to know of Tomás's crime. That was the reason Luis had lied to Quincannon, had been so frightened when the detective came asking about the statue. The gold figure had been a terrible burden to Luis all the years he had harbored it, and perhaps it had even been a relief when it was stolen.

My reasoning explained Luis's and his mother's behavior, but it still didn't answer the question of what had happened to those remaining artifacts. And the more I thought about it, the more I became convinced that nothing actually *had* happened to them. They had to be in their original hiding place even now; otherwise some of them would have turned up somewhere, at some time. There were too many of them, and most were too distinctive for them to have gone unnoticed and unrecognized.

206

Más allá del sepulcro . . . donde Maria. Beyond the grave . . . where Maria. . . .

I looked down at the picnic table where the other documents that had been in the package from the public library were spread: copies of the personal letters, the diaries, perhaps even photographs. But I'd save those for later, maybe for when Sam returned from wherever he'd gone; right now I was too restless and excited to go through them. I felt an urgent need to go to the ruins of San Anselmo de las Lomas once more, to stand in the graveyard as Quincannon had done, to try one last time to unlock the meaning of those haunting words.

I put the documents back in the big envelope and went around Sam's house to where I'd left my car. As I got into it, I thought briefly about leaving a note for the historian but decided there was no sense in that. I probably wouldn't be at the old graveyard long, and anything I needed to tell him would keep until I returned.

As I stood beside the remains of the church, the wind blew strong and chill. It rustled and moaned in the nearby grove of oak trees and made rain-dark clouds scud across the sky, their shadows moving over the ground and then vanishing. Today there was a sharp tang of eucalyptus in the air, as bitter as the knowledge of what had taken place here must have been to those involved. I glanced over at the oak-topped knoll where Quincannon must have kept his vigil and then been ambushed; I imagined how the shots must have sounded in the silence.

The desolation of this place not only took me into the past but also made me think of yesterday: someone had watched me here and then slipped away into these still-wild hills. Had it been the same person who had later broken into Sam's home? Or had that been mere coincidence? Whoever had stolen that report from Sam was probably just a treasure hunter, anyway. I doubted he would commit violence for the Velasquez artifacts; only Felipe's obsession had been strong enough for that.

I moved among the graves slowly, reading the markers more carefully this time, pulling aside the tall, tangled vegetation to uncover others. When I came to Felipe's plain stone, I stopped and contemplated it briefly. The fact that he had died a suicide explained both the lack of inscription and the way it was set apart from the rest. I allowed myself a moment of sympathy for this man whose heritage had both shaped and warped his life, then went on looking for Maria Alcazar's grave. In a short time, I had to concede failure. I straightened up and looked around, my excitement gone.

A hollow sensation settled in my stomach, and I turned from the graveyard. A rain-swollen cloud had blotted out the sun, and its shadow lay over the ruins of the church. I stepped over the crumbling foundation and began to walk down the nave to where the altar had stood, knowing I was doing this for the last time, silently saying good-bye. It was time I put a halt to my preoccupation with John Quincannon's search for the Velasquez artifacts, time I let go of the past. There were things I should do with the rest of my vacation: call a housepainter, mend my clothes, run errands, and—most important—make my peace with Mama.

But I didn't want to leave. Something held me in this lonely place, some indefinable but strong pull from the past.

I moved toward the front of the church to where the first rows of pews once had been, the leg of my pants snagging on the charred roof beam. Glaring at it as if it were an animal that had nipped at me, I kicked out irritably. A sharp twinge of pain in my sneakered toe reminded me I was being childish. I just didn't want to let go of the romantic past and immerse myself once more in a life that revolved around balancing the museum's budget, trips to the grocery store, and social obligations such as a shipboard wedding. Sternly I told myself that such mundane activities were the glue that held my life together, and that I'd better get on with them.

Before I left, though, I decided to allow myself one last self-indulgence. Apparently the church and the pueblo had gripped Quincannon's imagination as much as they had mine, because in his notes he had described them in greater detail than seemed necessary. And one of the things he had written of was finding another grave, that of the parish's first padre, in the floor in front of the altar. Many Catholic churches had allowed persons of importance to be buried within—although that practice had been more common in Europe than in the mission churches of California—and apparently the first priest of San Anselmo de las Lomas had been so honored. I couldn't help but wonder if the marker was still here.

The search was more difficult than I'd anticipated, however, because the broken brick floor was overgrown not only with weeds but with a carpet of that kind of wild grass that sends out a mass of tough, interlocking runners. I yanked at one plant, cutting my fingers and pulling it up, roots and all. To the left of the altar area, I got down on my knees, bracing my feet behind me, and tugged on a large runner. More of the shallowly rooted plants popped out from the cracks in the bricks, and I repeated the process until I had exposed a substantial amount of flooring and had found the edge of what appeared to be the grave marker.

My excitment returned as I crawled forward and removed more weeds and debris from the stone. When I was done, it was still covered by soil, and I shoveled it out of the way with my bare hands, until I could read the inscription. It was as Quincannon had described, an elaborate carving that had been made shallow and indistinct by more than a century of exposure to the elements. But the words were still decipherable: FRAY JULIO DEL PRADO, 1751–1826, HOMBRE DE DIOS.

Once again—in spite of my best intentions—I was there in the past with John Quincannon, looking down at that stone. The pull of those long-ago times was stronger than ever now. As strong as if someone were trying to tell me something. . . .

I stood, my eyes still on the grave. Then I glanced up at where the altar had once been. And then at the apse, the one to my left, where the wall was still intact.

Más allá del sepulcro . . . dondé Maria . . .

Maria!

I drew in my breath and stood very still. Then I released it in a rush as my heart started beating faster. I stepped around the padre's grave and hurried over to the apse. Its floor was littered with trash: paper bags and beer cans and wine bottles. Over by the stones that were piled against the wall, someone had made a charcoal fire, taking advantage of the shelter from the wind.

Stones?

I stared down at them, sidetracked from my purpose. What on earth were they doing here? I wondered. They were quite large and of the same type as those on the knoll where Quincannon had been ambushed. Someone had taken a great deal of trouble to move them all that distance and pile them here in the apse.

Because this was nothing like what I'd expected to find, I was momentarily disconcerted. Then I got down on my hands and knees and began to try to move the stones. They were cumbersome and didn't budge easily, both because of their weight and the way they'd been wedged together. How long had they been here? I thought. Not a great deal of time. There was nothing growing over them, and grass and weeds took hold quickly during the winter and spring rains.

A few of the peripheral stones had yielded. I grasped a big, jagged chunk of rock and pulled. It moved an inch or so, and a shower of smaller pieces rained down, one striking my knee. I paused to rub the place where it hurt, then grasped the rock more firmly. Leaning back against my heels, I pulled as hard as I could. The rock moved a few more inches.

At first I didn't recognize what was behind it. It looked like a polished piece of wood. Then I saw it was striated: brown alternating with lighter brown, and above it a curve of dark leather. It was the stacked heel of a woman's boot.

My heart began to pound as I leaned forward and looked closer. Above the shoe part of the boot was blue fabric. Denim. The leg of a pair of jeans.

A vague odor rose to my nostrils now, a kind of dusty decay. I pulled back convulsively. For a moment there was a ringing in my ears, a blurring of my vision. And then my senses cleared. I saw the boot and blue-jeaned leg with awful sharpness. Felt the prickling cold that was creeping over my skin. Tasted the metallic dryness in my mouth.

And heard the footfall behind me.

I swiveled around, wrenching my back, stones digging into one knee. Then I tried to stand but found my limbs had gone weak. Above me loomed the menacing figure of Gray Hollis.

TWO

GRAY'S FACE WAS an almost translucent white, the skin drawn taut over his cheekbones. His lips curled back like those of an animal about to attack. It was his eyes that frightened me the most: black holes in which pinpoints of fury glittered.

I got to my feet slowly, pain biting into the small of my back where I had twisted it. Gray stepped forward, and I smelled the sharp odor of bourbon. The liquor had not affected his control, however: he was steady on his feet, poised to spring at me, and the bunching of his fists at his sides suggested a brute strength.

He said, "Doing a little treasure hunting, lady?"

I said, "Yes, but there's nothing here."

"Nothing here." He laughed, a sound that abruptly cut off before it reached its crescendo. Goose bumps rose over my whole body, and I thought: *This is the way it was when he killed her.*

Gray said, "Nothing here but Georgia."

Involuntarily I glanced back at the cairn of rocks.

He smiled, but the feral set of his face turned it into a snarl. He said, "I see you've already met my wife."

The goose bumps rippled again, icy cold. My heart was pounding so hard I could hear its thrum in my ears. I took a step backward.

"Wha's the matter—don't you like my joke?" Gray lunged at me, but I sidestepped, and he staggered, then fell to one knee.

I turned and ran toward the other side of the ruins.

"Come back here, you goddamn bitch!"

I glanced over my shoulder. He had regained his feet and was running after me. Looking down at the ground, I saw a chunk of red tile. I scooped it up, and when he was within a couple of yards of me, I threw it hard. It missed his head but smacked into his left shoulder. He jerked his right hand up, clutched the place where it had hit, and the motion put his balance off. I jumped over the foundation and ran into the graveyard.

Something—a tangle of weeds, one of the low gravestones—caught my foot, and I fell heavily. For a moment I was stunned, face pressed into the grass. Then I heard Gray rush at me, overshooting the spot where I lay. I pushed up on both elbows and saw him stop, disoriented, midway between the graveyard and the grove of oak trees. As I got up, he whirled and saw me.

I expected him to run at me again, but instead he stood, fists clenched, feet spread wide apart. "Come on, bitch," he said, "what're you going to do now?"

I glanced around frantically, uncertain which way to go. Gray was blocking my path to the road—and the safety of my car.

He said, "Face it, bitch, you're caught. Thought you could run out on me, didn't you? Clean out the bank account and take off for Peru. Never come back."

Madre de Dios! I thought. He's lost his mind. He thinks I'm his wife.

"We'll see about that," Gray said. "Now we'll see."

As he started back toward me I turned and ran, not caring where. Pain stabbed at my back as I skirted the high headstone of Don Esteban Velasquez. At the edge of the cemetery my foot caught in a tangle of vines, and I stumbled almost to my knees but kept on going. Behind me Gray had also begun to run; his breath came in grunts and wheezes.

My own breath came hard, and I heard myself sob. The pain in my back was worse now, a fiery searing that brought tears to my eyes. I ignored it and raced across the field of wildflowers. Ahead was the stone *lavandería.* Perhaps there I would find some sort of weapon. . . .

Gray was gaining on me, only about ten yards away. I rounded the old well and looked inside. Nothing but stones and beer cans, and they were too far down to reach. Sobbing again, this time in frustration, I changed my course, running for the knoll where Quincannon had been ambushed. There were rocks up there. I could throw them at Gray—if I could run that distance. . . .

But before I could get very far, he hurled himself forward and dived at my feet. His outstretched hands grabbed my right ankle. I bent my left knee, flailed my arms for balance, tried to kick out at him. There was a wrenching spasm in my back, and I fell heavily to the ground.

Gray was on top of me now, his knees on my back, intensifying

212

the pain. His hands grasped my neck from behind, fingers reaching forward toward my throat. I tried to shake him off, but the pain prevented that. I screamed, my face pressed into the weeds, but the cry came out a mere gurgle.

Behind me Gray's voice was shouting: "Bitch! You'll never leave me!" The shouts were loud at first, then fainter, replaced by a buzzing in my ears. Tears were running down my face now. I tried to move my arms, but they felt numb. And there was the terrible, terrible pain in my back. . . .

A second voice began shouting in counterpoint to Gray's. The words were in Spanish: *"Basta! Basta! Hijo de puta!"*

Gray's body began to heave up and down, as if something were shaking it. His fingers loosened on my neck. For a moment his hands clutched at my shoulders, pulling my upper body away from the ground. Then he let go, and I fell flat. I felt him being dragged from me, heard grunts and scuffling. Then someone crashed to the ground beside me.

I tried to roll onto my side, but hands grabbed me again. Terror and rage flooded me and gave me the strength to scream. This time it came out a keening shriek. Above the sound, a man's voice said, *"Elena, Elena, está bien! Está Arturo. Está bien, Elena!"*

A hand, lean and long-fingered, touched my cheek. An arm supported me, helped me sit up. I cried out from the pain in my back, pressed my wet face into Arturo Melendez's rough wool shirt.

"Elena," he said, "are you all right?"

I hiccuped, cutting off a sob.

"Elena?"

I pulled back from his chest, scrubbed at my face with one hand. "What happened to—"

"For now, he is unconscious."

I opened my eyes. Arturo's face was directly in front of mine, made thin and pale by concern. He knelt beside me, one arm around my shoulders. Gray lay on the ground not three feet away from us, on his back, arms and legs splayed out. His eyes were closed, and blood trickled from a gash on his forehead.

"Elena," Arturo said, "what happened?"

"You didn't see . . . ?"

He shook his head. "I was walking on the far side of the hill, where I often go, by the ruins of the hacienda. I heard Gray shout. When I reached this side, he was chasing you across the field."

213

I sighed and brought both hands to my face, blocking out the sight of the supine figure. "Gray killed his wife," I said shakily. "That's what all this drinking has been about. She's buried over there under that pile of stones by the wall of the church. I found her."

Arturo sucked in his breath. For a long moment neither of us spoke.

Then he said, "We must go for the police."

"You go. I don't know if I can walk." And then I remembered what I'd been about to do when I'd discovered Georgia Hollis's body. "When you come back, I want you to help me with something."

"What?"

"Digging."

"For what?"

"You'll see."

Arturo looked puzzled, but merely said, "I will not leave you here with that *hijo de puta*. We will tie Gray up and both go for the police."

"What if he wakes up?"

"He won't, but I almost wish he would before we go." Arturo paused, and when he spoke again, his voice was low and ugly. "If he did, I would be only too happy to kick him in the head again. Or in the *cojones*, should you prefer that."

THREE

I⊤ WAS MIDAFTERNOON before the county sheriff's men were finished at the ruins of San Anselmo de las Lomas and later yet when Arturo, Sam, and I returned armed with a shovel, pick, and pry bar. We were curiously subdued for a trio of treasure hunters, shaken by the grim events of the past few hours.

Gray Hollis had been taken away immediately under guard in an ambulance, to be treated for a concussion and broken arm. Then the cairn of rocks had been opened, exposing the body of Georgia Hollis, wrapped in a tattered blanket. While investigators took statements from Arturo and me, technicians made their photographs and measurements, and finally Georgia was removed in a green body bag. The proceedings had a mechanical quality that chilled me; out of the improvised grave, into the bag, zip it up—and it was as if the woman had never existed. Even the horror and violence of her death had been negated by these routine and necessary actions.

In a way, I thought, the police procedure was very like the funeral ritual: a closing off, a signal that while one life had ended, it was time for others to get on with theirs. But there was one important difference: No one was here to mourn Georgia Hollis. As I watched the bag containing her body being bundled off through the grove of oak trees, I wondered if there was anyone who would claim Georgia and go through the formalities of grief.

When the investigators were done with us, Arturo and I had driven back to Sam's house. Earlier we'd called the sheriff's department from there, and the historian—who had just returned from mailing off the manuscript he'd been working on—had been left with the task of breaking the news to Dora Kingman. The ordeal had left him more angry than upset. Initially, he told us, Dora had gone into hysterics, but as she'd calmed down she'd begun to insist that Gray couldn't have murdered his wife. The more Sam had tried to convince her, the more adamant she'd become, and when he'd last seen her, she'd been on her way to the county hospital to try to help Gray.

"How can she do that?" Arturo had demanded. "How can she defend that *bastardo?*"

Sam shrugged. "She thinks she loves him. And the human animal only sees what it wants to see, anyway."

I had merely nodded, thinking of my affair with Dave—and of Mama's reaction to her illness.

But I had a more important concern than Dora and Gray, and as I explained to Arturo and Sam what I wanted to do, they brightened somewhat. At first Sam said that we would be tampering with a crime scene, but I assured him that I had already cleared it with the sheriff's department. There would be an officer on hand who would observe us and make sure we didn't destroy any evidence. Satisfied, Sam got the tools from the shed in his backyard, and the three of us returned to the ruins of the church.

The old pueblo seemed even more desolate than before. During the afternoon, the rain clouds had passed, but now the sky was dark once again, threatening a downpour at any minute. The sheriff's man had retreated to the warmth of his car, and he seemed sorry to see us; he donned a rain slicker before accompanying us to the ruins and sat down on the roof beam to smoke a cigarette.

As he set down the shovel he was carrying, Sam glanced at what remained of the cairn of rocks, and I saw a shudder pass through his body. Arturo was staring up at the sky; when he lowered his eyes, they met mine and I thought I knew what he was thinking: Let it rain; let it wash away the traces of this tragedy.

I shook my head, as if to clear it of such thoughts, and went directly to the foundation on the opposite side of the church from Georgia's makeshift grave. Lining my feet up against it where it turned at a right angle to form the apse, I paced off the distance: one, two, three, four, five feet. Then I went to the opposite side—ignoring the place where the body had been—and repeated the measuring in the apse whose walls were still standing. One, two, three feet. And a bit more. But not four feet.

I turned to Sam and Arturo; they were watching me intently. "Here," I said, "this is where we need to break down the wall." I stepped aside as they came forward with the pick and the pry bar. After a moment, Sam told me to move even farther back; the adobe wasn't yielding easily, and he didn't want to whack me with the pick. I'd already been injured enough for one day—Arturo had given me a muscle relaxant he'd had left over from when he'd hurt himself rock climbing last year, but my back still throbbed—so I retreated a few feet. But then I started moving closer again, excited now, sure of what they'd soon uncover.

John Quincannon had solved one murder, back in the 1890s. I'd discovered another, here in the 1980s. And now I was about to make the biggest discovery of all. I was about to find the long-lost Velasquez artifacts. . . .

Sam turned and glared at me. I was standing no more than a foot behind him. I gestured apologetically and went to sit next to the sheriff's man on the charred roof beam, annoyed that my back injury prevented me from helping. This was going much too slowly. Wasn't demolition supposed to be easy? Shouldn't that old wall just fall . . . ?

There was a cracking sound. Arturo shouted, and Sam grabbed his arm and pulled him away from the wall. Adobe bricks rained down, one chunk landing on Sam's foot. He began hopping up and down, his hand grasping Arturo for balance. The officer and I both jumped up and ran over there. I peered through the gaping hole in the wall of the apse.

Inside, the space between it and the outer wall was dark. The air was dry and musty. I put my hands on the waist-high opening and hoisted myself up, ignoring a dull throbbing that told me I was doing further damage to my back. My eyes quickly accustomed themselves to the darkness, and I was able to make out a number of lumpy shapes on the ground below.

"Elena?" Sam said. "Are they—"

"I think so." I let go of the opening and dropped back to the ground. "We've got to pull the rest of this wall down."

Sam and Arturo attacked it with renewed energy. Even the policeman helped. Now that an opening had been made, the rest of the bricks pulled apart easily. Of course this false wall would not have been built as sturdily as those of the rest of the church; there had not been time. But it still had stood for a hundred and forty years, miraculously spared from cannonballs, fire, and vandalism.

When they had made the opening large enough for me to reach through, the three men stepped back almost ceremoniously. I looked at them, suddenly reluctant to step forward, feeling like a child who has lain awake all night in anticipation of Christmas morning and now can't believe it is really here. They seemed to share the feeling, because they remained silent, staring at the opening.

I shook myself, laughed nervously, then knelt beside the jagged hole in the wall. Extending my arm through it, I felt around until my fingers touched a slender piece of metal. Pulling it out, I saw it was a gold crucifix; the metal gleamed dully, and the jewels at the tips of the crosspieces shone with a deep red fire. Fibers of fabric clung to it, as if it had once been wrapped in cloth that had now rotted away.

My lips parted, but I couldn't speak. I held the crucifix up for the others to see.

Arturo said softly, *"Jesus Cristo!"*

I smiled at the aptness of the exclamation.

Sam said, "You were right."

"Yes."

"But how did you know?" I'd outlined the entire story of the Velasquez treasure on the way here—including the first part for Arturo's benefit—but time hadn't permitted me to explain why I thought the artifacts had been walled into the apse.

I said, "It was in the letter Tomás Cordova wrote to his wife."

"But according to Quincannon," Sam said, "the last page was never recovered."

"That's true. And that was why he couldn't interpret it properly."

Arturo said, "But if this detective couldn't, why could you?"

"Because I'm Catholic, and Quincannon wasn't. The words on the fragment he found in Luis Cordova's hand were *'más allá del sepulcro'* and *'dondé Maria.'* Beyond the grave, where Mary something-or-other. Quincannon and Felipe interpreted the grave to be that of Maria Alcazar, Don Esteban's first wife. But its location had been obliterated in the destruction of the pueblo."

"And you found it?" Sam asked.

"I found *a* grave. Or actually, Quincannon found it." I pointed to the slab of stone in the church floor that I'd uncovered earlier. "It's the grave of Julio del Prado, the first padre of this church. And seeing it made me wonder: What if the grave mentioned in the letter *wasn't* Maria Alcazar's? What if it was really this one—the most distinctive one in the pueblo? And what if Maria referred to someone else?"

Arturo said, "Who, then?"

218

"The Virgin Mary."

Arturo began to smile, nodding in understanding. Sam and the policeman both frowned. Sam said, "I don't get it."

"That's because, like Quincannon, you're not Catholic. If you were, you would know that the statue of the Virgin Mary customarily stands in this apse, to this side of the altar."

Now understanding began to come into Sam's eyes, too.

" 'Más allá del sepulcro' actually meant beyond Padre del Prado's grave," I said. "And on the next page of the letter, the phrase 'donde Maria' was probably completed with something like the word 'stands.' "

Sam wasn't quite convinced, though. He said, "That's all very logical, but why didn't Felipe Velasquez realize it? After all, he was Catholic."

It was the one point that had originally troubled me and made me doubt my reasoning; but while the sheriff's men had been following their routine at the grave of Georgia Hollis, I'd had plenty of time to consider the tragic events that had befallen the Velasquez family, and I thought I had the answer. I said, "Felipe was fixated on 'Maria' meaning the grave of Don Esteban's first wife; he never considered the Virgin Mary or Padre del Prado's grave. He had probably forgotten all about the padre. He seldom came here in his last years—Quincannon made that plain—and even when he did, he had no reason to go inside the ruins. Besides, the marker was half-hidden by weeds and grass even then."

Sam's desire for historical accuracy was not yet satisfied, however. He said, "But why, in all the family's searches for the artifacts, didn't anyone notice that this apse had a false wall?"

That was another question I'd had to consider, and again I was reasonably sure of the answer. "For one thing," I said, "the workmanship on the false wall was very good. Even though there wasn't time to do a perfect job, it resembles the other walls closely. And during the siege by Fremont's troops, the other apse was destroyed; the size difference between the two wasn't as obvious as it might have been had they both been standing. There was nothing left to compare this one with."

Sam nodded, apparently accepting my explanation.

I turned back to the opening in the wall. The past had been dealt with; now I had a responsibility to the present, and—being a curator at heart—to these artifacts. They had lain protected in the wall for one hundred and forty years, but now the space was open to the elements, and a rainstorm was threatening.

"Come and help me," I said to the three men. "Let's get these things out of here before it rains." To Sam and Arturo, I added, "Later we'll go to Sam's house and call Sofia Manuela and tell her her family treasure has been found."

FOUR

"So," I said to Mama, "Mrs. Manucla told me she wants to donate the artifacts to the museum. She wants nothing to do with them, since they caused such tragedy in her family, and she has no heirs. Some of them are very valuable; there's even a small El Greco that survived undamaged. Imagine us with an El Greco!"

Mama smiled, looking pleased for me. She looked pleased with everything this morning, sitting on the edge of her hospital bed in a cheerful yellow dress and sweater, all ready to go home. Nick had gone downstairs to take care of the final paperwork, and once the nurse arrived with a wheelchair, we would be on our way.

I was about to tell her of my plans for an exhibit of the artifacts when she said, "Are you sure your back will be all right? Did you have Dr. George look at it?"

It took me a few seconds to grasp the shift of subject. "My back? Oh, yes, he looked at it. After a few days of taking it easy, I'll be good as new."

"See that you do, then." She gave me a look that promised dire consequences if I didn't, then added, "You really must be more careful, Elena. This whole thing, being attacked by that murderer, it's horrible. Did he really kill his wife?"

"Yes, he's confessed to it. Apparently he was at the ruins collecting rocks—I think I mentioned he owns a rock shop—and she came up there and announced she was leaving him. He went crazy and strangled her, then buried her body in the apse. I guess he figured it was a safe place, since nobody ever goes there except Arturo and kids who are looking for a place to drink and neck. And probably no one would ever have discovered her if I hadn't found Quincannon's reports and started snooping around there."

"And that's why he stole the report from Sam's house—to stop you from snooping?"

"Yes. He was watching me at the ruins one day—the day I

thought somebody was there and then found the cigarette butt—and he got this weird idea that without the report I'd simply lose interest and go away. It wasn't logical, but then drunks are seldom masters of logic. He also thought that if he had the report, he might be able to figure out where the treasure was himself." I laughed wryly.

Mama said, "What's so funny?"

"Not funny—ironic. Gray wanted to find the treasure, and all the time it was only a few feet from where he'd buried his wife."

"I see nothing amusing about that. He might have killed you yesterday afternoon!" She gave me a truly dark look this time, and I was afraid a lecture would follow. But then she fell silent.

I was silent too, suddenly uncomfortable. When I'd arrived this morning, Mama had been too happy about being released with a clean bill of health, and I'd been too full of my news about the artifacts to talk about the quarrel we'd had the other day. Now was the time, however.

"Mama—" I said.

"Elena—" she said at the same time.

"Go ahead," I told her.

She looked down at her clasped hands. "I just wished to say that I am sorry I spoke so harshly to you two days ago. I had no right."

"No, Mama, I had no right to speak that way to you."

She looked up again, her eyes reflecting my own relief. "There was a great deal of truth in what you said."

"And also in what you said."

She nodded, satisfied. "Then, we will speak no more of the matter."

We were saved from any sentimental gestures by the arrival of the nurse with the wheelchair. All business, she transferred Mama to the chair, plopped one of the plants from the dresser in her lap, handed me another, and began wheeling the chair out to the elevator.

While we waited for the car to arrive, Mama said to me, "This man who saved you, Arturo Melendez—what is he like?"

I smiled. "I told you before. About my age, although he seems younger. A very talented artist. Not handsome, but quite nice-looking."

"Melendez," Mama said thoughtfully. "One of our own people."

I knew what was coming next.

"And single," she added.

"But poor. I told you, he is poor."

She brushed the words aside. "Are you going to see him again?"

Normally I would have bristled at the question, but I was so happy Mama was well and going home and so relieved we'd made up our quarrel that I said, "Yes. We're having lunch tomorrow."

"Ah, you like him."

"I like him very much. But don't get all excited; we're only going to lunch to discuss a possible showing of his paintings at the museum."

The elevator arrived. The nurse pushed Mama's chair into it and turned it around so it faced me. Mama was smiling. "That's good," she said.

Astonished, I stayed where I was. "What do you mean—that's good?"

"It's good because I don't want you getting involved with him."

The nurse was holding the door open, looking impatient, but I stood still. "Why not?"

Mama held up one hand and began ticking off items on her fingers. "First, it's too soon after Dave. Second, like you say, he doesn't have any money. And third, you're only interested in him because he saved your life. You're interested in *anything* that has to do with murder and violence, and I don't think those are very healthy concerns for a young woman."

The nurse was smiling now. I rolled my eyes at her.

Mama added, "This Arturo looks exciting to you now, but after a while you'll realize he's no hero, and then we'll have another breakup on our hands—"

The nurse took her hand off the elevator's rubber safety strip. I reached inside to the operator panel and pushed the CLOSE button. As the two halves of the door moved together, I waved good-bye to Mama.

Maybe by the time I walked down to the lobby she'd have found a new topic of conversation. Whatever it was, I wouldn't have to put up with it long; I'd promised to have lunch with her and Nick at the trailer park, but then I had a date with Sam to read the remaining documents from the files of Carpenter and Quincannon, Professional Detective Services.

EPILOGUE
1894

IT WAS NOT until three days after the suicide of Felipe Velasquez that Quincannon finally returned home to San Francisco.

There had been much for him to do at Rancho Rinconada de los Robles. The most difficult thing was dealing with Doña Olivia, and not because of her grief. It was apparent that she had cared for her husband and that she mourned his death; but it was also apparent that her primary concern was her future and that of her daughter. A cool, practical woman, who was not deceived—as Barnaby O'Hare and the servants were deceived—by Quincannon's lie that Velasquez had shot himself in a fit of despondency over his terminal illness, rather than suffer a few more weeks of pain.

If she had not known of his cancer, she had suspected it. And if he had not told her that he'd murdered Luis Cordova, she had suspected that, too. In private she indicated as much to Quincannon and left him no choice but to reveal the truth to her. Once she had it, she demanded to see the two pages of Tomás Cordova's letter, which he had removed from Velasquez's desk after the shooting. She also demanded that he reveal none of his knowledge to the authorities or to anyone else, for the sake of her daughter and the family's good name, and that he prepare a full confidential report of his activities while in the employ of her husband, so as to ensure his silence. He saw no reason to refuse her, not even when she said in her haughty fashion, "You will be well-paid, Señor Quincannon. You have my word on that." He *would* have refused if she had demanded that he see to the private burial of Pablo at the ruins of the pueblo, a matter that would have to be attended to to preserve the facade she was erecting around Velasquez's death. But she seemed to sense that he would not go that far, and she made no mention of it. She would make the arrangements in her own way, as coolly as she would arrange for the public burial of her husband. Pablo, as far as anyone would ever know, had simply disappeared. Luis Cordova, as far as anyone would ever know, had died at the hands of an unknown assailant. And Felipe Velasquez, as far as little Sofia and the world at large would ever know, had died of natural causes; O'Hare and the servants would be sworn to secrecy just as Quincannon himself had been.

When he finally left the hacienda for the long ride back across the mountains to Santa Barbara, it had been with a sense of relief. But the relief had not lasted long; it had been replaced by an odd feeling of cheerlessness and frustration. Part of it was the events at the rancho, but a large part of it, too, was a sense of personal failure. None of what had happened was his fault, of course. Nor was any of it an adverse reflection of his skills as a detective. And yet the suspicion nagged at him that he had not done all he could have; that Don Esteban's artifacts *were* hidden at the pueblo, and that given enough time, and with enough effort, he *could* have found them. Groundless though the feeling might be—Velasquez had given up hope, after all, and he had had far more knowledge of the area—it continued to chafe at him. He should have found those artifacts, by God! Not for Velasquez's sake, nor for Doña Olivia's; for little Sofia's and for his own peace of mind.

Now it was too late, much too late. His involvement with the Velasquez family was finished, or it would be once he sent his report to Doña Olivia. There was no going back, even if he had wanted to. And he did not want to.

San Francisco, surprisingly, still basked in balmy spring sunshine. But neither the weather nor the familiar sights of the city cheered him as he rode a hansom from the train depot to Market Street. Even the prospect of seeing Sabina held little pleasure for him—until he entered the agency's offices and saw her.

She wore an attractive tweed suit this morning, her hair was piled high on her head in the rather exotic, Oriental fashion he liked, and her welcoming smile struck him as radiant. She came to greet him with outstretched hands that clasped both of his. Her touch was electric. It seemed to soften something within him, like heat softens a clot of wax.

"John," she said, "it's good to have you back."

"It's good to be back."

"Didn't the investigation go well? You look . . . well, melancholy."

"I'd rather not talk about it just now." His eyes took her in,

228

apparently with such intensity that her smile dimmed, wavered. There was more softening within him, and a sudden yearning.

"John?" she said.

He let go of her hands, caught her in a fierce embrace, and kissed her.

She struggled for a few seconds, then yielded all at once and for a few additional seconds she returned the kiss warmly, almost lingeringly. Then she pushed free of him and backed away two paces. Her eyes were wide, amazed.

She said a little breathlessly, "John Quincannon! Whatever has come over you?"

"A change of sorts," he said. "Yes, a change. Life is too short to waste in timid maunderings and impotent fantasies. Seize every opportunity to enjoy it, that's the ticket. I've wanted to kiss you for months. And now I have."

"Well, really." She was fussing with her hair and her clothing, even though neither was disarranged. "I must say I don't care for that sort of aggressive behavior. When I want to be kissed, I shall issue an invitation."

"Perhaps you'll issue one tonight, eh?"

"Tonight?"

"After we've had dinner at the Old Poodle Dog, opera bouffe at the Tivoli, and coffee and cordials at the Hoffman Café."

"Now, John . . . "

"I won't take no for an answer." He smiled at her roguishly. "I insist, my dear."

She averted her gaze, but only for a moment. When her eyes met his again, he thought he saw a tenderness in them, an indication of an inner melting of her own. "Very well," she said after a time. "But don't expect anything more than that."

"More than another kiss?"

"More than dinner and an evening on the town!"

His smile broadened. He felt better now, much better. The time he had spent in Santa Barbara and the Santa Ynez Valley, the frustration it had wrought, the specter of Don Esteban's missing artifacts, might well remain embedded in his memory. But if life had its unhappy aspects, it also had its ecstatic ones. Life could be good. Life could be very good indeed.

Sabina, dear sweet Sabina, was *definitely* weakening. . . .

1986

IT WAS A late afternoon in the middle of June, and I had fled to the conservation lab in the basement of the museum. Temporarily safe from both visitors and my staff, I perched on a stool, savoring the coolness and quiet. Above me in the nineteenth-century gallery, which had been closed to the public all week, I could hear bumpings and scrapings and occasional outraged voices.

As I sat there, Rudy's words came clearly through the floor: "I will *not* have that display case sitting in the middle of the space like that!"

Susana said, "It must be there. Otherwise the traffic will not flow properly."

"Who's curator here—you or me?"

"You are."

"Then let me set the exhibit up in my own way! I know how these artifacts should be displayed."

"You may be the curator and know about artifacts, but *I* am the public relations director and I know about people. If you do not have a display case there, they won't go in the right direction—"

I tuned out the argument—one of many that had been raging for days—and looked around the lab at the Velasquez artifacts. Each one had been cleaned and restored where necessary, and now they stood awaiting their debut before the Santa Barbara art community. Just seeing them there in their timeless serenity calmed me, made me forget the turmoil upstairs.

There was the Jusepe de Ribera *Madonna and Child*, the faces expressing a sweetness that saved them from pious pomposity. A silver censer gleamed from an energetic volunteer's many hours of polishing. A gold statue of Saint Katherine had been damaged when we'd removed it from the wall of the apse, but Rudy's deft fingers had restored it so the break was barely noticeable. There was the El

Greco, the prize of our collection. And the Bible in its jeweled cover. And many more. . . .

Tomorrow—*Dios mediante*—the exhibit would open with an evening reception. Sofia Manuela would be the guest of honor, attired in a gown that she and I had picked out after numerous consultations. Susana would attend with Carlos, seizing the opportunity to display the engagement ring she never tired of flashing; Rudy would be there with his new lover, an antiques dealer he had met at one of the auctions; and I would enter on the arm of Arturo Melendez, whose own show of paintings was not far off on our calendar. There would be friends and relatives: Sam Ryder, Jesse Herrera, Mama and Nick and Carlota, who was visiting from Minneapolis. There would be champagne punch and delicacies such as spicy beef and quesadillas prepared in the manner of *los ranchos grandes*. A band would play the festive music of that era. . . .

I shook my head, smiling wryly. I'd come down here to escape the pressures of overseeing and planning, and here I was making mental lists! In a way, it was ludicrous, all this fuss over a collection of religious artifacts. Especially artifacts that had brought the Velasquez family such tragedy and pain. But perhaps it was time that some good came of them.

I wondered what John Quincannon would have thought of all this.

Quincannon. In the month and a half since Sam and I had read the last of the documents from his agency's files, I'd been too busy to think much about the detective. Sofia Manuela's bequest had added much work to my days—insuring the artifacts, filling out the proper tax forms, aiding Rudy in the restoration—and my budding romance with Arturo had consumed my nights and weekends. Now I thought back to those documents—and my dissatisfaction with what they had revealed.

There had been a photograph of Quincannon, and he had looked surprisingly as I'd imagined him. And I'd been excited to discover that his partner in the agency had been a woman, Sabina Carpenter. A studio portrait of her had shown a handsome, black-haired woman who did not try to hide her keen intelligence. She looked like the sort of person with whom I would have much in common— after all, I'd done a bit of detection, too—and I was extremely interested in a woman who had broken the rules and become a detective in a male-dominated era. I wanted to know more about her and about her relationship with Quincannon, but there the documents frustrated me. For one thing, the librarian at the San Francisco Public Library had only sent items dated 1894; her letter—which I hadn't found until Sam and I had almost finished reading the materials—indicated she thought that year was the only one I was interested in.

It wasn't that the letters—which had been written and received by both of the partners—and the diary—which had belonged to Sabina—hadn't been absorbing. But apparently both of them believed in being circumspect on paper. Sabina's diary was full of notations of social engagements with "John." There were mentions of picnics and dinners, entertainments and carriage rides, and one "walk in the rain." But these were mixed with cryptic commentary on clients, cases, business appointments. And nowhere, both in that diary and the various pieces of personal correspondence, could I find what I really wanted to know: What had happened to Quincannon and Sabina? Had they remained partners? Fallen in love? Gotten married? Had children? Lived long and happy lives?

The romantic in me wouldn't let go of the story of these two people. I could feel my curiosity stirring even now.

From the librarian's letter, I gathered there were many more documents from Carpenter and Quincannon's files at San Francisco's California History Room. During the past two months, I'd often thought of calling there and asking if they would send copies of the remainder to me, but I'd kept getting sidetracked in the preparations for this exhibit. Now I decided maybe I should take some time off, go up there, look through the whole lot. Perhaps after Arturo's show opened, he would want to go with me; it would be a nice vacation for both of us. . . .

Once again I shook my head. Why was I planning such a trip? Did it really matter what had happened to the long-dead detectives?

Yes, I decided, it did. John Quincannon and I had shared an adventure; our lives were forever entwined. The detective had reached out beyond the grave—*más allá del sepulcro*—to me; he'd somehow enabled me to finish what he'd begun. And my life had changed for the better because of that.

There was only one more thing I wished I could do: I wished I could tell him the way it had ended. . . .

235

If you have enjoyed this book and would like to receive
details of other Walker mystery titles,
please write to:

Mystery Editor
Walker and Company
720 Fifth Avenue
New York, New York 10019